THE TOWER

ALESSANDRO GALLENZI

ALMA BOOKS

ALMA BOOKS LTD
3 Castle Yard
Richmond
Surrey TW10 6TF
United Kingdom
www.almabooks.com

First published by Alma Books Limited in 2014
This new, revised edition first published by Alma Books Limited in 2016
© Alessandro Gallenzi, 2016

Cover design: Jem Butcher

Alessandro Gallenzi asserts his moral right to be identified as the author of this work in accordance with the Copyright, Designs and Patents Act 1988

Printed and bound by CPI Group (UK) Ltd, Croydon, CR0 4YY

ISBN: 978-1-84688-376-7
eBook ISBN : 978-1-84688-343-9

The Tower

For Eleonora and Emiliano

1

"Any sign yet?" asked Peter Simms, glancing up from his phone at the Arrivals gate.

"No, Mr Peter. Not yet," replied the driver, a young Arab with short black hair and moustache. He was holding a board with an Italian name scribbled on it, which he lifted above the wall of bodies in front of him as a few more passengers straggled out into the main hall of Amman airport.

"It's absurd. Her plane landed an hour ago, and she still hasn't come out."

"Maybe queue at passport control, Mr Peter."

"Yeah." He looked at his watch, heaved a sigh and shook his head. Just as he was lowering his gaze back onto his phone, his eyes picked out a slim, tanned figure. Dark hair peeping from under her hat, tinted glasses pushed upwards for a moment as she scanned the room, she was his age or a little younger, maybe early thirties. Beside her, a brown-uniformed porter was pushing her trolley, overloaded with luggage and duty-free bags. She looked left and right.

"There," she said, pointing, and waved her hand.

"She here, Mr Peter," the young Arab said, turning a smiling face.

"Yes, I can see that."

"Giulia Ripetti," she said as she approached. "Pleasure to meet you."

"Peter Simms."

"I'm Majed, Miss Julia. I go and take the car. You wait there outside with Mr Peter, OK?"

Majed exchanged a few words with the porter, giving him a crumpled note as he dashed out.

Peter took a sideways look at her as she hunched over to put her passport in one of her bags. So this was his assistant – the philologist, the Latin specialist, the literary scholar. He'd thought this category of people only came in slightly hunched bodies wearing thick-framed spectacles.

Giulia took off her hat and glasses, and ran a hand through her hair.

"It's hot, eh? Even in September."

"I know. That's Jordan for you."

"It's hot also in Rome. But not so hot. So you are the investigator? I'll work with you?"

"Yes."

"You live here?" she asked, glancing at the small leather case at his feet.

"Me? No. I've just arrived too... you know... I live in London."

"Ah, OK."

He cleared his throat. "You're certainly planning to stay for a while?" he said, with a smile and a little jerk of the head towards the pile of suitcases on her trolley.

"What? Oh, I see."

Minutes passed. Car after car rolled by in front of them, until a faded-red Lada 21 screeched to a stop by the kerb and Majed jumped out.

"Jesus," said Peter, looking at the near-wreck as Giulia raised her eyebrows.

"Sorree. Sorree," Majed said. "Company car broken this afternoon. So I come with wife's uncle car. Sorree."

He opened the boot as the porter started to dismantle Giulia's luggage pile.

"Wait, wait, wait," called Peter, raising a hand. "Look." A makeshift repair to a loose corner of the number plate had resulted in a sharp, rusty screw sticking out three inches inside the trunk. "Don't damage the cases."

"No problem, no problem," said the porter, wedging the luggage in the boot one piece at a time. Peter shoved his suitcase in, as far as possible from the screw.

Soon they were out of Queen Alia Airport and onto the long stretch of road that cuts across the desert plain surrounding the city. They had only been driving a few minutes when the glow of a steep, truncated cone appeared on their right-hand side.

"Is that it?" said Peter, who was sitting in the passenger's seat.

Majed looked to his right. "Yes, Mr Peter."

"And what do you call it? I mean – in your language."

"What we call it? We call it 'Al-Burj'."

"*Al... Boorsch*. The Tower."

"Yes, Mr Peter. You know Arabic? *Hal tatakallamu alloghah al-arabiah*?"

"*Qaleelan*. I used to speak a few words. A long time ago. Now I'm a bit rusty. Do you know when they are going to complete it?"

"Al-Burj? Oh" – Majed leant over, taking his eyes off the road for an alarmingly long time – "perhaps two month, three month. Tower got big belly." He made the money gesture. "Eat blenty of dollars from Saudi and Qatar. They build quick, before oil run out." He gave a mad laugh and straightened up behind the wheel. "Many beople don't want Al-Burj. They say it's bad for Jordan, for Q'ran. Bring too much people from outside." He lapsed into silence, although it was clear he wanted to say more.

Al-Burj… Peter stared at the Tower in the distance. It looked like a runway of lights in the sky. But Majed was wrong if he thought that the money came only from Saudi Arabia and Qatar: it flowed from banks, from hedge funds, from private equities and from shareholders' pockets all over the globe. That was the invisible sap pushing up this rootless, preposterous one-thousand-metre-high tree in the middle of the desert.

He turned around to ask Giulia whether she knew any Arabic, but she had dozed off. He was just settling back into his seat when a car from the right lurched across their path – "Jesus!" – and missed them by no more than a yard.

Majed shook his head. "Donkeys," was his only comment. "These beople like donkeys."

When they arrived at the Grand Hyatt, Peter touched Giulia's arm to wake her from her doze. As they got out, the hotel boy opened the boot and began hauling their luggage out. There was the fatal rip of leather giving way to sharp metal. Peter went round the back of the car to look at his suitcase, a survivor of trips to Tanzania, Zanzibar and Belize. Why? Why *his* suitcase?

"Sorree, sir," the boy said, trying to patch the gash in the leather with his hand.

"Sorree, Mr Peter," said Majed.

"Forget it." He was angry, but less annoyed by the tear in his expensive travel bag than by the hint of schadenfreude in Giulia's smile of sympathy. "It's OK," he said, as the hotel boy flapped and flustered. "Majed, we'll see you in half an hour. Just give us time to take a shower and destroy a burger."

"Yes, Mr Peter."

And he flip-flopped towards the main revolving door, followed by Giulia and the contrite-looking boy pulling their luggage on a trolley.

* * *

The meeting was in a top-floor suite at Le Royal, in Amman's Third Circle.

They were shown into the suite's study, where a man of around fifty – pudgy, nattily dressed, with gold-rimmed glasses, crimped black hair and a goatee – sat behind a mahogany desk, his head immersed in a folio-sized book.

"Thank you for being here," their host said, rising to shake hands. "And sorry that it's so late. I wanted to meet you before you visit…"

"*Al-Boorsch*," said Peter.

"Exactly. Will you take a seat please? Anything to drink? No?" He sat down after his guests. "Had a good journey in?"

"Very good," Giulia replied.

"Super, Mr Al-Rafai," said Peter. The late-evening flight, the hour-long wait for Giulia, the clapped-out jalopy, the long, drawn-out ripping of his suitcase. "Super. Thank you."

"Good. Good. Well, first of all, I'd like to thank you both again for coming all the way to Jordan on this, ah, unusual assignment." He closed his book – a stamp collector's album. "Have you been filled in on any of the details?"

"No," said Giulia. "I got the letter from Amman University. All I know is that you need an expert on Giordano Bruno and his Latin works."

"I know a little," Peter added, "just what your lawyer mentioned to me on the phone."

"Oh yes," the man said, nodding, "my good friend, Henry Lancaster. We were at Westminster together, you know? Then Balliol. We play golf together from time to time."

"He said there's been a theft, a disappearance."

"A theft, yes, of a priceless manuscript. *And* a disappearance. Of a man. You'll find out much more tomorrow. I've summoned you here because I want to convey to you how important this is for me. You see" – he reopened his album with a slow gesture – "when you have assembled a collection, a collection such as mine, you don't want to see any of its pieces vanish – especially if they're rare or unique. That's what keeps the collector awake at night: the fear that his most treasured possession might be... mutilated in this way."

"Any idea who might be behind it?"

Al-Rafai closed his album again and smiled. "There are theories. There are always theories. I will make sure you are filled in. Mr Simms, Ms Ripetti, a precious item from my library has been stolen – and I want it back." Each of the last five words was accompanied by a gentle rap on the edge of the desk.

"Your lawyer said that the man who disappeared with your manuscript was a Roman priest."

"Yes, a Jesuit – Father Marini. That's somewhat tricky – and more embarrassing, is it not? He had been specially sent by the Vatican to analyse the documents and do some philological work."

"But you've reported the theft to the local authorities?"

Al-Rafai gave a pale smile, then looked towards his butler, who was standing at the far end of the room staring ahead of him with a blank expression. "Don't let me tell you what I think of the local authorities. This is a private matter – and it must remain private. Are you religious, Mr Simms?"

"I was until the age of five."

"What about you, Miss Ripetti?"

"I'm a Catholic."

"I'm Catholic too, a Melkite Catholic. There's a large Catholic community in Jordan, did you know? Almost three per cent of the entire population, I think. But this is a Muslim country, and religion and politics remain very delicate issues. You will remember all the controversy when the Pope visited the Holy Land last year? So be careful."

"Of what?"

"Of what you say, of what you do. You see, there is strong opposition, among the locals, to the presence of that tall building in our land." He made a dismissive gesture, then looked down and began to work the corner of the leather album with his finger. "It's run by Americans, after all – who are not famous for their sensitivity towards other cultures and religions."

"That's a mild way of putting it."

"Indeed. Indeed." He looked up with a gloomy smile. "But you must be exhausted." He got to his feet. "I shall see you in the next few days. In the meantime, I'll arrange for you to be briefed. Hopefully you'll have good news for me soon. Keep me informed, will you? And thank you again."

He shook their hands, and they were shown out by the butler, who escorted them into the lift.

"Fancy a quick drink?" Peter said as they descended.

"OK."

They made their way to the terrace restaurant on the tenth floor. It was too late to get food, but drinks were still being served. Peter ordered a beer and Giulia mineral water. The warm air, the synthetic palm trees and the creamy-coloured slabs of marble gave the terrace the artificial feel of a tourist village. There was no one else there apart from them. They sat on the balcony, from where a large swath of night-time Amman could be viewed. Far away rose the glowing outline of the Tower.

"This man, Mr Al-Rafai – who is he?" asked Giulia as she grabbed her glass. "There's nothing on the web."

"He seems to have found a way of eluding not just Google, but also the editors of *Forbes*," said Peter, laughing. "But my understanding is that he's worth a few billion dollars."

"Yes? And how has he made his money?"

"No idea. All I know is that he's paying me three times my going rate. Presumably it's the same for you." He took a swig of beer.

"A part of the Tower is dark," Giulia said after a long pause, looking into the distance.

"I think they're fixing the last panels of glass near the top."

"But it's already open to the public?"

"Parts of it. That's what I heard."

Giulia looked at her watch. "Perhaps it's time to go."

"Sure."

The waiter came to collect the empty glasses, and they settled the bill and went down to the lobby, where Majed was waiting to take them back to the Hyatt.

Peter proceeded to his room. He tuned the TV to BBC News and began to undress for a shower when he heard a light knock at the door.

"Yes?"

Giulia's face was strangely tense.

"I found this on my pillow," she said.

"A Bible?" he turned the book in his hands. "A strange courtesy in a Muslim country."

"Open it."

He did so and frowned. Along the fold line there was a dead earthworm, cut in half. Either side of it, the words "BOOK" and "WORM" were scrawled in what appeared to be blood.

"I'm not squeamish," Giulia said, "but I don't like this."

"Of course." Peter thought for a moment. "Perhaps it was left there by the previous occupant. Do you want to change rooms?"

"No, it's fine. I'm too tired now."

"All right. Leave it with me. I'll complain with the managers."

"OK. Goodnight."

"Goodnight."

He closed the door and had another good long look at the book and the dead earthworm. He was puzzled and unsettled by that strange message. As Al-Rafai had warned, they would have to be careful in their moves – very careful.

2

Rome, August 1569

The sun was rising when the coach left the dim outskirts of the Campagna Romana and rolled onto the first paved streets of the Eternal City. Giordano glanced at his travelling companion, old Father Ambrogio, and smiled: not even all the bumps and jolts of the carriage could shake him from his slumber.

They had left their monastery in Naples three days ago, summoned to Rome by Pope Pius himself. The previous year Giordano had presumed to send him a book, asking for permission to dedicate it to him. Now he feared that his work might have been misunderstood, and that His Holiness was going to reprimand him. Otherwise, why had he been sent for in such haste, after begging for an audience the year before? And why was he being escorted by the formidable Father Ambrogio Salvio da Bagnoli – basher of heretics, burner of books, Vicar of the Dominican Order and Provincial at San Domenico Maggiore?

Yes, there will be a rebuke, he thought, as he smelt the morning air, rich with the fragrance of mint and pine resin. But he knew he was innocent of any malicious or satirical intent, and so hoped to explain to His Holiness that this was only a treatise on mnemonics – an art, after all, which had always been dear to Dominican scholars such as the Pope himself.

He had not even been able to say goodbye to his fellow novices. He and Father Ambrogio had boarded the Papal *diligenza* well before the early-morning prayer. They had travelled through the deserted streets of Naples and out into the countryside in complete darkness, reaching the Appian Way between Arpaia and Capua at the break of dawn.

The warm season had helped them make smooth progress through the harshest part of the journey, from Capua to Terracina, though Father Ambrogio had to stop the coach several times a day, even between stages, because of his aching legs and back. Although he was still in good health, his seventy-eight years of active life were beginning to show in the bend of his frame and the dimming of his mind. Father Ambrogio had spent most of the journey shut in on himself, either dozing or in prayer. He was a silent, severe, impenetrable man – a solemn man of the previous century. Giordano looked up to him as a model of rectitude and austerity: at twenty, he found it difficult to believe he would ever be able to curb the exuberance of his mind and reach such heights of unflinching self-discipline.

The streets of Rome were now bathed in the light of dawn. The paving had become more even, the buildings more grandiose, and the smell of herbs and trees had been replaced by the pungent odour of horse dung and smouldering night fires. Only a few people – for the most part soldiers, labourers and homeless paupers – could be seen wandering around. Ahead, in the distance, the reddish bulk of Castel Sant'Angelo could be glimpsed, while to the north-west rose the white marble of St Peter's.

"La Minerva's over there, Iordanus," Father Ambrogio said, waving in the direction of the Pantheon on the right. "I was Master of Studies there, at the time of the Great Sack. It's over forty years ago now."

He chewed on his lip and fell silent again. Giordano thought that would be the last he'd hear from him until their arrival, but Ambrogio added: "They killed people in the streets. Buildings were pillaged and burnt down. Everyone ran away in fear. Even our cloister was empty. I was the only one who stayed behind. I put all our sacred things in big sacks and hid them in the crypt. Then I threw some clothes over my cowl and made my escape. To this day I don't know how I managed to survive."

"It was through the Grace of God, Father," said Giordano. "He saved you for higher purposes."

"Yes," said Father Ambrogio, with eyes that seemed to stare at nothing.

As the coach cut across the square in front of St Peter's, Giordano and Ambrogio raised their eyes to the unfinished dome. The shadowy figures of labourers at work could be made out in the hazy light among the wooden scaffolding.

"It's… divine," murmured Giordano, awestruck.

"Yes," said his superior. "A divine folly. The greatest waste in all Christendom. Only God knows when it is going to be finished, or why it was begun. All this money could have been used to fight the Turks or the heathens of the North – or to help the poor. Why did the old basilica have to be demolished? Rome has been turned into a building site."

They reached the gates to the Papal palace, where two guards with their long blue stockings, yellow-and-blue uniforms and red-plumed caps barred the entrance with crossed halberds. Another guard checked their travelling papers, then waved to the driver to proceed. The coach halted in front of a vast ochre-brick building, which was protected by two more soldiers. Giordano helped Ambrogio off the coach and gave him his arm to lean on as they clambered up the marble staircase and entered the building. Escorted by one of the guards, they trudged up two more flights of stairs and were shown into the antechamber to Pope Pius's private study, a large room decorated with dark paintings of saints and martyrs.

They were alone: Ambrogio sat on one of the chairs along the walls and immersed himself in prayer, while Giordano walked to the tall window overlooking the Papal gardens. As he let his gaze roam around the chirping foliage and the blue sky, he tried to master his anxiety, reminding himself that he had little to worry about: there was nothing controversial or irreverent in his book.

The gardens made him think of the summers of his childhood, when he played with his friends in the fields around Nola, throwing stones at trees or climbing up to the ruins of Castle Cicala in the afternoon, with his mother calling his name from their cottage at the close of day. He would answer the cry with a joyful voice and run back home through the warm blades of grass and sit with her at table, praying that God would protect their father from any harm in the fields of battle. Then, as the light died out, his mother would tell him stories of centuries long past – of knights and ladies, of saintly men and portentous miracles – and he'd close his eyes in peaceful sleep. Blessed were those days – blessed was that simple innocence and happiness – only too soon replaced by fasts and vigils, hours of meditation and arid study, his soul pent in a solitary cell, his mind forced to the ground or within itself, prevented from reaching out to the true light of the universe...

The guard came back and asked them to follow. They were ushered into a smaller room, not dissimilar in style from the one they had just left. The door was closed behind them as they uncowled their heads. Pope Pius was sitting in a red velvet chair near the far wall, wearing a scarlet camauro and mozzetta over his white vestment. To his left stood a portly cardinal. The Pope shifted in his chair, as if about to get up and greet them, but Ambrogio extended an arm and advanced towards him with little hurried steps, while Giordano kneelt on the cold stone and bowed his head.

"*Dilecte fili et frater*," Pius said.

The two men embraced, as tears welled in their eyes. The Pope stepped back to look at his friend. "*Bonum iter fecisti? Sine cura?*"

"My legs are not what they used to be, dear Father," Ambrogio replied, still in Latin. His familiar tone, apparent even in that ancient tongue, surprised the young novice near the door. "I am old. I even doubted I could make it to Rome to answer your summons."

"I wouldn't have troubled you unless it was necessary to God's work," Pius said. "We need your help, brother. The Venerable Iohannes Baptista, Bishop of Nardò, has passed away. We cannot delay a new appointment, and we have decided that you should continue his work in those lands."

"But Father," said Ambrogio, struggling to his knees in front of the Pope, "you know how old I am – my strength is failing. I was reluctant to accept when you made me Provincial, and now…"

"Rise, brother, and take heart. You have always been prompt in answering God's call: this is not the time to hesitate or refuse."

The great evils afflicting the world, the threat from the Lutherans in the north, the danger from the infidels in the east, the laxity of morals, the aberrations of philosophy, the temptations of sin – Pope Pius urged Ambrogio to remember his calling.

"You are one of the pillars of our Church," he continued. "You are indispensable to us."

Ambrogio's protests soon died down, and they began to talk about the time when they studied under the same tutors in Bologna and worked together in Como. The two saintly men, thought Giordano, without glancing up, must have known each other for close to fifty years.

"And that young man knelt over there," resounded the voice of the cardinal standing next to Pius, "is he the novice who sent His Holiness that most curious book concerning Noah's Ark?"

Giordano blinked, not knowing whether to reply.

"Yes," answered Ambrogio, "he is the most brilliant *puer* in our school. *Propius huc accede, fili.*"

Giordano rose to his feet and walked up to join Ambrogio in front of Pope Pius and the cardinal.

"Remind me, my son, what is your name?" asked Pius.

"Iordanus Bruni, Father."

"Iordanus…" Pius narrowed his blue eyes and seemed to consider this for a moment. "I'm told you excel in the art of artificial memory?"

"He's a true marvel of nature, Father," intervened Ambrogio, who had been Giordano's master for over a year. "He can memorize any text he's given. You will show His Holiness your skills, Iordanus."

"Scipio, please pass me that Bible," said Pius.

He opened at random the tome that the cardinal handed to him and pointed a finger to the recto page.

"Psalms," Pius said. "*Fundamenta eius in montibus sanctis.* Will you recite it for us? You can read it once, if you wish, to refresh your memory."

"There will be no need, Father," said Giordano.

CHAPTER 2

"And if the page I opened was from Joshua, from Ezekiel? From Galatians?"

"Any page, Father. From any book."

The Pope stared at him. "Well, then, recite it, this page from Psalms."

"In Latin or Hebrew, Father?"

Pius gave a little smile and exchanged a glance with the cardinal and Ambrogio.

"Hebrew."

And the room was soon filled with music – the music of the language of ancient scriptures. Without any hesitation or interruption, with a soft tone that gave his voice an almost celestial ring, Giordano brought back to life those dead verses as if conjuring them up by magic from the depths of an invisible source. The three prelates were spellbound.

"Extraordinary," Pius said. "Truly extraordinary. And how do you intend to use this skill of yours, my son, and all the knowledge that you can acquire by it?"

"In the service of the Church, Father."

"Very good, my son. Very good."

"I believe that thanks to my new system of memory, it will be possible one day to absorb, with little effort, all the fruits of human lore, past and present."

"All the fruits?" Pope Pius glanced at Ambrogio. "Earthly knowledge is not the ultimate aim of our Church or our Holy Religion. Our true objective is to defend our faith against the serpent of heresy."

"What I meant, Father, is that, you see, all this knowledge *can* be used to the greater glory of God, to make our Holy Church even more impregnable and invincible against its enemies."

"I see," Pius mused. "And this little book of yours…"

"*Noah's Ark*," said the cardinal.

"*Noah's Ark*, yes... Is it wise, my son, to choose a biblical subject for a book on mnemonics?"

"I meant no offence to religion..."

"Perhaps you meant nothing at all. It sounds so obscure and far-fetched."

"I can explain, Father."

"I am sure you can. I am sure you can. And you'd like to dedicate this work to me?"

"Only if it pleases Your Holiness." Giordano lowered his eyes to the floor.

"Well, it may please us once we have had time to read it and examine it properly. You see, my son, we are seldom granted the leisure of study and meditation these days. We are living in difficult times – times that require all our energy and courage and prayer."

"Yes, Father."

"And all our efforts must be directed towards the defence of our faith. Do you understand, my son?"

"Yes, Father."

"And you should never allow your eyes to be deflected from that aim. If you observe the precepts of our Holy Mother Church and remain true to the doctrines of our Sacred Scriptures, you may be worthy one day of rising to the highest offices in the service of God and His religion. Just take the man standing next to you as an example."

"Yes, Holy Father."

"Now off you go." Pius put his arm on Giordano's shoulder and gave him a gentle shake, so as to make him look up. "Cardinal Rebiba will take you to our library, which is the real repository of human knowledge, as sanctioned and approved by our

Holy Office. I am sure he will want to hear a great deal more about your new methods of mnemonics." The cardinal gave a slow nod of the head, and Giordano bowed and left with him.

Pope Pius watched the door close on the novice and the cardinal. He took hold of Ambrogio's arm. "There's something I don't like about that young man. He—"

"Father—"

"Imagine if someone like him – with such great powers of mind – were to deviate from the true path." He scrunched up his pointed face and stroked his beard. "Before you leave for Nardò, ensure that appropriate measures are taken to watch his movements and record anything he says, reads or writes. I'd like to receive regular reports on his conduct."

Ambrogio stared at his old friend with champing lips. "Very well, Your Holiness."

In the evening, Giordano and his superior returned to Santa Sabina in the coach of Cardinal Marcantonio da Mula, the chief librarian of the Apostolica.

"But you are too young to understand!" The cardinal was explaining a small theological point that Giordano understood very well. "You must realize that – oh no, not again."

The path of their carriage was blocked by a cortège of dark-frocked men wearing pointed hoods that concealed the whole of their faces except their eyes. They advanced with small, measured steps, chanting sombre litanies. At the head of the cortège, three bearers carried a large crucifix covered by a black veil. Among the column of people was a small wooden pushcart carrying a bare-headed man. Two hooded men flanked him, while a third kept shoving an effigy of Christ to his face for him to kiss.

"All these processions are a real nuisance," said the cardinal. "You cannot go anywhere these days without being impeded or delayed. This morning it was a procession of penitent whores from Trastevere."

Ambrogio cast a sideways glance at the cardinal: he didn't like the glibness of his tone, and found him too talkative for a man of his calling.

"Who are these people, Father?" asked Giordano.

"These must be from the Confraternity of St John the Baptist," the cardinal replied. "They're leading that poor man to his place of execution – just over there, on Campo di Flora."

"And who is he?" Ambrogio pointed at the bare-headed man in the cart with his wooden staff, a parting gift from Pope Pius.

"No one of note – some heretic, perhaps. There hasn't been an idle day for our brother inquisitors of late. You can smell it in the air."

The witticism was met with coldness by the two friars. Giordano followed the chanting procession as it inched down the street in the dimming light. The pushcart came into full view. Giordano leant out, trying to see the face of the condemned man, who kept jerking his head away from the image of Christ in a gesture of unrepentance. The hooded men continued to advance in a straight line, singing their gloomy Misereres, until the tail of the cortège cleared the way and the coach began to move again. Then, just before the cart disappeared behind the corner of a building, the prisoner turned slowly towards Giordano, stared him in the eye and gave a wan, chilling smile.

3

Giulia skipped breakfast and came out of the hotel an hour later than agreed. Peter sensed she'd passed a difficult night.

"How are you, Miss Julia?" Majed said, fussing over her. "Slept good?"

"What was all that yowling in the middle of the night?"

"You mean the morning prayer, Miss Julia? The Imam wake you up?"

The door was closed with a thump, so he turned to Peter with an embarrassed smile.

"It's OK, Majed," he said, opening the passenger door. "She'll sleep in the car. Let's go."

Once they were driving, Majed began to fiddle with a variety of switches, knobs and buttons on the dashboard.

"You see, Mr Peter?" he said. "Good car today. Back to future!" He gave one of his mad laughs. "We got air conditioning. Satnav."

Thank God it was as cool in the car as in the hotel: outside, wherever Peter looked, he saw signs of age-old aridity. The bright light blanched the roads and the buildings, the fierce heat shimmered over the tarmac, and the air was filled with a fine dust which seemed to infect the few living creatures around with a sense of drowsiness.

Al-Burj remained visible throughout the journey – it was difficult to steer the gaze away from it. But only when they were close enough to make out tiny helicopters flitting around it did he understand just how massive it was.

The approach was from one of the four bridges that linked the green island on which the Tower rested to the small city rising around the shores of an artificial lake. Hotels, high-rise business centres surrounded by cranes, a futuristic glass structure still under construction reminiscent of the Sydney Opera House – buildings that could have graced the financial district of any European capital – were dwarfed by the gigantic pyramidal skyscraper towering over them.

They went through a succession of checkpoints, until they reached a vast parking lot scattered with a handful of long cars. Once they got out, the sweltering breath of the desert engulfed them. Shielding his eyes, Peter examined the Tower from base to peak, then wiped his brow and followed the other two towards one of the entrances.

"What's that?" Peter asked, pointing at a train approaching from the south-west bridge.

"That is shuttle from airport, Mr Peter. Run every ten minute."

"It's empty."

"Hopefully full one day, Mr Peter."

Inside, the temperature was almost ice-cold. The immense open space resembled the nave of a giant cathedral, but it had the feel of a luxury-hotel lobby. Soft classical music was piped in across the hall, while flat-screen TVs hung at every corner, broadcasting corporate presentations about the construction and layout of the building. Staff roamed around in listless fashion, most of them wearing the green uniform of Biblia, the American company that ran the place.

After obtaining a pass from the registration office, they went through security and its full-height turnstiles.

"I leave you here," Majed told them. "I come back at five, Mr Peter?"

22

"Just before you go…"

He handed him a plastic bag with the Bible discovered by Giulia in her room.

"Please tell Mr Al-Rafai we found this in the hotel. I'll call him or send him an email later to explain."

"Yes, Mr Peter."

"Well, good morning!" A man in white trousers and a yellow shirt was greeting them. Bald and red as a cooked prawn, he wore a trimmed beard and a thick gold chain.

"So you guys are here to see Chris Dale, our VP?"

"We are indeed," said Peter.

"Welcome to Biblia Tower. My name's Chad Rogers. Come with me. You wanna go the fast or the scenic route?" he asked as they followed him.

"Scenic," said Giulia.

"Fast," said Peter.

"In that case, I'll take you up *scenic* and down *fast*."

They boarded an empty double-decker glass lift that could have taken a hundred people. Chad swiped a card and pressed button 199. A moment later the doors closed and they began to ride upwards at high speed. If this was scenic, Peter wondered, what was "fast" like?

For a minute or so they were surrounded by concrete, before emerging into blinding sunlight. An ever wider horizon revealed the city of Amman as a rippled vision in the distance.

On level 199 there was a suspended tunnel bridge with two long travelators moving in opposite directions. Chad guided them onto one of them, and they reached a circular hall enclosed by raised galleries of offices and surmounted by a floating roof. Behind the window of the galleries, rows of identical desks could be glimpsed, together with the shadows of their occupiers.

In the middle of the hall loomed a stunted quadrangular structure, around ten metres high, with a tinted-glass dome on top.

"The two-hundredth floor," Chad announced, pointing.

Another swipe of the card, further security procedures and a brief trip in a smaller lift took them to the VP's office. Chris Dale cut a gangly figure under the subdued natural light percolating through the glass cupola. He was pacing around as he talked into his headset, while composing a message with his thumbs on a tablet.

"Let's make a decision when the Big Board opens. I wouldn't… No, I don't think it's… Uh-huh… uh-huh…"

He gestured to them to sit down in front of his Plexiglas desk. From his sprawling position, Peter studied the man. Chris Dale looked to be in his early thirties and, like Chad, had very little hair to account for on his head. He was wearing a strange style of glasses – Google Glass, Peter suddenly realized. Through the transparent panels of the dome, Peter looked round at the surrounding offices and the people who worked in them. From that height, their watery figures were more clearly visible.

"Right, right," Dale was saying, as he continued to type. "Right. Listen, can I call you back? All right."

He looked over and smiled.

"Hi there. Mr Simms? Miss Ripetti? Good to meet you. Look, just give me two seconds while I answer an email and then I'll be with you."

At his desk, Dale tapped on his keyboard with nimble fingers, the shadow of a smirk creeping up his face.

"I'm all yours now," he said, folding the laptop and pocketing his device.

"Busy morning?" asked Peter.

"Oh, it'll get busier later on."

"When the Big Board opens."

"Right." He nodded. "So, Mr Simms – the mysterious disappearance."

"Yes."

"Well, we are as baffled and distressed as Mr Al-Rafai is – and we'll do anything we can to assist you in your inquiries. Now, first of all, let me tell you what we're about here."

"There was very little I could find out about you when I agreed to the job," Peter admitted.

"We haven't launched this new operational site yet, so we don't want to give away too much information to our competitors."

"I understand. Well, as you know, we are bound by a confidentiality agreement with our client, so you can tell us without fear."

"Sure." He took a long pause. "Our operation in Jordan is part of a much larger project. Our ambition is to have all the world's books, magazines, newspapers, pamphlets and manuscripts digitized by the year 2020."

"Really? Everything?"

"Everything. We started a few years ago with English material, and now we are moving on to content in other languages."

"So this is your Arabic outpost?"

"You could call it that."

"Big outpost," said Giulia.

"Oh, this will be the hub for many other projects. Chad will show you around the building in a while and explain."

"So," Peter said, straightening up on his chair, "back to the 'mysterious' disappearance."

"Right. We signed contracts with a number of private collectors – to get exclusive reproduction rights on some non-printed material, you know. The batch we received from Mr Al-Rafai contained, together with other books and manuscripts, some Latin papers."

"And Father Marini was sent in by the Vatican to have a look at them."

"Yes, Father Marini arrived two weeks ago to study these documents. He's an expert on… on…" He snapped his fingers twice.

"Classical philology," said Giulia.

"Right. So, around ten days in, Marini just vanishes with some of the papers."

"He didn't take the whole lot?" Peter said.

"Just one manuscript, marked in the collection 'nine hundred', or 'CM' in Latin."

"Nine hundred?"

"That's right."

"Is it possible to have a look at the rest of the material?" Giulia asked.

"Sure. Chad will take you down to the library rooms later on."

"And do you reckon it was Marini who stole the manuscript?" asked Peter. "Couldn't someone have kidnapped Marini and stolen the papers?"

"We don't know. Four days ago, Marini checked out of the building at 3.30 p.m. – and since then he hasn't come back or made contact. He hasn't returned to his hotel in Amman either."

"The Vatican?"

"They say they've not heard from him."

"You alerted the border authorities?"

"We called the airport the morning after he disappeared."

"He could have gone through the Iraqi border across the desert." Dale chuckled.

"What?"

CHAPTER 3

"Sounds a bit adventurous for a priest in his seventies."

"You never know."

"Sure. Well, we have informed all border authorities. It doesn't look like he left Jordan."

"Did he use a mobile phone?"

"A cell phone? We don't think so."

"Mr Dale—"

"Yah."

"Does the word 'Bookworm' mean anything to you at the moment?"

Dale grinned. "Bunch of crackpots."

"Sorry?"

"Oh, it's a group of… what do they call themselves, Chad?"

"Neo-Luddites."

"Right. Neo-Luddites. In the US and Europe. I believe they're against the digital revolution."

"And the digitization of books," added Chad.

"I see," Peter said. "And have they come knocking on your door?"

"A few times," said Dale. "Back home. They're not active over here."

"We got a threatening communication from them yesterday night."

Giulia turned to look at Peter.

"You did?" Dale's eyebrows arched above the rim of his eyepiece.

"Do you think they have anything to do with Father Marini and the missing manuscript?"

"I guess it's a possibility. I think that's all I've got. Are we done?"

"Yes, OK, thanks." Peter and Giulia rose from their seats.

"Been a pleasure to meet you both," Dale said, flipping his laptop back open as they left.

"You just met the new Steve Jobs," Chad said as they crossed the hall towards the fast lifts. "He was headhunted by Facebook and Microsoft, but he chose to stick around with Biblia. Real smart guy."

"How old is he?" asked Peter.

"Twenty-eight? Twenty-nine? He started working for the company straight after his PhD."

"Harvard?"

"Mm-hm. Promoted three times in two years. Now he's the second-in-command of the entire group."

The ride back to the entrance hall lived up to its billing. As Chad explained some technical detail of the Tower's construction, Peter and Giulia grabbed at the handrails with their hearts in their mouths and a vague feeling of plunging into the void. They were glad – and a little dizzy – when they stepped out of the lift.

"Shall we go straight to the library rooms?" asked Chad.

"I need a coffee first," said Giulia.

4

Naples, March 1576

That day was the beginning of spring, the season of Aries –
the time of year when, according to the ancients, the world
was created. It was also his birthday: "You were born with the
spring," his mother used to tell him when he was a child. How
appropriate, then, to start a new life on that day.

Giordano was fleeing from his monastery in Naples, from
eleven years of study, privations and pointless disquisitions,
never to go back. He had been accused of harbouring heretical
beliefs and, threatened with disciplinary proceedings, he felt
he had to leave.

He had left behind a few dear friends – brothers Pietro,
Bernardo, Lorenzo, the good old Prior Iacopo and his deputy,
Sebastiano – and a large number of enemies: chief among them
Bonifacio, that filthy sodomite, with his following of little
puers. Since his first appearance at San Domenico, Bonifacio
had made Giordano's life a torment. Whether it was envy
that moved him, or just stupidity coupled with a malicious
nature, was hard to know. Perhaps Bonifacio had even darker
motives too.

Although the allegations levelled against him were serious,
putting him in great danger, Giordano felt a certain relief at
the thought of leaving that sordid world, that weasel's nest.
He had developed a profound disgust for all the theological

subtleties of scholasticism – that stultifying verbal experience of the Godhead. As if human language could aspire to capture anything but a dim shadow of the Almighty!

More than anything else, he despised the ignominious brood of friars – for the most part coarse, corrupt, greedy, illiterate and duplicitous. How could he forget the things he had heard and seen within the cloister's walls – the jealous glance, the lustful smile, the blatant swearing, the unctuous praise? How could he forget the Most Reverend Father Nincompoop pacing up and down the lecture hall, "full of unbounded, noble wonderment" – as Petrarch would say – with the *Commentary* under his arm, shuffling the hems of his learned gown around, shaking his feet about, thrusting his chest left and right, flinging an invisible flea to the floor with his fingers? The Most Reverend Father would furrow his forehead in deep thought, then raise his eyebrows in amazement to gasp out to the sycophants surrounding him: "*Huc usque alii philosophi non pervenerunt* – no other philosopher has ever reached these heights!"

Giordano was sick of his brothers' pettiness, their bestiality, their blind, superstitious worship of empty rituals and wooden icons, their faith in the dead memory of books rather than in the powers of the living mind. Whenever they saw him sitting in his cell studying or writing, they'd scoff at him and taunt him with the words of the Scripture: "*Abiit in regionem longinquam*" – he's left for some faraway land... Oh, if only they had known how much he longed to see other countries, other ways of life, how much he craved to put an end to his walled-up existence, regain his lost freedom and devote himself to the true quest for knowledge!

A few days ago, Brother Sebastiano had come to his cell after compline, when the corridors and dormitories of San Domenico had fallen silent. His face was ash-pale.

"You must leave at once," he had whispered.

"Sebastiano! Why?"

"They are starting proceedings against you."

"Who?"

"Father Vita, the Provincial, with the help of some informers. I'm not sure who they all are, but I'll try to find out. I heard him talk to the Prior this evening."

Giordano felt the cold stones of the wall behind his back.

"What charges are these?"

"Heresy."

"Heresy?" There was scarcely a worse charge that could be made.

"He mentioned that old incident when you were a novice. But also some more recent things. There are a hundred and thirty separate allegations against you."

Giordano gave a soft laugh.

"This is not a laughing matter, brother."

"But I have done nothing, Sebastiano, I swear. Unless they have read something in my mind or in my eyes."

"Or in your papers and your books." Sebastiano nodded towards the desk, where a volume of St Jerome's *Works* with annotations by Erasmus laid open. Giordano had bought the banned text from a bookseller for a full *tarì* – which is what it must have cost the monastery to pay a diligent friar to excise all the dangerous material from the library's copy.

"Is it possible you're exaggerating?"

"No. Remember what happened to Brother Raimondo. You could be sent to prison, to the galleys – or face the inquisitors."

"I could defend myself."

"You know that is impossible. Take my advice and leave."

Giordano's eyes darted around his cell.

31

"How?"

"Go about your things as usual tomorrow morning. I'll let you slip out after Mass. If anything goes wrong, you didn't see me and you didn't talk to me tonight."

"Sebastiano—"

"God be with you." Sebastiano turned and disappeared down the corridor.

Giordano stared into the void for hours, sleepless in the night, then got up and started bundling up his papers. He took the St Jerome tome and another book that was deemed pernicious and padded through the darkness to the latrine, where he flung both of them down the hole. As he went back to his cell, he thought he saw a shifting shadow at the far end of the corridor. He returned to his bed and stayed awake until daybreak.

Later, when Sebastiano helped him out of the monastery's doors and he stepped into the teeming streets of Naples, he looked back at the high walls of San Domenico feeling like a stray dog: he did not know what to do or where to go. His first impulse was to board a vessel to Rome or Genoa, but that is what they would expect when they searched for him – it would be better to wait a few days before embarking. Or perhaps he could travel by road to the north, and then across the Alps? But that would be expensive, and he had almost no money. So he decided to walk back to Nola, his native town: he could ask his parents for help, and take the opportunity to say his last goodbyes before leaving the Kingdom.

It was late in the afternoon when he reached the main square of the town, with the imposing Palazzo Orsini overlooking it and an implacable sun still beating down. The Palazzo now belonged to the brethren of the Society of Jesus, and for a moment Giordano thought he might knock on their door and ask for some water – but he could already see ahead of him, not far away, Mount Cicala and its ruined castle, near which lay his parents' cottage, so he decided to continue on his way.

His father, white-haired and bare-chested, was tilling the fields in front of the house. Looking up, he dropped his hoe and ran up to embrace him.

"Filippo!"

Filippo – his old name, before he had taken his vows. Giordano's eyes welled up to see a tear streak down his father's face into his beard. They had not seen each other for years.

"Fraulissa!" he shouted. "Fraulissa!"

His mother appeared at the door and gave a little cry. Her expression changed from surprise to delight, and then to concern.

"What brings you here, all of a sudden?" she said, embracing him.

He didn't want to lie, but didn't want to make them worry either.

"I am leaving for Rome – perhaps even Lombardy."

"When will you come back?"

"I may be away for a while, so I thought I'd pay you a visit."

They had a simple supper in the open air, and his mother informed him about the doings of the town. Martinello's son had married Costantino's daughter. Albenzio's wife, Vasta, had had a bad fall in the fields which had left her with a limp. For the first time in many, many years, Giordano felt the rays of the setting sun on his skin, smelt the fragrance of the grass from the fields. He had no prayer to make other than the one that gushed spontaneously from his heart when he extinguished the candles in his old room. And instead of fear, what filled his mind were lines of poetry, and plans for great works of philosophy.

He made his departure on the third day. His father came to him in his room and gave him a small purse with some money in it.

"It's all we can give you, son," he said. "I have been out of service for weeks. I may get another call, but I am not getting any younger, you know."

"Thank you, Father."

"Write to us, if you can."

"I will." It had always been hard to speak to his father – a man of very few words and a bit surly, like himself – and now, with a gulf not just of years but of learning between them, it seemed more difficult than ever. "I may never return, Father."

Giovanni Bruno nodded and turned aside to stare at the ground. "Do what you have to do, son, and don't look back."

His parents walked with him to Nola and saw him off on a hired donkey bound for Naples. When he got there, he paid a short visit to a friend, a bookseller near the Church of Sant'Angelo a Nilo, and entrusted him with a message for Brother Sebastiano, telling him where and to whom he should send his letters if he wanted to contact him, then jumped on the first cart for Rome.

After an arduous two-day journey, he reached his destination, the monastery of Santa Maria sopra Minerva, where he hoped to see one of his old mentors, Father Michele. Perhaps his friend could help him get an audience with the prior, the famous theologian Sisto Fabri – or even with the new Pope, Gregory – so that he could defend his name against his enemies' aspersions. If that was not possible and he was unable to obtain protection in Rome, then maybe he could remain as a guest for a few weeks, lying low, before setting off again for the north of Italy or France.

Michele greeted him like a long-lost son, but within moments a cloud of anxiety seemed to descend over him.

"You should know, two brothers from San Domenico, Antonio and Dionisio, arrived on Tuesday."

"I know them. What of it, Father?"

"The same day Father Serafino Cavalli, the Master of the Order, left for Naples."

"I doubt it's anything to do with my escape."

"It could be. You cannot risk staying here for long. The inquisitors may soon be on your tracks."

Giordano spent two fretful weeks in the monastery, burying his head deep in his cowl, getting out early and returning late in the evening, always careful not to be seen by the two Neapolitan friars, who were still staying at La Minerva. To try to speak in these circumstances to Father Fabri was out of the question, although he went to see him lecture at La Sapienza more than once.

One evening there was an unusual amount of chatter in the refectory. One of the brothers visiting from San Domenico was dead.

"They found his body this morning in the Tiber," a Dominican was saying.

"With all the killings and robberies happening in Rome these days," said another, "one should not get out at night."

"There was a witness. It looks like it was another brother who pushed him into the waters."

"They come from Naples and think they can pick up men on the street like they do there in that filthy city. What was his name?"

"Antonio, I believe."

Giordano, with his head down, chewed on his bread and avoided Michele's gaze.

After a sleepless night, they met soon after dawn in the cloister. Michele had two letters for him.

"They've just arrived from San Domenico."

The first was unsigned, but was from Brother Sebastiano.

I hope God has granted you a safe passage to Rome. The day before you left, Brothers Antonio and Dionisio were dispatched to La Minerva with the charges against you. Now the General is here. A brother must have seen you throw the books in the latrine, because they have been retrieved, and have been added as a proof to your list of indictments. Leave Rome at once. I confided to one of your trusted friends, and he asked me to enclose a note from him. I am writing this in great haste and at the risk of being discovered and betrayed. Please destroy this letter as soon as you've read it. May God be with you.

The second was written in the familiar hand of his young friend Lorenzo.

Dear brother, I know your enemies: they are Bonifacio and Antonio. They have been spying on you, finding every pretext to slander your name and instigating the Provincial to inform the Holy Office. I believe they may have also been sending letters and reports to Rome. Yesterday Bonifacio was strutting his big belly down the corridors, laughing and crowing out loud: "The Nolan's left for some faraway land!" His little friend may still be there at La Minerva, so be watchful. May God rescue the lamb from the jaws of the lion.

Bonifacio's little friend was dead and probably burning in hellfire by now, but there was no shortage of enemies who could do him harm. As for that fattening calf, Bonifacio – he would pay for his sins one day, in this life or another…

"I must go," Giordano said, crumpling the letters in his palm. "The pack of demons is at my heels, and they are planning my destruction."

"Where will you go?"

"I don't know. Genoa, Venice perhaps."

"No, not Venice – I have heard the city is scourged by a plague: they may close the gates of Rome soon too. Make your way to the north-west – and across the mountains, if you can."

"I will. Farewell, dear brother."

"Farewell. May God help you in your journey."

When the door of Santa Maria sopra Minerva closed behind him, Giordano stood still for some moments, staring at the cobbles under his feet. He was alone in this world, naked like a newborn baby, like our old father Adam – or rather like the Sage Bias, with only his mind to give him support and consolation. Where did his path lie? Wherever it was, it would have to lead as far as possible from the oppressive and vindictive hand of the Church of Rome.

5

"They don't call this thing coffee in my country," Giulia was saying, as they sat in an almost empty Starbucks the size of a baseball field.

"No? What do they call it, then?" asked Peter.

"They don't call it anything. We just don't drink it."

"So," Chad said, rising from his chair, "I'm gonna show you our editorial centre first, then I'll take you to the library and finally to our Project Earth rooms."

This time their journey was downwards: the lift took them to the fifteenth floor below ground, around halfway down the hidden base of the Tower. They followed a labyrinthine series of empty corridors and rooms to emerge into a huge circular open-plan space bustling with activity and noise, similar to a newsroom. A belt of large plasma screens ran around the walls, showing broadcasts from dozens of TV channels around the world, while rows and rows of operators stared at monitors, typing away on keyboards, tablets and phones.

"This is where it all happens," Chad said, with a swipe of his hand. "Or at least a great part of it – the scanning takes place on a lower level."

"What are these people?" asked Peter. "Editors?"

"Well" – Chad swung his head from side to side – "we call them 'content processors'. They receive the content in raw digital form, work through it, run some prep scripts, tag it and then disseminate it through all the available channels. Their biggest task is to make the content searchable and visible on every Internet platform. Come with me – I want to introduce you to someone who may be useful to your inquiry."

The man in question was perched on a kneeling chair in his own private office, surveying the images on four ultra-thin screens arranged in a semicircle around his desk. Probably in his late twenties, he had a shaven head, thick black-rimmed glasses and a wooden, shard-shaped earring. He mumbled a hello as they trooped into his office, but didn't look up.

"Hi Jim," Chad said. "How are you?"

"Busy."

"These are the guests I told you about. Jim is in charge of all our IT, including the old NICK system."

"Network, Information and Communications Kernel," Jim explained, looking up at last.

"*Old Nick*?" Peter smirked.

"We've got a new NICK on the way."

"Old Nick means the Devil," Peter told Giulia, who wasn't getting the joke.

"If you have any technical questions about our programme or operations," Chad continued, "Jim's the person to ask. Jim, you'll join us on our tour of the library and Project Earth, right?"

"I'm actually in the middle of something. Let me ask my colleague next door."

He got up from his chair and with three long strides was out of his office. He came back with a disappointed look.

"Not around," he said. "Let's go."

They took the lift and went down a few more floors. This time, the corridors and rooms they walked through were lined with lockers, racks, trolleys and movable shelving units full of bundled manuscripts and time-worn books of all sizes, from folios to duodecimos. Even in that dry, aseptic environment, the smell of musty paper – of real or imagined dust – seemed to catch in the throat.

"Most of this material," Chad explained, "is from some of the major libraries and private collections in the Middle East and the Gulf. We already have a deal in place with Google and other companies to access their content, so there is little duplication of work. We are more interested in rare publications and manuscript material. Our aim is to become a one-stop-shop resource for readers, students and academics all over the world."

They reached a vast room that was immersed in near-total darkness, from which emerged sudden flashes and scattered pools of white light. The haloed, chiaroscuroed faces of people handling books over glass-topped lecterns became more and more visible the nearer they got. There were dozens of them: they placed the open volumes face-up on the glass surface in front of them, waited for the beam of light to sweep across, lifted the book, turned one page and repeated their actions.

"This is one of the scanning rooms," said Chad.

"There's five scanning rooms," Jim explained, taking off his glasses and rubbing the bridge of his nose. "Each room has a hundred Fujitsu scanners, operated round the clock on four six-hour shifts."

"How many books is that a day?" asked Giulia.

"An experienced operator can scan around six pages or spreads every minute, which means three hundred and sixty scans an hour. With fatigue, machines going out of service and technical failure, the actual productivity is about seventeen per cent lower. With that taken into account, our target is 2.75 million scans a day—"

Peter whistled.

"Or a billion scans a year. That's several hundred terabytes' worth of memory."

"Wow. Busy bees. Then what happens?"

"Digital ingestion."

"Which means, in simple terms?"

Jim massaged his eyelids. "It gets prepped up, OCR'd, double- or treble-key verified depending on accuracy requirements, and so on."

"But it's the library you really want to see, right?" Chad said.

"The library, yes," Giulia said.

Located three floors below, it was modelled on the Rijksmuseum Research Library – all wooden shelves, iron pillars and glass cabinets – but on a vast scale.

Giulia turned around, feeling tiny in that immensity, gazing up at bookcases ranged on three levels, taking in the staircases, the balustrade galleries. "But this must be four, five times bigger than the Biblioteca Nazionale in Rome."

"Yup," Chad confirmed.

Scattered far apart were large reading desks where, in the churchlike silence, scholarly figures sat in deep consultation, made pencil notes on paper or wrote on their laptops.

"Rare Books and Manuscripts section," whispered Chad. "For older texts and handwritten documents that can't be digitized using optical-character-recognition software but must be manually transcribed. The people you see here are scholars who specialize in a particular field – Egyptologists, Sanskritists, Semitic-language experts… Wait, great, there's Helen."

He led them to an office where a woman was waiting by the door.

"Helen Barnet, head librarian," Chad said, as she ushered them in and closed the door.

"Pleased to meet you," Peter said.

"Likewise."

"I think," Giulia said, shaking hands with her, "it's you who will be most important to us."

"I'll certainly do my best. I've got something to show you." She led them to a table in the corner of the room that was laden with material. "Everything here is the collection Father Marini was working on before he disappeared," Helen explained.

"May I?" Giulia said, reaching out her hand.

"No need for gloves?" asked Peter.

"No, it's OK," Helen said. "Human skin's better than latex or cotton. It's important not to lose the sense of touch when you handle fragile or brittle papers."

The octavo-sized volume Giulia had picked up was bound in vellum, with a ribbed spine which showed, written in ink, the title at the top and the date at the bottom. It was the *editio princeps* of one of Giordano Bruno's so-called "mnemonics" works, *De umbris idearum – The Shadow of Ideas* – published in Paris in 1582. The front and back covers were worn out at the edges and presented clusters of tiny holes that pierced through the vellum and the inside paper lining, but did not seem to affect any of the pages of the book. On the verso of the front board were scribbled some numbers in seventeenth-century script, and on the title page, under the dedication, was scrawled "P. Isar. O.P.", probably the name of some long-dead librarian or collector. The laid paper was yellow and blotched, and the strong, smudgy black type showed through, often in embossed relief. The binding was surprisingly sturdy for such a slim volume, with thickly knotted head and tail bands, and the sewing was visible in the gutter of each folded signature. For Giulia, it was an object of beauty.

"There are twenty-one printed books in this collection that Marini was looking at," Helen said, "including a nine-volume edition of Aquinas's *Summa*, and a large number of unsorted papers, as you can see. They are mostly in Latin, but some of the material appears to be in Italian. It's very difficult to read. Father Marini took all the documents marked 'CM', which amounted to over seven hundred sheets of various sizes."

"How could he have stolen such a sizable part of the collection without anyone noticing?" asked Giulia.

"The thing is," Helen said, "Father Marini is a renowned scholar – and a religious man. I trusted him. Everyone trusted him. We think he may have carried off the material little by little during the time he was here."

"Is it possible to start the work now?" Giulia said.

"I'm afraid we'll be closing soon. But we're open all day to-morrow, from 8.30 a.m. until 4.30 p.m."

There was just enough time for a quick visit to the Project Earth programme, some thirty floors below ground. It was Jim who took them there, as Chad was called back to his office on some urgent matter.

"We are still running it as a pilot," Jim was saying, as they stepped out of the lift. "It's a kind of rudimentary time-space machine" – Peter laughed – "using 5D technology."

"Jesus Christ, I am getting old. I thought there were three dimensions, four at pinch. What's 5D?"

"You've got your traditional 3D framework, and then you add sensory and interactive."

"OK, I'll give it a go."

In separate chambers, they were strapped into cockpit-like seats and fitted with masks and headsets.

"So, you've got all these options," Jim's voice said through their headsets. Different places in different times were scrolling before their vision. "Just make your choice and then…"

"And then what?" Giulia asked.

"Then enjoy…"

"Video games!" Peter exclaimed, as his senses were assailed with sights, sounds, movements and – yes, it was true, even smells.

London, in the year 2084. He was piloting a flying car in the middle of heavy air traffic. "*Star Wars*, here I come," he said. While he navigated his way in the sky, trying not to crash into other aircraft or the surrounding skyscrapers, he looked round for some landmark. But London was almost unrecognizable: wherever he turned his eyes, futuristic buildings rose up, beaming lights from their windows and images from colossal screens attached to their glass walls.

"St Paul's!" he said at last. "Still standing…"

Giulia had chosen "Florence in the time of Leonardo". She was walking through empty streets and low, elegant buildings, meeting the occasional passer-by dressed in quaint Renaissance style. "*Ma che…*" A stray digital dog limped past. It was like being suspended inside Piero della Francesca's Ideal City – a cold, geometric place with no life in it…

"Ha!" A big sign saying "Museum" was just one of the inaccuracies and anachronisms she was beginning to notice. What next, a Pepsi-Cola logo? She followed a red arrow and was guided into a vast hall where pale copies of paintings by Raphael, Titian and Giorgione hung among the works of other artists of the Rinascimento. Tut-tutting – was this a glimpse of the kind of artificial, solipsistic world people would inhabit one day? – she moved on to an exhibition of sculptures, Michelangelo's *Pietà*, Donatello's *David*, Cellini's *Perseus* – and was about to enter the building's library when the vision disappeared.

"Just a little taster for you both," Jim said. "Come on out."

"Impressive," Peter was saying.

"My favourite one," said Jim, "is Rome in Nero's time. You can actually smell the buildings burning and feel the heat of the flames. And these are just rough pilots. In future you'll be able to access just about anything: visit all the world's monuments, wade across rivers, descend into mines, catacombs – even enter your own dreams."

"I hope I am dead by then," Giulia said.

"You don't like it? Everybody loves it."

"Sure." She laughed. "I'm sorry, but I don't get it. If you can smell, touch and see things for real, why do you want to do it through a machine?"

"Because it's fun."

"Fun, yes. Everything has to be fun today. People must be entertained all the time. But it's not good. It's not good to kill your senses and your imagination, no? People today prefer to escape reality and feed with fake visions."

"*On* fake visions," corrected Peter.

"OK, so I'm Italian," she said, shrugging. "When your understanding of Italian prepositions is better than my understanding of English ones, then you can correct me, OK?"

Chad hurtled out of the lift at the farther end of the corridor and rushed up to them.

"They found Father Marini," he announced.

"Fantastic," said Peter. "Where is he?"

"Hanging from the North West bridge."

6

London, 14th February 1584

"Could they speak Latin?"

"Yes."

"Were they gentlemen?"

"Yes."

"Of good repute?"

"Yes."

"Men of learning?"

"Of a *little* learning."

"*Doctores philosophiæ?*"

"Yes – at least judging by their long velvet gowns and white beards. One of them was bent down under the weight of two neck chains. Real gold, not brass. The other had a dozen gold rings on two fingers. When he moved his hand, you were dazzled."

"Were they familiar with Greek?"

"Yes, with Greek wine – and beer too."

Master Smith burst out laughing at Giordano's quip. They were walking back from the Change to the French Ambassador's residence in Salisbury Court, where Giordano lived on the top floor, overlooking one of the most crowded areas of London. The sun had already set: the fog and the persistent drizzle gave the badly lit streets and their straggling inhabitants an eerie, almost infernal look.

"Well then, who won the disputation?" asked Smith in his heavily accented Italian, as they crossed the Fleet ditch coming from Ludgate.

"No one did. No one ever wins a disputation. A man takes up black and another man white, and they beat themselves bloody with words. But neither of them moves one inch from his convictions or gets any wiser. Do you know the story of the two blind beggars who sat by the entrance of the Archbishop's Palace in Naples?"

Smith shook his head.

"One of them claimed he was Guelf, the other Ghibelline. So they started to give each other a taste of their sticks – until a man stepped in between them and said: 'You wretched fools – tell me: what does *Guelf* mean? What does *Ghibelline* mean?' The first one didn't know what to say, the other mumbled: 'Well, I'm very fond of my master – and he's a Ghibelline.'"

Smith chuckled. "And did you come to blows with the noble and learned personages?"

"No. It was a much more civilized affair – unlike last year in Oxford." Giordano darted a smiling glance at his companion. "I did most of the talking: the others just sat listening, grinning and scoffing. They looked at me as if I was a madman. But they are the fools."

There was a short pause, then Smith said: "What brought you to our country, Signor Bruno?"

Giordano shrugged his shoulders and gave out a long sigh. Everyone asked him the same tiresome question – and he had no answer that satisfied him. He had been fleeing from city to city and from nation to nation out of necessity, not choice.

"I've come in search of freedom," was his clipped reply. Then he added as an afterthought: "Which is precious, as he must know who gave his life for it."

"Dante."

"Dante." There was a long pause. "The heroic mind would rather fall trying to achieve a lofty goal than reach perfection in vile endeavours." He stopped and looked to his left. "I can see the roofs of my lodgings. Please do not trouble yourself: I can walk there on my own."

"It's been an honour to have your company and enjoy your conversation today."

"Your Italian is excellent, Master Smith. I wish I could express myself with the same fluency and elegance in your language."

"This is a great compliment coming from you, Signor Bruno." Then he added in English: "Thank you."

Giordano bowed. "Goodbye."

Giordano quickened his pace across the dark cobblestones of Salisbury Court. His mind was racing through a tangle of ideas, images and events: the outline of new works, fragments of Latin dialogue, the obstacles and the expense of getting his books printed in England, the few friends and the many enemies he had made, his worn-out clothes, his awkward situation as an uprooted exile in the household of the French Ambassador – a man who had problems of his own, with his wife gravely ill and King Henry delaying the payment of his salary. He felt his head burning and his heart pounding. Was his a heroic life or just a desperate one – like that of the blind multitudes around him?

He was surprised to see Giovanni Florio pacing in front of the entrance to the Ambassador's house, with his friend Matthew Gwynne standing by the door.

"Is anything the matter, Master Florio?" Giordano said.

"Ah, here you are, at last! We've been looking for you everywhere."

"Why?"

"Why? Don't you know what day it is today?"

Giordano thought for a moment. "Ash Wednesday."

"Yes, and Sir Greville has invited us to supper. Your prodigious memory has failed you, for once."

Matthew Gwynne, who understood Italian, smiled.

"I had not forgotten," said Giordano. "How can one forget being invited to a meal on the first day of Lent? I waited until after noontime, but heard no news, so I thought the engagement had been cancelled and went to see some friends."

"Well, never mind. Let's go: we're late. There are many learned gentlemen and distinguished scholars waiting for you, determined to dispute the night away – including your namesake, Dr Browne."

"What, now?"

"Yes, now."

"At this time of night?" He laughed. "I was expecting to settle the matter by daylight, not candlelight."

"Some *cavalieri* wanted to come," said Gwynne, in shaky Italian. "They couldn't earlier, so they came for supper."

"It's beginning to rain," protested Giordano.

"This pitter-patter has never been called rain in England before. Come on."

"Where are we going?"

"Not far – we'll be there in no time."

He followed John Florio and his friend through the dark alley. He expected them to turn left in the direction of Fleet Street, but instead they made towards the river front.

"It will be much quicker," said Florio.

They soon reached the pier of Lord Buckhurst's palace, and Gwynne started shouting "Oars! Oars!" in the hope of finding a rowing boat to take them upriver to Whitehall. They stood there in the cold and rain for longer than it would have taken them to go on foot at a leisurely pace.

In the end, two boatmen replied from afar and slowly approached the river bank. After a long exchange as to where the gentlemen were going and why, and how much they were going to pay, the boatmen docked by the lowest step of the short pier. The younger of the two – who looked over sixty years of age – helped Gwynne and Florio onboard, while the other, even older, possibly his father, reached out a shrivelled hand to assist Giordano. As he stepped in with a cautious foot, the boat gave a loud crack.

"Good Lord," he said. "I hope to God this man's not Charon." Gwynne and Florio laughed.

"This vessel," he continued, resting on the gunwale, which creaked at the touch, "must be as old as Noah's Ark. Surely it's a relic from the time of the Flood. Now I believe the story of the singing walls of Thebes: just listen how it whistles when the water seeps into its cracks – hear the melody of piping reeds…"

They all laughed again – but it was nervous laughter.

The craft pulled away from the shore and began to contend with a resolute current, under the faint shimmer of a lantern. The boatmen bent and straightened their backs with great effort, but the boat only seemed to crawl forward.

"I think we're going to be here for a while," Giordano said.

"Then maybe we should put our time to some use," said Florio, "and sing to the accompaniment of these Tartarean tunes. I am sure these two old oafs won't mind."

"One of them won't even hear," Giordano said.

"Ha!"

Florio threw back his head to intone the lines of a madrigal from Ariosto:

"Deh dove, senza me, dolce mia vita,
rimasa sei sì giovane e sì bella?..."

And Giordano, ignoring the surly mutterings of the two oarsmen, responded with the grieving Saracen's lament against the fickleness of women:

"Oh femminile ingegno, egli dicea,
come ti volgi e muti facilmente,
contrario oggetto proprio de la fede!
Oh infelice, oh miser chi ti crede!"

They were still making slow progress over the dark waters of the river. On the right-hand side they recognized the banks of the Temple: not yet a third of the way to their destination.

"This is absurd," said Giordano. "We're going to be here all night. Can't you ask them to hurry up?"

He heard Florio cajoling them, pleading with them – and then swearing at them as they started to steer the boat towards the shore.

"What are they doing?" said Giordano. "Catching their breath?"

Gwynne and Florio were berating the boatmen, then Florio told Giordano:

"They're setting us down. They won't go any farther."

"What? Why?"

"They say their lodgings are around here."

"Offer them more money."

"I tried."

"Try again. We're in the middle of the Styx. We'll get butchered."

A few more urgent expostulations followed, but to no avail: the three passengers were offloaded without ceremony, the agreed fee was insisted on and, to avoid further problems, the boatmen were even thanked for their services.

Giordano watched the dim light of the boat's lantern glide away from them. "Now what?"

"They said that if we go straight ahead we'll reach the main road."

"You mean we'll have to wade through this muddy wasteland?"

"It doesn't look like there's a way round it," said Gwynne.

"That's a pathway fit for a pig. Well, come on then, follow me…"

He set off, and within five steps found himself ankle-deep in mire.

"I can't move my legs! *Aiuto!*"

Gwynne tried and failed to hold back a throaty chortle, then the three of them burst out laughing. They wobbled through the mud like drunken men, hoping to get through to firm ground, but were soon faced with a high brick wall. They trudged along it for a while, only to be stopped by another wall.

"We're doomed," said Gwynne.

"What a wonderful Garden of Delight to be trapped in!" said the Nolan.

"I can't see where we're going."

"We're lost."

"At least it's stopped raining."

"I'm knee-deep in sludge," said Gwynne.

"Poor Candido," Florio said, using his friend's nickname. "You'll get all sullied…"

But the jesting was becoming strained. They pressed on in silence and, with despair looming over them, cursed under their breath.

"We might as well be blind in this darkness," Giordano said. "Since our eyes can't help us, let's follow each other's feet."

At length they reached shallow marshland and were able to climb up the river bank, until they came across a runnel that afforded some dry ground on one of its pebbly sides. They staggered up the slope for a while, and finally they heard voices and saw the feeble reflection of light: a road at last.

"*Tandem læta arva tenemus!*" cried Florio.

"A real Elysium after our ramblings in purgatory," said Giordano.

"But where are we?" said Gwynne.

They looked around, trying to find their bearings.

"I don't believe it," said Florio. "We're not even fifty yards from where we left..."

"What are you—"

"That's Salisbury Court, just over there – isn't it?"

The laughter, washed with curses, swept over them like a wave, and if it subsided from one of them, it broke again on another, until they were weak with the exertion of fighting it.

"Shall we try to get another boat?" Florio said.

"Shall we just drown ourselves instead?" Giordano asked. "It's been a long journey, and I'm tired. I think we should make our way back to our lodgings, Giovanni."

"What do you mean? Those gentlemen are still waiting for us. It would be ill-mannered to disappoint them."

"It was ill-mannered of them not to send us horses or a boat at such a time of night and in such foul weather. If we are of so little importance to them, I doubt they really care whether we go or not."

"We'll go on foot. It would be a great discourtesy to ignore Sir Greville's invitation. Come on – in twenty minutes we'll be there."

"Are you in earnest? We're drenched, and so covered in mud we can hardly walk. And it's too dark and cold to be around on the streets. We've had enough bad omens tonight: we should go back."

"Giordano!"

"*Mejor es perder que más perder*, as the Spanish say."

"Well, it will be a great loss indeed if you don't go. There's a gentleman there you'll be delighted to meet."

"And who would that gentleman be?"

"It is meant to be a surprise, so I cannot tell you. Will you come?"

Giordano sighed and groaned, brushing at the mud on his cloak.

"Let's go back to the Ambassador's house, Giordano. We'll wash our faces and have a change of clothes. We shall dignify our appearance."

Giordano sighed. "I have no other clothes."

"I'm sure we'll find something for you."

So they walked back to Salisbury Court at a quick pace – Florio and Gwynne singing more cheerful lines from Ariosto, Giordano brooding, his weary mind full of dark thoughts.

7

Chris Dale, VP of Biblia, looked at the pictures as Chad handed them to him, then passed them one by one on to Peter and Giulia. "Poor man. Did they find anything on him?"

"Nothing," said Chad.

"God knows what happened to the manuscript."

"Perhaps he sold it," said Giulia. "It's very valuable."

"Or perhaps it's somewhere in Amman," said Peter. "There's no way to know at the moment. We'll have to sit tight and wait until we have more elements." He turned to Giulia to his left. "Have you decided what you want to do? I hope this awful death and what happened last night haven't put you off?"

The Italian gazed at him for a few seconds. "I want to stay. For now. Though if the papers weren't so interesting I'd be on the first plane to Rome."

"Well, in that case," said Dale, "it may be sensible for you to review some of your practical arrangements. We have some wonderful suites on the top floors. You are more than welcome to stay there during your research and investigation. This will save you travelling each day from Amman."

"And it will be much safer," added Chad.

Peter looked at Giulia, who nodded.

"All right," he said. "We'll check out of the Grand Hyatt tomorrow morning, then."

"Great. And if there's anything else you need during your stay here, just let me or Chad know."

A young woman in green uniform came into the conference room and leant over to whisper something in Dale's ear.

"Seems your driver's here," he said, "so we'll see you tonight."

"Tonight?" Peter said. "You mean tomorrow?"

"No: tonight. Aren't you going?"

"Where?"

"Today's the birthday of Mr Al-Rafai's son – and we're all invited to his party."

"A party? How old is his son?"

"Ten."

"Ah."

One hundred and ninety-nine floors below, in the vast lobby of Al-Burj, Majed ran up to Peter and Giulia when they emerged from the lift.

"Sorree, sorree, Mr Peter," he said.

"About what?"

"You give me plastic bag and I forget."

"You forgot to give it to Mr Al-Rafai?"

"No, I forget to tell you he invite you to his home tonight. For celebration. Sorree. Sorree." He struck his palm on his forehead.

"That's all right, Majed. Let's go."

In the car, Peter and Giulia considered the death of Father Marini. Had the Jesuit been killed? If so, by whom? Would the killers be linked to the people who had put the Bible with the "BOOK WORM" message in Giulia's room? And why would he have been killed? For contravening some agreement? For refusing to give up the manuscript he had stolen? For knowing too much? Or had he hanged himself out of guilt or remorse, or because something had gone terribly wrong?

"I doubt he killed himself," said Giulia.

"Why?"

"A religious man wouldn't do that. It's a sin."

"So is theft."

"Suicide is a mortal sin. The worst sin."

"Maybe you're right." Peter squeezed his eyes almost shut, thinking it through. "What could prompt a reputable scholar like Marini to steal those scripts? They must be very important. It would be good to know what these documents were."

"Perhaps when I look at the other papers we can find out."

Majed picked them up again from the Hyatt just after nine o'clock. They drove for over half an hour – first through the streets of Amman and then north, across the dry open plains surrounding the city – until even the lights of Al-Burj became invisible.

They wound their way up a steep road and reached the gates of a walled compound, joining a long queue of cars waiting to be admitted.

"Many beople tonight," said Majed as they crawled forward. "Rich beople."

Armed guards could be seen patrolling the grounds along the perimeter of the wall as the muffled throb of music echoed in the distance and multicoloured laser beams swerved across the night sky.

Majed parked the car inside the compound and told Giulia and Peter he'd wait for them there.

"We shouldn't be too late," said Peter.

"Not worry. Enjoy yourself."

They followed the other guests down a paved path across a lawn so improbably green that it might have been airlifted that morning from Scotland or Wales. A cluster of white-uniformed waiters holding drink trays welcomed them into the gardens of

Mr Al-Rafai's mansion, which rose in floodlit majesty to their left. Round tables laden with flowers, candles and ice sculptures were scattered around the edges of a monumental swimming pool, which was surrounded by even rows of palm trees and gas lamps resembling flame-topped Greek columns. At the farther end of the gardens was a large concert stage, complete with megascreens on both sides, where the members of a rock band busied themselves strumming on guitars, pogoing and squawking into microphones.

Peter grabbed a glass of white wine and walked with Giulia towards a small group of Biblia people with Chris Dale at the centre of it, still wearing his fancy eyepiece.

"Hi guys," Dale shouted, raising his wineglass. "How's it going?"

"Any news?" Peter said.

"About what?"

"About Marini."

"Oh well." He gave a little laugh and sipped at the wine. "I try not to bring work with me when I step out of the office. I like to switch off." Just then his phone rang. "Will you excuse me?" And he peeled out of sight.

"One of the security guards," Chad chipped in, "was saying that it was probably suicide."

"How does he know?"

"He's heard it from a friend who works in the Jordanian police."

"That will have to be verified." Peter turned to Helen, who was wearing a liberally cleavaged blue dress, and blinked. "Did you smell any alcohol when he was around?"

The librarian shook her head.

"Do you know which hotel he was staying in?"

"I think it was the Marriott," said Chad. "The one in the Shmeisani district."

"Has his room been inspected?"

"Yes. No trace of the manuscript."

"It may be worth running some other checks."

"Such as?"

"Minibar bills – that sort of thing."

"Long shot."

"Well, we don't have very much at the moment, do we?" Peter emptied his glass, which was immediately refilled by a passing waiter. "What are the Vatican saying?"

"Nothing, as far as I know. They've issued no statement."

"Have they confirmed the identity of the man in the photos?"

"I believe so."

"So what will happen now?"

"I guess they'll get the body repatriated."

"Will they send someone in to investigate or to continue Marini's work?"

"I doubt it. Not in the current situation."

"And with the papers still missing."

"Right."

Chris Dale rejoined the group with the phone still in his hand and a pained expression on his face.

"Enjoying the party?" Peter said.

"What's that?" Dale said, tapping a message as he spoke.

"I think I'm going to have a look around. See you later."

Weaving his way through the crowd of guests, Peter walked from table to table to take a look at the melting ice sculptures of swans, angels, sirens and dolphins – until he reached the opposite side of the pool, from where he could watch unob-served the two women laughing and talking to each other, Dale fidgeting with his phone and Chad standing next to him with a sorry look on his face.

There was a break in the music so that food could be served from long tables placed under the portico of Al-Rafai's villa: lobster, crab, shark's fin, fatty tuna, dried scallops, Cornish oysters, abalone, Almas caviar out of gold tins, Kobe-beef carpaccio, quail's eggs and other extravagant delicacies.

Peter finished one glass of wine and commandeered another. "Do you do burgers?" he asked one of the waiters.

The man did not reply and proceeded to serve another guest.

He sat on the marble steps of the main staircase, eating smoked salmon on toast and drinking Château Lafite, until the concert stage came alive again with floodlights and a loud roll of drums. From a cloud of smoke emerged the podgy figure of a boy wearing a suit and sunglasses, flanked by two wiggling teenage girls dressed in white miniskirts and high-collared tops. As the drums died down and the first notes were played, it was clear that the treat in store was Mr Al-Rafai Junior dancing and lip-syncing to 'Gangnam Style'. And to be fair, thought Peter, as the boy bobbed up and down with crossed arms and arched legs and then did the lasso move, it wasn't a bad impersonation at all. It was obvious that professional choreographers and wardrobe experts had been employed – every detail of the original video was copied, including the Chinese-looking Superman in the background, the man in yellow suit and sleek black bob and the flaming-red convertible Mercedes.

More white-dressed girls and boys appeared onstage, joining the frantic dance in a crescendo of special effects, until a big shout erupted:

"E-e-e-e-h, sexy lady!"

The party guests clapped their hands, singing and dancing along. As the song came to its end, the cheers of the audience changed into shouts and exclamations when an explosion of fireworks above a shower of glittering confetti drowned out the last notes.

All the lights went out – and among the occasional cry and wolf whistle, the reassuring melody of 'Happy Birthday to You' resounded through the gardens, accompanied by Arabic chanting. A phosphorescent cake surmounted by sparkling candles floated in the darkness and landed onstage as an outsized "10" rose in the background.

The chanting came to a climax, a single spotlight was trained on the puffed cheeks of the boy, the candles flickered and went out to a roaring cheer from the crowd. Then the lights came on again so that servants could present the boy with his father's gifts: an electric motorbike, medieval armour and a lion cub. Mr Al-Rafai and his blonde wife went onstage to embrace their young performer amid a frenzy of flashes from cameras, mobile phones and tablets.

As the guests returned to their food, drinks and conversations, Peter followed Al-Rafai. He was making a meandering journey back to the house, punctuated by hellos, handshakes and pats on the shoulder.

"Mr Al-Rafai!" Peter ascended the main staircase after him. "Excuse me, Mr—"

Since the tall French windows were open at the top of the stairs and other guests were socializing in the house, he drank the last from his glass and went in: this seemed as good a time as any to have a quick chat with the man.

Inside, the air conditioning gave him goose pimples. Al-Rafai was crossing the drawing room on his right. He greeted a couple on a sofa before disappearing behind an open doorway at the far corner. Peter followed, nodding at the couple on the sofa and smiling at a gentleman who was examining the paintings hanging on the walls.

A long corridor stretched in front of him, with several doors on each side.

"Mr Al-Rafai?" he called, but there was no reply.

He advanced with a cautious step and, leaning against the door frames, peered into the open rooms. There was an indistinct voice at the end of the corridor. It came from a study that resembled the one in the suite at Le Royal – though bigger and lined with bookshelves from floor to ceiling. Al-Rafai was sitting on the edge of his desk with his back to the door, leafing through a large book or album, talking on the phone.

"Take him out," he rasped in a dry tone. "La la, la."

Peter knew enough Arabic to understand his host was not singing to himself but saying "No".

"Out," he continued. "Out!" And he replaced the receiver.

"What can I do for you, sir?"

Peter turned and froze. The butler was staring at him with his customary blank expression, which could equally mean cordiality or murderous intent.

"Come in, Mr Simms," said Al-Rafai.

Peter glanced at the butler, who gave a faint nod and withdrew.

"Please, take a seat." Al-Rafai's eyes were bloodshot, his voice husky. "Drink? A cigar? I have some decent malt."

"Thank you."

Al-Rafai filled two large tumblers.

"Did you like the show?"

"You have a popstar in the making."

"I know. I know," Al-Rafai said, sitting behind the desk. They looked at each other over the glasses they sipped at.

"I gather there have been developments today. Have you made any progress?"

"Yes. It's still early days, but I think we are on the right scent."

"Are you" – Al-Rafai made small circles with his glass – "are you confident you can recover the manuscript?"

"Yes, I am." Peter had a long sip at the whisky. "I think it's too important to be burnt or thrown into the Dead Sea. My only worry is that someone may ask for a ransom. Did you have the collection insured?"

Al-Rafai looked at him and nodded. "Yes. But the manuscript is irreplaceable. It's not a question of money, as you know. It's unique."

"Of course."

There was a long pause.

"By the way" – Al-Rafai drew out the bag Peter had sent him – "what am I supposed to do with this Bible and the worm inside?"

"Ah, yes. We found it in Miss Ripetti's room. I want to check if the words are written in blood. Human blood. Do you know anyone who can help? Discreetly?"

"I do."

"I thought you might. Good." Peter finished his drink and stood up. "We'll be in touch soon, then."

"Enjoy the rest of the party, Mr Simms."

"Thank you."

Peter left Al-Rafai's study and stumbled back to the party. He had drunk far too much, mixing white wine with red and then spirits. The first symptoms of sickness were stirring in his stomach.

Outside, it was unbearably hot. The music had started again, and people were dancing to disco classics from the 1970s and

'80s, interspersed with crowd-pleasing tunes from the current charts. Wearing a medieval helmet, Al-Rafai Junior was riding around on the electric motorbike. Zigzagging on the grass among palm trees and lamp-posts, he honked, laughed and shouted, cheered on by the guests' applause and the proud smile of his mother.

There was the whirr of a helicopter circling above. As Peter looked up, his head began to spin. God, he really felt wasted now. Short of breath and sweating – shivering too. Was he going to retch? Perhaps he should go back inside the house and look for a bathroom before it was too late.

Just then, a blurred patch of red advanced towards him.

"You're here," Giulia said. "You disappeared."

"Met some old friends over there."

"Are you all right? You're looking pale."

"I'm fine. I'm good. Cut some shapes?"

"What is 'cut some shapes'?"

"Fancy a dance?"

"I'm too tired," said Giulia. "And tomorrow we get down to work. Shall we go? It's starting to get cold."

"Just one last drink, then."

Peter staggered to the drinks table and ordered a glass of red wine for himself and a tonic water for Giulia, then joined her near a table by the pool. The ice sculpture of Neptune and Triton suspended over the middle of it had all but melted away.

"Cheers," he said. "To our research."

"*Salute.*"

The helicopter was still describing wide circles on the night sky. Some of the guests were beginning to leave.

"Ooh," Peter said, and emptied his glass. "Time to go." He tottered as he took his first steps.

"Great!" Giulia groaned. She offered him her shoulder to lean on, and they advanced down the lawns in an erratic pattern.

"Just a bad oyster," Peter slurred.

When he saw them approach, Majed jumped out of the car wide-eyed.

"No, Mr Peter," he said. "No! Why do this? Why do this to me?"

"I'm fine, I'm fine, Majed. Done what?"

"Noo, Mr Peter, noo! Not fine, not fine." He kept slapping his forehead with the palm of his hand. "I go to jail. You go to jail. She go to jail."

"Don't keep doing that. You'll get brain damage."

"What can I do, Miss Julia? What can I do?" said Majed, flapping his hands.

"Take him off my shoulders."

"Sorree. Sorree."

Opening the back door, he relieved her of her burden and tried to manhandle Peter in.

"Lie down, Mr Peter."

"I'm not going in the back. I want to drive. I can drive better than you."

"No, Mr Peter, no! Not time for jokes. Blease lie down and sleep. Bleeze!"

"Give me the key, I'm not drunk."

He lurched forward and tried to thrust his hands into Majed's pockets, but the Arab stepped back and Peter collapsed to the ground. A comical scuffle ensued as Peter, on his knees, fumbled at Majed's pockets and Majed strived to push him towards the car.

"*Ehi!*" shouted Giulia, freezing a departing couple in their steps. "*Basta!* You're making a spectacle. I'm exhausted, and I want to go back to the hotel. Majed, pass me the key: I'll drive."

"But, Miss Julia—"

"No buts. Sit in the back with him and make sure he doesn't move. *Capito?*"

The two men exchanged guilty looks and clambered into the back.

Not far down the main road, Peter dozed off. His wheezing snore accompanied the muttered incantations of Majed, who was probably praying that the Englishman would not be sick in his car. Soon they were back in the night-time traffic of Amman, with Majed whispering instructions to the driver:

"Left, Miss Julia. After next circle, right."

They were almost within sight of the Grand Hyatt when Majed moaned. There was a roadblock ahead.

"Police!" he whispered. "Police! Miss Julia. They find Mr Peter here, drunk, we go to prison!"

"I handle this. You stay still and don't say a word."

She slowed the car down and lowered the window.

"*Markaba.*"

The policeman studied her for a while, as if it was the first time he had seen a woman at the wheel, then peered through the window of the back door. Majed had sunk a little lower and shrunk into the darkest corner of the back seat, holding his breath and hoping that Peter's snoring could not be heard outside. Giulia handed over her passport.

"Italy?" the policeman asked.

"Grand Hyatt," she said.

"Italy? Italian?"

"Italy."

"Bizza?"

"Pizza."

"Spaghetti?"

"Spaghetti."

"Grand Hyatt?"

"Grand Hyatt."

The policeman returned the passport and stepped back. "Go."

As they drove away, Majed kept glancing back, laughing and smacking his hand on his thigh. "You're the best, Miss Julia! You're the best! Gelato... panini... Go!"

"Shut up, Majed."

By a sort of sixth sense, as soon as the car stopped in front of the hotel, Peter came to and sat up. He looked around, bewildered.

"8 a.m.," Giulia said. "We'll meet at eight."

He mumbled something that even he didn't comprehend, then opened the door and made a dash for the entrance. He was going to be sick. Swallowing hard in the lift, his body shaken by tremors, he followed the rolling numbers on the digital display, willing them on past 4, 5, 6 to 7, until the doors opened. He darted down the corridor, slotted the key-card into his door and just made it to the bathroom. He remained on all fours for two long minutes, squealing like a pig being throttled.

"What an idiot," he said out loud, spitting in the bowl. "What an idiot."

Feverish and dizzy, but beginning to settle down, he rinsed his mouth and groped his way towards bed and the welcome comfort of the duvet. He closed his eyes – then opened them with a sense of unease. A thin shadow was flitting across the dim red light of the smoke alarm overhead. Wasn't it? No. Yes. No. He blinked a few times.

"What the hell..." he whispered, reaching out in the darkness for the bedside lamp.

His hand, on its journey through darkness, met with something soft and furry.

"Aaah!"

He turned on the bedside lamp. The lifeless lump of a rat was hanging from the ceiling.

8

London, 14th February 1584

Giordano's mood had not improved with a change of clothes. As he stepped out of the Ambassador's house dressed in white from head to toe and saw Florio and Gwynne's smirks, he snorted in irritation.

"You look quite the gentleman," Florio said, trying to keep abreast with him.

"Just walk," Giordano said, pressing ahead in the darkness.

They reached the main road, lit by the occasional lamp and candle. Against the rising mist of that cold night, their shadowy outline could hardly be seen.

As they came onto the Strand, where the lighting was brighter and more people were astir, a drunken man staggered out of a tavern and ploughed into Gwynne.

"Move on," Florio said, as the man made a clumsy effort at hitting them with something he had picked up from the ground, cursing at them all the while.

"Give him a lesson with your sword," Giordano shouted.

"It's not a good idea to mix up with this sort."

Other passers-by, seeing the scene and suspicious of their foreign language, started to obstruct their path and bump into them on purpose, laughing and jeering.

"Donkeys," Giordano hissed.

"Walk on and don't speak," whispered Florio, grabbing him by the arm and pushing him along.

They proceeded at a brisk pace for a while, often stepping onto the dirty road to avoid incoming groups of night walkers who refused to give way on the pavement.

"Have you heard what happened to poor old Citolini?" said Florio as they came to the end of the Strand and began to push their way through the boisterous crowds around the Charing Cross monument.

"Didn't someone knock him to the ground?" said Gwynne.

"Yes, and he got a broken arm for his troubles, while everyone around was mocking him."

"Didn't he complain to the magistrate?"

"Of course he did, but he laughed at him too. He said something like that couldn't have happened – not in the open space where he was walking."

"The boors."

Just as Giordano said it, he received such a violent blow on his shoulder that he clattered into the wall. He looked back and caught the grimace of the gentleman who had treated him with such civility.

"Thank ye, master!" he shouted, using almost all of his English vocabulary.

"Walk on!" whispered Florio, seeing that the man and his five burly companions had stopped to consider the diminutive foreigner in white dress behind them. "These people can slit your throat for a giggle."

"I thought I should thank him for not hitting me with the spike of his buckler or the one on his helmet."

"Walk on, I said. And thank God that we're still alive."

The crowds thinned out as they continued towards Whitehall, and without further problems or obstacles they soon reached their destination, an imposing building on the banks of the

River Thames. After a light rap, a motley gang of servants, guards and hangers-on welcomed them with hardly a nod of acknowledgement. A lazy hand pointed at a door. The three visitors went through it and walked up a double flight of stairs to the building's noble floor.

A large room lined with oak panelling opened in front of them. Nine gentlemen sat around the table, eating, drinking and talking. They fell silent at the sight of their visitors bowing to the assembled company.

"We had given you up for dead, gentlemen," said the host.

"Sir Philip, we gave ourselves up for dead more than once on our journey," Florio answered. "Forgive the late hour. I bring with me my friends, Mr Gwynne and Signor Bruno."

Florio made the introductions, first pointing at their host Sir Philip Sidney at the far end of the table and then working his way round to the distinguished man nearest him, Sir Fulke Greville, who had organized the gathering. Giordano was glad to see his friend and disciple, Alexander Dicson, among the guests, but irked by the presence of two Oxford doctors – the very fellows he had wrangled with earlier at the disputation in the Ambassador's house – whom he had nicknamed Torquato and Nundinio, from the Latin words for "necklace" and "market-seller". As Florio had anticipated, Browne was there too, as well as three other young fellows he had never met or heard of, who were sitting near Sir Philip.

"They apologize for having started eating," said Florio, "and for having almost finished. They'd been waiting for a long time and thought we wouldn't come."

"I cannot blame them," said Giordano.

Florio was invited to take a seat at the near end of the table.

"Oh, this is far, far too high an honour, sir," he said, with affected reluctance. "I can sit somewhere else – wherever you like."

Greville and Sir Philip exchanged an embarrassed look.

"They want you to take that seat," Gwynne whispered to him in Italian, "because it's the least prestigious place at the table. They can't have Bruno sitting there. It would be discourteous."

"Oh. Ah."

Florio smiled awkwardly and sat down, facing Sir Philip at the other end of the table. Greville took a seat to his right. Dicson, Giordano and Torquato, the doctor with the gold chains, sat to Florio's left, while the other Oxford lecturer, Nundinio, faced the Nolan.

Giordano let his eyes roam round the room and the table, taking in the scene – the fine wooden carvings and the family portraits on the walls, the bright light from wax candles, the glasses full of wine, the silverware besmirched by the well-picked bones of beast and fowl. It was all suffused with a dreamlike aura. He was sorry not to be sitting next to the fine gentleman at the far end of the table. He had heard great things about him when he was in Milan and Paris. Florio was right in guessing that he would be delighted to make his acquaintance.

The potent images of the last few hours were playing against each other in his mind, turning and combining on the mystical wheels of his imagination. Wasn't there a secret correspondence between this night and the journey of his own life? Had he not been dragged away from the safety of his home, from the straight way he was supposed to follow, onto a tortuous, meandering path in the dark? That ancient, creaky boat full of holes, was it not an image of the sinking Church or Rome – and those two decrepit, Charon-like boatmen with their pale tallow

CHAPTER 8

candlelight of superstitious faith, didn't they resemble St Peter
and the Pope, who had promised to take him to the light as he
sang of poetry and love, going past the very Temple of Christendom, and left him instead in a mire of error and sophistry,
only fit for monkish swine? Yet he had found the way back to his
home, his pure soul. He had thrown away his old clothes and,
despite the many dangers and difficulties – the blows delivered
by fate and the brutish people around him – he had managed to
reach his intended destination: intellectual freedom, the banquet
of true minds, the internal sun.

As the wheels continued to turn and lock in his mind, he
thought he could grasp even more obscure and ineffable connections with the secret fabric of things, which lay beyond the
reach of humans and was only foreshadowed by the intricate
order of the stars in the sky. He was the first living man of any
religion or philosophy to have had a glimpse of the true light
and captured these hidden correlations. He had developed a
unique language and a new system which – although not perfect
yet – he was sure one day would give him the key to unravelling
the deepest mysteries of the universe.

"Would you like some wine?" Dicson asked in Latin.

Bruno cast an uncomprehending look at the cup his friend
was offering him. For a moment he thought it was one of those
beakers he had seen elsewhere in this country, being passed from
mouth to mouth – full of grease and motes around their rims.
This time he was relieved to see that each guest had his own cup.

"I will," he said. "It was so cold outside."

"Please take this," the young man whispered, pushing a pamphlet into Giordano's lap as he passed him some wine. "I only
got it a few days ago from the printers. It will set Oxford and
Cambridge on fire."

Giordano peeked under the table and, reading the title, he couldn't conceal a smile: *De umbra rationis.*

"I look forward to reading it," he said.

"I am sure you will be delighted by it. Have you decided when to publish your great work?"

Giordano looked around to make sure no one else was listening.

"Well, I am not even sure I will ever commit it to print."

"Why?"

"Because… it's imperfect. And even if it were perfect, words are a weak and slow medium for the operations of our mind, as you know: instead of getting us into the heart of things, they create a distance between ourselves and reality. Their meaning is questionable and unreliable: they will always lead to endless disputations, misconceptions and misunderstandings. The only true and effective language for man is the language of images. Think how long it takes to describe an image in words. We must train our mind to think through images and only through images. No human alphabet is powerful enough to depict them or evoke them. A whole new system must be invented, and—"

A loud burst of laughter made him turn round – he was being observed by the rest of the company. Nundinio, the Oxford doctor sitting in front of him, put his bejewelled hands on the table and cleared his throat.

"*Intelligis, domine, quæ diximus?*"

"No. Why were you laughing?"

"You don't speak English?"

"I'm afraid not." Giordano gave a wan smile. "I've only learnt two or three words since I arrived here."

"And may I ask why you make no effort to learn our language?"

"Most of the people I want to talk to can speak Latin, French, Spanish or Italian – including your most gracious queen." He bowed his head.

"Well, in that case, sir," Nundinio continued, stroking his beard, "let me translate for you what caused our mirth." He threw a sidelong glance to Giordano's right, where his learned colleague was sitting. "My honoured friend here was telling us a joke that has been circulating among our Oxford students since you abandoned your lectures last year. They say they know why you are so keen to promote Copernicus's opinion that the earth goes round and the heavens stand still."

"Yes? And why would that be?"

"It's because your own mind never stands still and your head keeps spinning with all those Lullian wheels…"

"Very amusing, sir." Giordano's features remained poised.

"And we know that Copernicus himself did not believe that the earth moves, as this is clearly impracticable and impossible. If he affirms that it's the earth that moves rather than the eighth sphere, it's only for the ease and convenience of his calculations."

"Are you telling us that Copernicus's system is only a mathematical or geometric one, bearing no relation to reality?"

"Well, that's what is stated in his book," intervened Torquato, turning a fierce look on Giordano, "in the notice to the Reader."

"You are wrong, sir. You would know that if you had cared to read and understand the author's own words after that notice, which must have been put together by some ignorant, arrogant dunce. Copernicus knew well what he was saying, and demonstrated his theory to the best of his abilities."

"Are you suggesting, sir, that we are all wrong – that generations and generations of learned men from different nations have been blinded by error? And that only you and Copernicus are right?"

"Many ancient philosophers, as well as some recent ones – the excellent Nicholas of Cusa, for example – held the same opinion. Most of those you call 'learned men' have simply followed what was taught to them with a superstitious faith and a misplaced worship of words, logic and dialectic."

"Then perhaps," said Fulke Greville, "you will be kind enough to explain to everyone here, in simple terms, why you believe the earth moves."

Giordano bowed his head again. "I'll be delighted to do so."

He handed back Dicson the pamphlet under the table, stood up and began to talk. With wide gestures and a clear voice that carried across the room, he begun to expound the main tenets of his new philosophy.

The sun was larger than the earth. If the moon were farther away from us, it wouldn't eclipse the sun and would appear less bright to our eyes. Neither the earth nor the sun were at the centre of the universe, because the universe was infinite and had no centre and no boundaries, contrary to what Ptolomeus and Master Aristotle had thought. There were innumerable astral bodies in the universe – stars like our sun, worlds such as our earth and the moon, with living creatures on them, each occupying its own place in the boundless expanse of God's creation, each moving with its own speed and trajectory, as if infused with a life, soul and mind of its own.

The two doctors kept throwing in questions and interjecting – "What is the substance of these bodies?", "Are they all of the same size?", "Are they hot or cold, with intrinsic or induced brightness?", "This is pure madness!" – but this didn't halt the flow of the man from Nola, who seemed to be drawing from an inexhaustible well of knowledge and learning. He spoke with fervour, quoting from the works of ancient philosophers, conjuring daring images, drawing diagrams in the air with his hands so that even if they did not heed his argument they felt its beauty. Sidney looked on with burning eyes; the others sat in confused admiration.

The Oxford men had also fallen silent. Nundinio was gazing at Bruno with the stupefied stare of someone who had just seen a portent of nature. Who gave this small, contemptible foreigner, this miscreant rejected by his own fold, such assurance, such ardour, such authority? Why was it that his preposterous ideas seemed to make sense on his lips – even the most abstruse formulations and wildest fantasies? The infectious enthusiasm with which he spoke was as dangerous as the evil ideas he professed: it could not be allowed to take root in the minds of Englishmen. The disputation he had initiated was turning into a humiliating defeat. Nundinio assumed a sarcastic expression and began to chuckle.

"May I ask you what it is that you find so amusing, sir?" Bruno asked.

Nundinio darted his eyes around.

"These other worlds you talk about, sir... similar to the one we live on... seem to be taken straight from Lucian's *True Story*, if I may say so... Ha!"

Giordano slammed a fist on the table.

"I'm sorry you feel that way, sir," he said. "But the first rule of honest disputation is not to offend the rival and not to make fun of something one doesn't understand. If I don't laugh at your fantastic notions, then I would expect you to do the same when you hear my ideas."

Torquato stood up, his nostrils flaring. "Whose notions are fantastic? Who does not understand what? Do you presume to be the new master of all philosophers?"

"What are you getting at, sir? What are you getting at? What if I am the new master of all philosophers? What if I do not yield to Aristotle or to anyone else any more than they would not have yielded to me? Will that make this earth the immobile centre of the universe? Give me some reasons, some facts, and demonstrate why the old masters are right and the new master standing next to you is wrong." Giordano smirked. "Or are you bristling with wit but shorn of argument?"

"Hear! Hear!" shouted some of the guests.

Torquato played with the gold chains round his neck and cast a faltering glance around the table.

"Well, then," he said, clearing his throat. "How can you explain, sir, if the earth moves, that Mars at times looks bigger and at times smaller?"

Giordano smiled. "This is due to the motion of the earth and Mars along their relevant paths, which makes them closer to each other or farther away from each other as the case may be."

"Oh yes? Then perhaps you would care to show us the various courses of the planets and the earth?"

"I am not here to give you a lesson, sir, but to reply to your questions."

"I think I've just asked one, have I not?"

"If I were to answer this, we'd be here the whole night and there will be no disputation. I think we all agree on the shapes, positions and courses of the planets' movements – which have been known since antiquity. This is not the subject of our debate, and I do not intend to contradict the mathematicians or argue against their theories and calculations. What I am interested in

80

is the nature of these movements and what can be inferred from them – and whether they confirm our beliefs or the commonly held opinions of the philosophers."

"Perhaps," said Browne, "if you state the ideas you are defending, our esteemed friend will be able to present his arguments against them."

"I think I have already given enough explanations and topics for argumentation," was Giordano's sharp reply. "But since you're asking – very well."

He repeated that the universe was a boundless ethereal space scattered with innumerable planets and stars such as the earth, the moon and the sun, originating from the Godhead's infinite power – the thousand thousands ministering unto Him, the ten thousand times ten thousand standing before Him, as the Scriptures said. These were the great animated bodies which, thanks to the light they emanated, were visible all around us. Some of them, such as the sun and other blazing orbs, were hot, while others – such as the earth, the moon, Venus and numberless other planets – were cold. These bodies, in order to communicate with each other and to participate in one another's vital principle, performed their circular movements at given distances – some around others – as shown by the seven planets circling around the sun. And the earth was just one of them: it rotated around itself from the west to the east over a period of twenty-four hours, giving the impression that the universe was spinning round it. Not only did the earth turn around its own axis – producing the alternation of light and darkness, day and night, cold and heat – but it also circled around the sun, giving rise to the changing of the seasons: spring, summer, autumn, winter...

Torquato was staring at Giordano, but no longer listening to what he said. His mind was blank, his ears were ringing. All he wanted to do was to put an end to the stream of fantastic ideas spouted by this venomous little man.

"To the point! To the point!" he shouted.

Giordano burst out laughing. "These – these are the points I'm making!" He sat down and levelled a finger at his opponent. "It is your turn now, sir, to add something *to the point.*"

Torquato turned to the other guests. "*Anticyram navigat…*" He chuckled. "It's clear, my dear friends, that his head is still spinning." He turned to look down at Giordano. "Maybe it's your empty stomach and the wine, sir. You should have eaten something before launching into so much talk." He flashed a smile at his colleague. "But perhaps you're abstaining from food today? Although I thought you were no longer following the dictates of your old religion…"

"Someone should take those neck chains, sir, and put a halter instead round your neck."

"What? How dare you?"

"And give you forty lashes on your back to commemorate this first day of Lent."

"Sir!"

Bruno turned to Greville. "Sir, I hope next time you'll be able to produce better and more civilized speakers."

There was commotion around the table. As the guests brayed and bustled and jumped to their feet, Sidney watched with an amused smile.

"Bruno, please, contain yourself!" Florio was urging. "Do not be offended, Sir Fulke. Gentlemen all, I—"

"*Pazzi,*" Bruno said, pushing towards the door, "*pazzi asini barbareschi.*"

"Please, Giordano," Florio pleaded. "You're offending our host and his gentleman friends. Please apologize to them."

"Apologize to them? I don't think so." He gave a soft laugh and whispered in his friend's ear. "Don't worry, Giovanni: these old donkeys won't smart – their skin's too thick."

"Do it for me. Make an apology and let us leave this house in good order."

Giordano heaved a deep sigh and turned to Torquato. "Brother," said the Nolan, as silence fell on the room. "Don't think for a moment that I'll be your enemy just because of your flawed beliefs. I'm not angry with you: I just pity you and wish to God that you'll come to see the truth one day. After all, I was as ignorant once in my youth as you are now in your old age."

"Is that an apology?" Dicson whispered to Gwynne.

The two Oxford doctors, without sparing another glance for Bruno, bid their goodbyes and took their leave.

"Oh, please," Florio said, following them close behind, "please stay. My friend is a bit short-tempered at times, but he meant no offence. Sirs!"

Soon the other guests made their way downstairs – among them Dicson, who handed back his pamphlet to Bruno before giving him a warm handshake and wishing him goodnight. Giordano thanked Sir Philip for inviting him to his table and Greville for arranging the debate. He gave his farewells, made an awkward bow and followed Gwynne out of the room.

Florio was waiting out on the street, by the front door. The night had got colder and gusty: wisps of breath swirled and trailed from his mouth.

"They won't accept an apology from you," he said.

"I didn't intend to apologize," said Giordano.

"This will hardly swell the number of your friends, Fastidito."

"Who cares, Florio? Let's go home, it's late."

They walked back to the main road. Four tottering men were improvising a round dance. A youth was urinating against the stones of the Charing Cross monument. They wrapped themselves in their mantles and hurried back along the empty Strand to Salisbury Court, under a sky that remained dark and impenetrable.

9

Peter woke up with a head-splitting hangover. He tried to make out the time from the TV display. "Jesus, nearly nine…"

He switched on the bedside lamp. The dead rat – was it a dream? No: he could see the slight bulge of the laundry bag, where he had put it the night before.

He checked his phone and saw a message from Giulia that morning: "8.15 and you're not here, so I go on my own. Majed will come and pick you up later."

Good. He took a long shower, drank an entire bottle of water and went down to have breakfast.

Majed was less friendly than usual. He placed his suitcase in the boot, opened the back door and waved him into the car with professional politeness and a neutral smile under his moustache.

"How are you today, Majed?" Peter asked as they drove out of Amman.

"Fine, Mr Peter."

"Sorry about yesterday."

"No problem, Mr Peter."

"You're not offended, are you?"

"No, Mr Peter."

"Good weather today, uh?"

"Yes, Mr Peter."

Chad was waiting for him in the circular hall on the hundred and ninety-ninth floor. Once they were in Dale's office, he invited him to sit on one of the chairs and offered him a drink.

Dale arrived ten minutes later, with his usual harried face and his phablet glued to his ear. As he passed by Peter, he nodded to acknowledge his presence, then walked over to his desk uttering soft grunts of assent and whispering unintelligible words. When he ended his conversation, he said, "Give me just *one* second," went through his tapping-and-clicking routine on his laptop and looked up with a strangled smile.

"So," he said. "Did you enjoy the party yesterday night?"

"I enjoyed it too much. Can I show you something?"

"Of course."

Peter laid out his newspaper on the table and placed his laundry bag on top.

"You want us to look at your dirty pants?"

"Wait."

Peter lifted the bottom corners of the bag and let its contents roll onto the newspaper with a thud.

"God!" Dale shouted. "What the heck is that?"

"What does it look like?"

"A dead rat."

"Quite. So imagine my feelings yesterday when I returned to my hotel and found this little beast hovering over my bed in the dark."

"Someone killed it and hung it in your room?"

Peter fixed his gaze on Chris Dale. "Unlike Father Marini, there's no doubt that this little fellow didn't commit suicide."

"Another gift from Bookworm?"

"Yep."

"What's the message?"

"This is the message," Peter said, pointing at the rat. "What they are trying to tell me, in a cut-worm, dead-rat sort of way, is 'Don't get involved in this, get the hell out of here, now'.

I'm going to send it to the same people who are checking out the dead worm."

"So you reckon it's a threat?"

Peter surveyed Dale's bald head, fancy eyepiece, tiny ears, upturned nose, bloodless lips and dimpled chin. "I believe that much is clear. I want guards posted outside my suite and Giulia's."

"Right."

"I don't think we are in any immediate danger, but it might be a good idea as a precaution – at least for the next few days."

On his way to the library to see Giulia, Peter stopped at a McDonald's. He was still munching his second burger and finishing off the Coke when he entered the librarian's office.

"Hi, Helen," he said, licking his thumb.

The librarian blanched and pushed him out of her office.

"How did you get past the attendant?"

"What do you mean?"

She pointed at a sign on the wall: "STRICTLY NO FOOD OR DRINKS IN THE LIBRARY".

"Oh." He licked his other thumb. "I'm sorry. But don't worry, I'm not here to smear your incunabula: I was trying to track down the Italian lady."

Helen stared at him and shook her head. "She's been here all morning and left ten minutes ago."

"Do you know where she is?"

"Presumably eating proper food in one of the appropriately designated areas."

"OK, OK, got it. Bye."

He found her in Starbucks, sitting at a lonely table with her back to the entrance, drinking from her espresso cup. He walked towards her with a big smile that faded as he drew near.

"Are you crying?"

She looked up with smudged eyes.

"Hi," she said, sniffling. "Slept well?"

He sat down in front of her and touched her arm.

"Are you all right? Giulia?"

Two teardrops fell on the table.

"Something's happened?"

"Nothing," she said. "Nothing... I'm just..." She blew her nose, wiped her eyes and looked up. "I'm just too happy."

"You're too happy?"

"Yes."

"And you're crying?"

"Yes."

"Why?"

"Bruno."

"Your boyfriend?"

"No!" She laughed. "Giordano Bruno."

"Giordano Bruno? Oh..."

"Come with me, Mr Last Drink, we're going to a bar. I want to celebrate."

Ten minutes later they were sitting in a cocktail lounge on the mezzanine overlooking the entrance hall, clutching glasses of prosecco.

"You know nothing about Giordano Bruno?" she taunted him. "Eh?"

"I read the Wikipedia entry a few days ago. Never heard of him before."

"Well, he is a very famous philosopher. In fact, one of the greatest. He published many books during his life, but some of them – how do you say? – have not survived."

"How come?"

"It's because they were printed in little numbers and because he was persecuted for his ideas. Most of the copies were taken by the Church—"

"Taken? Confiscated?"

"Yes, confiscated or destroyed by the booksellers or the owners. There was a book called *L'arca di Noè* – *Noah's Ark* – and two others, *On the Signs of the Times* and *Hell's Purgatory*. He talks about them in other writings, so we know he wrote them, but they can't be found anywhere. Lost for hundreds of years." She gave him an expectant look.

"What's so great about that?"

"They've been found now. They're part of Mr Al-Rafai's collection." There was a pause. "Well? You don't seem very excited."

"Well" – Peter scratched his neck and concealed a smile – "I am sure this is all very important for you and a bunch of other scholars – no offence, Giulia – but in real, practical terms..."

"I don't think you understand."

"Maybe I don't."

"Let me explain to you, then. There are very few existing manuscripts of Bruno's works – only six or seven in total, I think. And there are even fewer specimens of his handwriting, because he dictated his books. There's one in the Public Library in Geneva, one in Wrocław in Poland, one in Wittenberg, if I remember well, another one in Stuttgart, then the famous Wolfenbüttel letter, the Norov codex – and that's it, I think."

"OK. So they're worth tens of thousands of dollars?"

"Hundreds of thousands. Millions, perhaps."

"Really?"

Giulia had a sip from her glass. "Because autographed documents by Bruno are so rare, any fragment that comes to light has an inestimable value. Mr Al-Rafai has in this collection not merely lost books by Bruno, but hundreds and hundreds of pages written in Bruno's own hand."

"So, in terms of the theft, it adds weight to the possibility that money is the motivation?"

Giulia shrugged. "That's your job to find out. If I were you, the question that would interest me most is this: what was in the stolen papers? It must be something even more valuable than what Father Marini left behind."

"I have another one for you."

"What is it?"

"How did this material end up here in Jordan?"

"This is difficult to know. There are a few possibilities. After he left the monastery and gave up the habit, Bruno began to travel around Europe. At one point – I think it was 1585 – he was crossing the English Channel to France with the French Ambassador. Their ship was attacked by pirates and all their possessions were taken. But why would a pirate be interested in books and private documents?"

"Right."

"A few years later, when he was in Venice, his papers were seized and given to the authorities, but I think it was only a few well-known books and a short manuscript. What we have here is much more important."

"What is your theory, then, about this collection?"

"This seems to have been put together by someone who wanted to have a record of everything Bruno had ever written."

"Who could that be?"

"The Holy Inquisition." Giulia ran a hand through her hair. "Either as a proof for the trial against him or as an archive copy when they put his works on the Index and ordered their

90

destruction. Many scholars find it strange that the minutes of his trial and his written statements cannot be found on the shelves of the Vatican Library."

"What are you saying?"

"I think you know what I'm saying."

"That Father Marini stole all the documentation of Bruno's trial? I guess it's a possibility." Peter emptied his glass of prosecco. "Not bad for a few hours' work."

"Hopefully I can find more information about the missing documents when I read the manuscripts."

"Good. Let me know as soon as you find out anything else. And please, don't tell anyone about this for the time being – not even Helen, the librarian. Not Dale, not Mr Al-Rafai – not anyone."

"OK. Only one drink today?"

"Only one drink."

They kissed each other on the cheek and went their separate ways. Peter returned to his room and stretched out on the bed. He was tired, and his mind was teeming with thoughts. Should he tell Giulia about the dead rat? Not for now, perhaps. It would just kill her happiness and enthusiasm. He switched on the TV, and a corporate documentary about the Tower's construction came up unsolicited.

"Welcome to Biblia Tower," announced a blonde in a strong American accent. "Since time immemorial, man has aspired to the greatest heights. The ancient pyramids and the temples built on the top of hills and above cities are a clear example of our desire to be 'closer to the gods'. In more recent centuries, religious buildings have been replaced by daring military or defensive structures, and in our secular times by commercial or residential high-rise buildings."

The woman gave a short history of modern skyscrapers, from the 1931 Empire State Building and the 1972 World Trade Center in New York to the "supertall" Sears Tower in Chicago, completed in 1974, Kuala Lumpur's 1998 Petronas Twin Towers and the "megatall" Burj Khalifa in Dubai, completed in 2010, which at nearly 830 metres would remain the tallest skyscraper in the world until the completion of Biblia Tower later in the year.

Biblia was described as the leading company of the digital age, with a turnover three times the combined revenues of Google and Microsoft and over fifteen thousand employees scattered around the globe. Founded in the late Noughties by Jerry Dyson and Fred Mortensen, with headquarters in the Silicon Valley and offices in one hundred and forty-six countries, it had quickly risen to prominence through a series of double- and treble-digit growth years, until its flotation in 2015, when it became the first company with a market capitalization of over $1 trillion.

In recent years Biblia had emerged as the largest content supplier in all languages and across all media and platforms. The firm was also one of the world's driving forces in the digitization of all human knowledge, which was scheduled to be completed by the end of the second decade of the twenty-first century. Not since the first mission to the moon had there been such an ambitious goal in sight.

Biblia Tower, built in less than five years at a cost of around $3.5 billion, was the flagship project in the company's programme. Once fully operative, the building would host a resident population of 35,000, with projected daily visitors in excess of 10,000.

"Jesus," was Peter's comment.

The woman continued with a virtual tour of the structure, its architectural details, technical specifications, services – which included fitness centres, swimming pools, tennis courts, shopping malls, offices, restaurants, cinemas, interactive museums, concert halls, parks and even a small zoo and aquarium – its vertical network of lifts and the sophisticated electronic systems that controlled every aspect of its life.

As the documentary went on to illustrate the large development of buildings surrounding the Tower, with its shuttle service to the airport and its train link to Amman, Peter stopped listening and tried to remember where he had read these words: "Thoughts are things: when you imagine a thing, you're making a thing." That immense tangle of concrete and steel had been, for a long time, nothing but a thought, an idea living only in the mind of its inventor – and now it was reality, and his living body inhabited it, his mind created new things...

He dozed off. He dreamt of a cowled figure dressed in black wandering through the corridors of the Tower. Then he saw a woman in white, with a diadem and a sceptre. She had long hair and resembled Giulia, but was not her. The woman took him by the hand and kissed him on the cheek. He looked to the right, and there was a long stretch of railway disappearing into the night. Something advanced from far away, running on four legs over the tracks at an even pace. It was a dog – a hound with diabolical eyes. Peter picked up some sharp white stones from the ground and threw them at the dog, but missed it, and the beast turned its head slowly, bared its pointed teeth and proceeded to maul him.

Peter shook himself awake. He still felt a bit rough. The documentary was now showing Biblia's involvement in several charitable causes: the fight against poverty, children's learning disabilities, the promotion of numeracy and literacy through the funding of schools in deprived areas of the world... To listen to this, Biblia was not in the business of making money, but was the corporate version of Mother Teresa. He picked up the remote and switched off the TV.

He checked his email, and one of the messages was from Al-Rafai's office, saying that the blood on the "worm" message was human. He replied to warn him that something else was on its way for his friend's lab, giving him a short description of last night's mishap at the hotel.

After a long shower, his dizziness disappeared altogether. He changed clothes and left his room. He had not made two steps when he started back.

"Good afternoon, sir."

The voice was from a man with a convict's face but wearing a reassuring green uniform, who was stationed between the door to his room and the one to his left.

"Afternoon," Peter said.

One of the things from the documentary that had caught his attention was the existence of a navigation system for getting around in the Tower, which he could download onto his phone. So he stopped at one of the many information points scattered about the building to get the free application. As he was registering for the service, he was asked if he agreed to make his location visible to others and trackable.

His finger hovered over "No", but then he selected "Yes" and had an idea. What if Marini had also used the navigation system? Perhaps it was possible to follow his whereabouts in the building before his disappearance.

He went to see Jim, the IT director, in his office. Sitting next to him was one of his colleagues, Boris, with a laptop on his lap. Peter said hello and asked Jim whether he could look up the friar's details and retrace his movements in the Tower.

CHAPTER 9

"Don't think so," Jim said.

"How do you know?"

"The old man was a technophobe."

"Was he?"

"He made a big point about only ever using pencil and paper and not owning a mobile phone or a computer."

"I see. Oh well. Thought it was worth a try." Peter made to leave, then turned back. "But he must have had one of these, right?" He held a magnetic card in his hand. "An entrance pass."

Jim turned with a look almost of annoyance on his face. "Right."

"He'd have used it to check in and out of the building, get into rooms, the library, operate lifts… right? Is there any chance you can have a look for me?"

Jim exhaled. "I don't want to sound dismissive, but I'm sort of busy right now. There's seven hundred people on this floor alone reporting to me, each sending me fifty emails a minute. And we found a bug in our system."

"Perhaps your colleague can help me? It won't take long, will it?"

Jim shrugged and turned to Boris. "Have a look for him. But quickly: we need to get this fixed today."

Boris tapped the keyboard of his laptop with nimble fingers. After a while, the typing slowed down and a single touch of the return key brought up a long list of codes and numbers.

"What are these?" Peter asked.

"Marini's entrance-pass logs."

"Not easy on the eye."

"I'm afraid that's all we've got," said Jim.

"Is there a key to the various codes?"

"Not to hand."

"Can you get me one?"

"Sure," said Jim. "I'll have an instruction manual dropped at reception tomorrow."

"How about today?"

Jim drew a long breath. "Today."

"One last favour. Can I have a printout of Marini's logs?"

"Sure." A printer in the corner whirred and Boris passed him a few sheets.

"Cheers. Well, I'd better go. I know you're busy. Bye for now."

"Bye," said Boris.

Jim didn't reply, and his gaze continued to roam over the screens in front of him.

Peter was on his way back to his room when he heard his phone beep and vibrate. He was surprised to see a message from Giulia. It only said: "Dinner tonight?"

10

Venice, 22nd May 1592

"*Ars longa, vita brevis*," thought Giordano as he turned in his bed. He opened his eyes and looked at the bright moon casting its light through the window. His head was overflowing with thoughts: perhaps he should light a lamp and commit some notes to paper. At times he found that ideas coming to him clearly at night would be lost in shadows by the following morning. Still, he felt he was at the height of his intellectual powers. Over the last few years he had written two dozen works, enough to secure his name among the great – but this was only a very small fraction of what teemed in his mind.

He gave a long sigh, turned again in his bed and closed his eyes. Perhaps he should write and publish yet more, as his disciple Besler encouraged him to do. But writing was demeaning his vision, bringing it down to an imperfect medium – and as for publishing… well, that was like fixing half-truths and mistakes in stone, leaving equivocal words open to infinite misinterpretations by people of different times and languages. No one could understand his ideas better than himself – no mouth could express them more accurately than his own live one.

But Besler meant well, and was probably right: although limited and defective, books were a useful tool to disseminate thoughts across countries and generations – and perhaps he should finally reconcile himself to publishing his great work in progress and present it to the new Pope, Clement. But how? Tossed about by Fortune, he was again on his own and with very little means. After leaving England and fleeing France, after wandering for years throughout Europe and being forced to leave Germany, he had moved to Padua full of hopes, with a chest brimming with manuscripts ready to be published. There he could read, study, give lessons and write. But Besler had to return to Nuremberg after the death of his uncle, who was paying for his studies; Forgács and the other students were drowning in debts and unable to help him or offer him any kind of protection. So he'd had to accept work as a tutor to Giovanni Mocenigo in Venice.

He, Giordano Bruno of Nola, who had radiated with the brilliance of his mind across the purview of princes, queens, kings and popes, was now reduced to teaching an ignoramus, a pompous fool who hoped to learn nothing less than the art of memory and the occult sciences from him! If there was any consolation in such a thankless endeavour, it was that he could often poke fun at the stupidity and superstition of his new pupil. Like the other day, when he was travelling with Mocenigo to San Giorgio Maggiore:

"Do you believe that Jesus performed miracles, Bruno?"

"Of course I do."

"By which arts?"

"Oh, I know well by which arts," he had said, smiling. "So it's no wonder that he came to a bad end. He must have known that he'd end up on the gallows. But his knowledge of the Hebrew language was nothing like mine, so I can conjure up much greater miracles and portents than him."

Ah, if only Besler or one of his students could have seen the dumbstruck expression on the face of the Venetian gentleman – his staring eyes, the gaping mouth! But he knew he should be careful. The bookseller Ciotti, who first introduced him to Mocenigo, had warned him: "Giovanni may look dull, but he is a venomous snake. Ask poor Leoni, his old friend, what it's like to be under his thumb." Sometimes Giordano even suspected that his pupil might be conniving with the Holy Office. Otherwise why these prodding questions about his beliefs? Why such insistence about being taught the magic arts? Was it a treacherous trap to elicit unorthodox statements from him? It is true that he always replied in jest and tried to be circumspect, but he knew he was playing a dangerous game.

That was one of the reasons he had decided to pack his belongings and go to Frankfurt. He had already given instructions for his chest to be shipped, and he would be on his way as soon as it was practicable. Mocenigo was furious when he heard he intended to leave.

"And what is the reason for this sudden departure?"

"I must get some of my works printed in Germany."

"You can't go: you have not taught me half of what you promised."

"It takes time. Have some patience. I'll be back to complete my lessons."

"You're lying. Have you found some other rich student to dupe?"

"No, sir. And I am telling you the truth. I have to take some important papers to the printers."

"Why do you need to be there?"

"To help them with the composition and the proofing. You know how illiterate these press hands are. I don't want my books littered with errors."

"These are excuses. I won't let you go until you have fulfilled your obligations."

"I'm sorry, sir, but leave I must and leave I will."

"Well, if you don't want to stay out of your own goodwill, I'll find a way to keep you here."

Giordano turned again in his bed. Mocenigo could stamp his feet as much as he liked, but no one was going to hold him in that city a day longer: he had work to do. He would set off at dawn and, all being well, he would be in Frankfurt in less than two weeks if the weather was favourable and the roads negotiable. He was sure that his friend, the Prior of the Carmelites' monastery, would offer him a safe shelter again – and perhaps Besler could come to see him from Nuremberg and help him with all the revisions needed before publication?

He extended a hand towards the moon – so far away and yet so close as to be contained between two fingers. His journey on earth had been long and tortuous, but despite all the hardships and adversities, he had not shied away from probing the darkest depths of the universe. Now the secret language of the stars and the human soul was within his reach. At times he thought he could see it in his mind's eye – if not in its entirety, at least the light it gave off, like the reflection of the sun against the face of the moon. All he needed now was to translate that divine shimmer into intelligible signs: then his destiny would be fulfilled.

There was a creak outside, a gentle knock, and the door opened to reveal Mocenigo's bearded red face shining above a flickering candle flame.

"We must talk, Bruno," he said, stepping over to Giordano's bed.

"Can't it wait until tomorrow?"

"No, not tomorrow: now."

"What is it?"

"Bortolo told me you've packed your stuff and given orders to dispatch it."

"I have."

"I thought we had already discussed the matter. You're not going anywhere."

"With all due respect, sir, I'm my own master and will decide what to do with myself."

Mocenigo raised the candlestick and slammed his palm against the wall. Giordano froze as something tumbled onto the bedsheets.

"A spider," Mocenigo said.

"A spider?"

"Well, a dead one now."

"Why did you do that?" Giordano was almost shouting.

Mocenigo laughed. "I didn't know you cared so much about spiders. We can arrange a proper funeral, if you want." He brushed the little creature onto the floor and crushed it under his boot.

"To kill one of God's creations like that – you have committed a crime."

"Ha! I will burn in hell for a spider?"

"I wouldn't laugh about that, sir. Maybe in that little spider lived the soul of an old friend. There is a soul in every living creature – and even in planets and stars. Once we're dead, our souls don't vanish, but move from one body to another."

"And how do you know? Have you been in this world before?"

"Yes, I have. And I'll return many times in the future after my death in the body of another man or animal."

"Ho! Will you? Maybe as a wasp or a rabid dog – or a ghost."

"Every life is precious. Perhaps the life of that spider is more precious than your own. Now, sir, if you don't mind, I'd like to go back to my sleep."

"And you still intend to leave for Frankfurt?"

"The question is closed, sir."

"Bortolo!"

Mocenigo's servant entered with six other men – gondolieri, to judge from their clothes. Giordano pulled himself higher up his bed.

"Follow us, sir," said Bortolo.

"Where are you taking me?"

"Your black arts don't tell you?" Mocenigo said, sniggering.

They pulled him out of bed in his nightshirt and guided him out of the room with their candles. They walked through a series of dark corridors, went up a flight of stairs, then down a long passage, until they arrived at the foot of a ladder leading up to the garret.

"This is where you're going," said Mocenigo.

Giordano shook his head. "You're not in earnest?"

"Step up the ladder, sir," said Bortolo.

"I demand to leave this house now," shouted Bruno.

"Up." Bortolo unsheathed his dagger and pointed at the gaping trapdoor.

Two of the gondolieri grabbed him by the arms and pushed him up the ladder and into the garret.

"You'll be sorry for this," Bruno bellowed. "I'll make you pay for it."

The trapdoor was shut and fastened, and the ladder removed. Giordano's cries could be heard through the ceiling.

"What's that, Bruno?" said Mocenigo, laughing. "Speak louder."

"Let me out! In the name of Christ! Cursed dog!"

Mocenigo smiled and darted a quick glance at Bortolo and the others, then whispered: "Have you heard? Have you all heard how this godless man insults our Saviour? He just called him a cursed dog."

The men nodded.

"Bruno!" he shouted. "Do you hear me?"

"I do."

"I have a proposal for you. If you agree to stay in my house and teach me all the terms used in the art of memory and in geometry, as you had promised to do, then I'll let you free. If not…"

"Then what?" yelled Bruno.

"Then I'm afraid something unpleasant is going to happen." Again Mocenigo glanced a smile at the others.

"I have taught you as much and perhaps more than was appropriate," came the cry from above. "I have fulfilled my obligations, and I don't deserve to be treated in this manner."

"You must complete your lessons, or I'll denounce you to the religious authorities."

"What do you mean?"

"Have you forgotten all the evil things you said about our Lord Jesus Christ and the Holy Catholic Church?"

"My conscience is clear: I have nothing to worry about."

"So you're not scared of the Inquisition?"

"No, I'm not. I'm not hurting anyone with the way I live, and I don't remember saying anything bad. And even if I did, it was said in jest among ourselves, so I have nothing to be afraid of. Even if you deliver me to the Inquisition, what could they do? Force me to take up my habit again?"

"Oh, so you *were* a religious man once…" Mocenigo gave out a loud laugh.

"I only had my first orders. And in any case, any past quarrel with the Church can be easily mended."

"Oh yes? And how, if you don't believe in the Holy Trinity, if you say so many blasphemous things about our Lord Jesus Christ? How, if you declare that our souls are made of mud and everything in the world is governed by Fate? What you need to do first is to mend your ways and opinions – then all the rest can be easily mended. And if you are willing, I can help you to achieve that, so that you can see that although you broke all your promises and have been ungrateful to me, I still want to remain your friend."

Mocenigo grinned and nodded his head in the direction of the trapdoor.

"Let me go, sir," came Giordano's voice, plaintive this time. "Please. If I've packed my belongings, it doesn't mean that I wanted to leave tomorrow."

"Why did you do that, then?" Mocenigo said, stroking his beard.

"To curb your impatience to be taught more; to show you that I was prepared to leave if you kept pressing me."

"I see." Mocenigo considered this for a while. "And what will you do if I let you free? Will you continue your lessons?"

"Yes, I'll teach you everything I know. I'll reveal to you all the secrets of the works I have written and intend to write – some of them truly extraordinary. I will be at your service for no other remuneration than you have already given me. And you can keep all my things, if you want – they are all yours anyway."

"Everything? Including your books and papers?"

"Yes," Giordano said. "Except perhaps a few diagrams I am working on just now."

"That must be his book of conjurations," Mocenigo whispered to the others. "Very good, Bruno, very good. I'll think about it. Let me sleep on this, and we can talk again in the morning."

"You will keep me in this dismal place for the whole night?"

"Oh, I'm sure you'll be fine up there, among the souls of so many of your old friends…"

He broke out into laughter as he turned to leave with his men. They had only taken a few steps when they heard the sound of stamping, banging and shouting above.

"You hear, my fine fellows? He's possessed by demons. We did well to lock him up there, out of harm's way."

As they descended the stairs to the first floor, a feeble light met them on the landing.

"Cecilia," Mocenigo said. "What are you doing here? Why are the girls up?"

His wife was wearing a white nightgown and bonnet; a scarlet mantle covered her shoulders and those of his two young daughters, who were looking on with half-suppressed smiles that betrayed their excitement.

"It's impossible to sleep with all that noise and shouting upstairs," she said. "The girls were scared."

Mocenigo gestured to Bortolo and the other men to continue downstairs, and the seven of them filed past him with nods of their heads and mumbled "Goodnights".

"We've locked that man away in the attic. He is not very happy, as you can imagine."

"How much longer do we have to put up with this?"

"Not much longer, Cecilia. I have already spoken to Saluzzo, the Father Inquisitor. I'm turning him in tomorrow."

"Four months of carnival we've had in this house. How many times have I told you? You should never have got involved with that man. There is nothing you can gain from him. I still don't know why you invited him to stay under our roof."

"There are many things you don't know, Cecilia – many things. But you don't need to worry about that. Now you all go back to your beds, and sleep well. Tomorrow is another day. *Come se dise? Passerà pur la notte, e vegnerà doman.*"

11

The appointment was at 7.30 p.m. sharp at the Goccia d'Oro restaurant on the seventy-fifth floor. Peter took Giulia's "sharp" literally, not the Italian way, and by ten to eight he was fidgeting with the menu and his napkin. Two text messages to Giulia received no reply.

When she finally sauntered into the restaurant, she greeted the maître d' and stopped to examine an aquarium full of exotic fish and lobsters. Peter glimpsed at his watch: five past eight. She waved hello with a big smile and walked towards him, dragging a trolley bag behind her.

"Take your time, Giulia," he said, when she reached the table. "Don't rush."

"Sure."

They kissed each other on the cheek, and she sat down, standing the trolley bag up by her side.

"Have you decided to leave?" Peter asked, nodding in the direction of the bag.

"I've brought something to show you."

"You're stealing papers from the library too?"

"No, these are the reference books I used this afternoon." She patted the trolley. "The waiter's coming. Do we order some food? I'm hungry."

Peter grinned. "Me too. What are you having?"

"I don't know. A salad?"

"A salad? And?"

"That's it. Just a salad."

"Just a salad," Peter repeated, glancing at the menu. "OK, you're being dainty. Me, I'm having beef carpaccio to start and a Fiorentina steak as a main. And a bottle of house red. Thank you," Peter said, passing the menus back to the waiter. "So," he continued, turning with a smile to Giulia. "Have you made any other discoveries? Have you found out what the missing papers are?"

"I think I have a hatch," Giulia said as the waiter left.

"A what?"

"A presentiment. What do you call it?"

"Oh – a *hunch*. And what is it?"

"It's complicated. I must explain to you a few things. So be patient, OK?"

"Sure."

She took out five large tomes from the trolley bag and put them on the table, on one side. "These are Bruno's Latin works. We don't need them now." She fished out three more volumes, worn and yellowed. "These are his Italian dialogues. Good editions, very old."

As she rummaged, Peter looked around uncomfortably. "Do you think we need the entire British Library on our table?"

"It's OK, I put them away in a minute. These are the ones I wanted to show you." She handed him two books and placed the others back in the bag. "The one in Italian is about documents by Bruno. Turn to the page I have bookmarked."

He did so and saw the reproduction of a manuscript sheet. He looked up at her.

"This is the longest existing document in Bruno's handwriting. It's a letter he wrote to the vice chancellor of the university of Helmstedt in Germany. The reproduction is not great, so it's difficult to see the detail. Now look at these photos I have taken in the Biblia library with my phone. They are from Al-Rafai's collection. Don't worry, I have asked for permission."

She passed him her phone, and Peter examined the two images for a while.

"Look at the capital A, the J, the B, the H," she said. "Look at the small 't's and the ligatures."

"Well, I'm not an expert, but they seem—"

"Identical. It's Bruno's hand."

"Well done." He gave her back the book and the phone.

"Of course, I knew in my heart the works were authentic, but it is essential to validate that with scholarly evidence. And this is very important for what I have to tell you next. Now, the other book, in English, is by a famous scholar, Frances Yates."

"*The Art of Memory*."

"Yes. It's about Bruno, but not just about Bruno: it's about the memory techniques from classical times to the Renaissance. Yates, she was the first one to… to… how do you say?… revaluate Bruno and—"

"Re-evaluate."

"Yes, and understand the meaning of some of his more obscure works. I am sorry I have to be a bit technical, but I'll try to make it simple for you, OK?"

"Go on. We're still waiting for our food."

"Perhaps you know already that Bruno had an extraordinary memory. In fact, that's how he became famous. People thought he was a kind of *mago*, a sorcerer. He could read the page of a book and say it backwards without looking at it."

"Really?"

"People admired this, but were also scared. You see, he had developed a new powerful system of memory. It was based on the methods of ancient and medieval philosophers, for example Ramon Llull, who believed you could conjure up all human knowledge in your mind by making combinations of a small number of logical concepts and universal truths accepted by everyone – virtue, goodness, divinity, eternity and so on."

"Like a kind of rudimentary mind machine."

"Precisely. This was a time when paper was very expensive and difficult to find. So if you wanted to memorize a long speech or take part in a disputation, this technique was very useful. Llull called his philosophical system *Ars magna*. Remember this name, OK?"

"I'll try." He looked up thankfully at the waiter, who had arrived with his wine.

"Now, the Dominicans were the masters of this art of memory. Bruno was of the same order, so he was well trained in it – but he took it to a much higher level with his new system, a new language to help not just to memorize things, but also to discover the hidden truths of the universe. This was before the great flowering of science, of course."

"Ambitious."

"Yes. He wrote many books on this subject, all in Latin. Some of them are explanations of Llull's method, others are dedicated to his own system of mnemonics. His first important work is *De umbris idearum*. I think he found the idea for the title in a book by a medieval necromant – is that how you say? – a sorcerer who was burnt at the stake – so he knew he was playing with fire and might end up in fire."

"Fascinating."

"What Bruno was trying to do was to create a new mind technique to replace the old one based on Aristotelian philosophy, in accordance with his own Neoplatonic and Copernican vision of the world."

"Giulia, I've got the message. But how did his system work? – I mean, if it's not too complicated and it's not going to take for ever to explain."

"Well, no one knows exactly: there are different theories, and we can only guess. Bruno didn't like rhetoric and sophistry. He was sceptical of words as a means to express high concepts, so he never explained properly. He also didn't trust printed books: he was curious about them and used them with caution, but they were a recent invention. He was ambivalent about them all his life. He thought that fixing a series of signs on a page was like dumbing down the faculties of the imagination, which is powerful and ever-moving, like nature. Perhaps this is why many of his works were never printed in his lifetime, and even the ones he published are often messy, full of mistakes and fragmentary."

"Was it a question of being unable to use the new technology?"

"I don't think so. He simply – how can I say? – he simply thought that human language is weak, limited. He believed in the power of images."

"Images?"

"Yes, mental images. That was his new language. He believed that man should think through images, not words. But here's my salad and your carpaccio. *Finalmente.*"

The arrival of food didn't slow down their conversation. The restaurant was now almost full, and a pleasant hum in the background drowned the loud outbursts from a noisy American party.

"I hope I'm not boring you," said Giulia.

"No, not at all." Peter took a sip of wine from his glass. "This is all very romantic."

Giulia burst out laughing. "Yes, I know. Now we come to the more difficult bit. I have to show you some drawings to explain. Llull's system consisted in a series of concentric wheels, like this one.

"He divided each wheel into sections and put a letter of the alphabet or a word in each of them. The top wheel remained fixed and the other ones turned this way and that, you understand? So he could make a number of combinations and connections, you see? It was a tool to boost the power of the intellect."

"I get it."

"OK, now Bruno developed much more sophisticated memory wheels. In his book he describes two main methods: the first one makes use of three turning wheels, the second one five. When you had mastered the easier technique you could move on to the more difficult one. The advance on Llull is that instead of simple letters or words he uses adaptable mental images to create a huge number of combinations. It's like he is saying: 'The universe is bigger than we thought, life is more complex than we knew, learning is expanding, so we need to train our mind, our imagination, to understand and memorize the infinite variety of nature, language, history, etc.' With the first method he could produce 27,000 combinations, but with the second…"

"A lot more?"

"Almost seventy-six billion."

"Jesus. And I don't even remember what day it is today. What was he trying to memorize?"

"There are different opinions about this. According to some recent scholars, the first method was used to remember syllables and the second one words. It was a kind of mental software to evoke any possible word or concept in your psyche."

"It sounds like a lot of work just to commit a few words to memory. Don't you think this is all slightly over-engineered?"

"Yes, that's what everyone thought in Bruno's time too. No one could understand why he had created such a complicated and obscure system. Many complained that it required so much effort and didn't deliver what it promised to do. But Frances Yates – she thought there was something else behind it."

"Like what?"

"She believed that the wheels, with all their sections and subdivisions and all the references to the Zodiac, the planets and the decans, had some other religious, cosmic and magical significance – which by the way you can find also in Llull's *Ars magna*. So Bruno was not just trying to create a universal memory machine, but wanted to establish a link between the mind of man and the workings of celestial powers – including angels and demons – and between the sublunar world of appearances and the unchanging realm of the Godhead."

"A kind of alchemy of the imagination."

"That's it. His aim was to forge a godlike mind who could grasp and remember every possible combination of the lower world – all the creatures and objects, all human discoveries, thoughts and events – and in this way come to understand and control the laws of the universe. He thought that the stars and the planets were intermediaries between us and the divine unity beyond. So if you could mirror in your mind the mechanics of the astral forces, you'd be able to connect with God – to *be* God, in fact."

Peter let out a deep sigh. "This sort of talk makes me feel so dumb. Our lives and ambitions seem insignificant, almost comical by comparison." He drained the last drops from his glass. "Interesting man."

"Yes, and dangerous too. Now you understand why the Church wanted to get rid of him and his works. But let's go back to the missing documents." She finished her last mouthful of salad and placed her fork on the empty plate. "When I heard that the papers stolen by Marini were under the title or heading 'CM', I thought: 'Um, nine hundred – that's a typical Brunian number.'"

"Why?"

"Why? Because nine hundred is thirty times thirty, and Bruno was obsessed with the number thirty. His memory wheels are divided into thirty segments: if the top wheel doesn't move and one of the others turns, you can create nine hundred combinations, you see? Also, thirty are the statues in his *Lampas triginta statuarum*, thirty the seals in *Explicatio triginta sigillorum*, thirty the sections of the first two parts of *De vinculis in genere*."

"Why is the number thirty so important for him?"

"It must have some magical or cabbalistic significance, possibly to do with the ability to evoke demons or link up with them. But I don't think CM has anything to do with the Latin number nine hundred – or if it has, it's just a coincidence."

"What is it then?"

"I studied the original edition of *De umbris idearum* this afternoon and I saw a reference by Bruno to one of his works that have not survived, called *Clavis magna*."

"Like Lull's *Ars magna*."

"Yes. The *Great Key*, the *Key to Everything*. Many scholars think Bruno never wrote this work. Others believe it's just a collective name he used for some of his books on mnemonics, or an early treatise on memory that was only available as a manuscript. However, there are others who think that *Clavis magna* did exist, but that Bruno decided not to publish it."

"Why?"

"Who knows? Perhaps because he preferred to keep it as a work in progress in his mind instead of seeing it as a book, set and fixed for ever on paper. Or maybe it dealt with dangerous things. In any case, it's the Holy Grail of Bruno's philosophy. If that's what was in the missing papers, you can understand why Marini was tempted to steal them. It could be priceless in monetary terms. Priceless too, for human knowledge. And if it achieves what its title claims – even now, you can see the Catholic Church wishing for it to disappear."

"Mmm, excellent. This is taking a very intriguing turn," Peter said, stroking his chin. "Have you told anyone about your findings?"

"No one apart from you."

"Good. May I ask you to keep this between ourselves? Even the walls have ears these days."

"Of course."

"Perfect. Shall we order some coffee now?"

They had their espressos and continued to talk, joking and teasing each other, until they were the only ones left in the restaurant and realized that it was time to go.

"I'm looking forward to more discoveries tomorrow," Peter said, paying the bill.

"Tomorrow's Friday, so the library is closed. I'll continue on Saturday."

"Oh, I forgot about that. Have you got any plans for tomorrow? There is some work I have to follow up, but I can take off half a day. Perhaps we could go to Petra or Jerash? Or Umm Qais? Madaba?"

"That would be nice."

The maître d' approached their table. "Sorry to disturb you, sir."

"Yes?"

"Mr Al-Rafai's personal assistant called and left message for you."

"Oh, right." He unfolded the piece of paper that was handed to him, read it and sighed. "He wants to see me first thing tomorrow morning. Typical, uh? No sleep for the wicked." He glanced up at Giulia and said with a smile: "We'll catch up tomorrow night or Saturday morning. Enjoy your day off."

12

Venice, 26th May 1592

On the first floor of a building near San Domenico di Castello, which housed the prison of the Holy Inquisition, were gathered the papal nuncio Ludovico Taverna, the Patriarch of Venice Lorenzo Priuli, the regional inquisitor Giovanni Gabriele di Saluzzo and Luigi Foscari, one of the three Wise Men on Matters of Heresy. They had spent a large part of the morning discussing two written denunciations of Giordano Bruno, a friar from Nola, by the aristocrat Giovanni Mocenigo. Now, after a rich lunch that had made Foscari slightly drowsy, they were ready to hear the witnesses in order to prepare the case.

The first to be called in was the Sienese Giovanni Battista Ciotti, the owner of a printing and bookselling business near the church of San Giuliano. The young man was made to swear on the Bible and reminded about the consequences of false testimony.

"Would you please tell this tribunal," Saluzzo asked, "if you know a certain Giordano Bruno – how you got to know him, what manner of a man he is and what is his profession?"

Ciotti wiped his brow and cleared his throat. "Yes, I do know this man. I think he's from Nola or Naples. He's a short fellow, scrawny, with a sparse dark beard – about forty years of age, I'd say. I met him for the first time in Frankfurt, in Germany. I was there for the September book fair – it'll be two years this coming

September. I was staying in the monastery of the Carmelites, as I usually do when I go to that city. I remained there for about two weeks, I think – and this man, Giordano, was also lodged there, so I had the opportunity to talk and discuss things with him several times. His profession was, I suppose, that of a philosopher: he seemed very cultured – a man of great learning." He wiped his brow again. "Then I met him again here in Venice. He came to my shop many times to browse and buy books."

"Very well," Saluzzo said. "Proceed."

Ciotti told the tribunal how he had introduced him to Giovanni Mocenigo and how Bruno had later become the nobleman's tutor in science and the art of memory, first living in a rented room and then in his house. He listed all the works by Bruno he knew of and said he'd heard from many people that the Nolan had given philosophy lectures in Paris and in many cities of Germany.

"Do you know," asked Saluzzo, "if this man, Giordano, is Catholic and lives as a good Christian?"

"Whenever I spoke to him here or in Frankfurt, he never said anything that make me doubt that."

There was a long pause.

"Is there something you would like to add to this?" said Saluzzo.

"Well, not long ago," said Ciotti, "just before Easter, I saw Signor Mocenigo, and he asked me if I was going to Frankfurt for the spring fair. I told him I was, and he said: 'That man' – he meant Giordano – 'has been living at my expense for a while. He promised to teach me many things, and I've given him a great deal of money and gifts for that. But I can't get him to complete his lessons,' he said. 'I'm starting to think he's not an honest man. So, when you go to Frankfurt,' he said, 'I'd be very grateful if you could find out if he's someone to be trusted and if he's likely to keep his promise.' So when I was in Frankfurt I spoke with some of his former students who'd heard him lecture during his time there and who'd had a chance to spend time with him and talk to him. Well, in short, they told me that yes, Giordano did claim to be a master in the art of memory and suchlike secret techniques, but no one had seen any demonstration of it. In fact, all the people who'd had dealings with him about this kind of thing said they'd been very disappointed. And they also said: 'I wonder how he can live in Venice, because people over here regard him as a man without religion.' That's what they said. And when I returned from the book fair and told Signor Giovanni, he said: 'Well, I have the same misgivings. But I'll try to get from him some of the things he promised me, then I'll leave him to the censure of the Holy Office. This is all I know and can tell you about Giordano Bruno – and if I knew more, Fathers, I would tell you."

The officiating clerk reread the minutes, and the witness confirmed his deposition and was asked to take an oath of silence.

Later that afternoon another bookseller, Jacobus Brictanus, originally from Antwerp, was brought in. He confirmed that he had known Bruno for three years, having first met him in Frankfurt and then in Zurich and Venice.

"What was his profession when you first met him?" asked Saluzzo.

"Well, according to the prior of the Carmelite monastery, he spent most of his time writing, daydreaming and racking his brains about the most unusual things." He gave a soft laugh.

"And then, in Zurich?"

"I think he gave lectures to some doctors."

"Heretical doctors?"

"Well, they're all heretics in that city – aren't they, Father?"

"What kind of lectures was he giving?"

"I'm not sure. I only know what he told me, and what he told me was that he was giving lectures to some doctors – but I don't know if these were lectures on philosophy or some other science, because I didn't ask him and no one told me."

"What else was he doing there?"

"I have no idea. But… come to think of it, he mentioned a few times that he was working on a book. He said all knowledge would be revealed in this book, once he'd finished it."

"And after Zurich?"

"I've heard that during the time he was in Padua, before coming to Venice, he was giving lectures to some German students – but again, I don't know what kind of lectures they were."

Brictanus was asked if he thought Bruno was a good Christian.

"I have seen nothing unchristianlike in him."

"Have you heard any comments about him?"

The bookseller screwed his face up as he pondered. "The prior of the Carmelites in Frankfurt – I once asked him what he thought about Giordano, and he said he was a man of talent and learning, a great polymath, but he thought he was someone without religion. 'Bruno claims he knows more than the Apostles did,' the prior told me, 'and that if he just put his mind to it, the whole world would be under one religion.'"

"Anything else?"

"Nothing apart from what I've said already." He turned to the clerk. "May I go now?"

"What is the name of this prior?" asked Saluzzo.

Brictanus exhaled. "I don't know his name, but he's still in Frankfurt and he's prior for life. He has been there these last sixteen years, since I first went to that city and that monastery."

"Do you know if this man, Giordano, also lived in Paris and in other cities of Germany?"

"According to what he told me himself, both in Frankfurt and here, he lived in many cities of Germany and France, in particular Paris, Toulouse and Wittenberg – as well as other places, as I've just said."

"Do you know if Giordano has any close friend in this city – anyone who might know about his life and conduct – or who could provide information relevant to our case? Have you seen and read any of his works? Could you tell this tribunal what you think of them, what these works are and where they were printed?"

Brictanus grimaced. He had left an inexperienced apprentice at the shop, who would probably be losing customers. And he hated acting as an informer for the Church of Rome, whose authority he secretly despised.

"I don't know anyone, in this city or elsewhere, who might be his close friend. The only one who can give you some information about him is the prior I mentioned before."

He gave them details of three of Bruno's books he had seen but not read. He said that he had heard his works praised by everyone for their brilliance and originality.

"I think he gave me a list of all his books himself," he added. "I'll have a look around in my shop, and if I find it I'll bring it over to you immediately."

"Very well," said Saluzzo.

The clerk reread the bookseller's statement and, after confirming it and swearing to secrecy, Brictanus left in a rush.

It was now the defendant's turn to be questioned. Bruno was taken from his prison cell and led into the room by two guards: his pallid face bore the signs of sleepless nights and ill-contained anger.

He was made to stand in front of the prelates, the Patriarch and Foscari, and as the clerk held up the Bible in front of him and began warning him that he should tell the truth and nothing but the truth, Bruno dismissed him with a gesture:

"I shall say the truth indeed!" The Patriarch flinched; Taverna and Saluzzo exchanged a concerned look. "I've been threatened many times with being brought before the Holy Office – and I have always laughed it off, because I'm quite ready to give a full account of myself."

Saluzzo waved his hand, and the clerk retreated to his table and began to take down notes.

"Will you tell this tribunal how you came to be in Venice?" asked Saluzzo.

"Last year, when I was in Frankfurt, I received two letters from a Venetian gentleman, Signor Giovanni Mocenigo. He wrote to me asking if I could teach him the mnemonic and inventive arts. He promised he'd treat me well and said I wouldn't be displeased with him. So I came to Venice – it must be seven or eight months ago now. I taught him several terms relating to both sciences, first living outside his house and then under his own roof."

Bruno went on to relate how he had decided to return to Frankfurt to see some of his works printed, feeling he had taught Mocenigo enough and fulfilled his obligations. On Thursday last, he had asked leave to go, but the young nobleman had refused. He described the terrible scene that ensued the following night, when he was locked in the garret and left there until morning.

"Then an officer arrived, with some other men I didn't know, and he asked them to take me down to a storeroom on the ground floor. I was left there till night, then another officer came with his assistants, and they led me to a prison cell in this building. And I'm sure it's through some slanderous accusation of Giovanni Mocenigo that I'm here. He must have a grudge against me for the reasons I gave you."

The Patriarch leant to his side and, covering his mouth with a hand, whispered something into the ear of Foscari.

"Would the defendant state his name and surname," Saluzzo said, "and tell this tribunal who are or were his parents, where he was born and what is his profession, as well as his father's?"

"My name is Giordano, and my family name is Bruno, from the town of Nola, around twelve miles from Naples. I was born and brought up in that town, and my profession has been and is that of man of letters and sciences. My father was called Giovanni, and my mother Fraulissa Savolino. My father was a soldier. He is dead now, as is my mother."

"Continue."

"I'm around forty-four years of age: from what I heard from my parents, I was born in the year '48. From the age of fourteen I was in Naples, studying humanities, logic and dialectics. I used to attend the public lectures of a man called Sarnese, and received private lessons in logic from an Augustinian friar, Teofilo da Vairano, who went on to lecture on metaphysics in Rome. When I was sixteen or seventeen I took up the Dominican habit at the monastery of San Domenico Maggiore in Naples."

The clerk raised his hand while continuing to write.

"Could the defendant speak more slowly and louder?" said Saluzzo.

Bruno nodded. He recounted how he was clothed in the habit of the order by the prior of San Domenico, Ambrogio Pasca; how after the probational year Father Ambrogio had allowed him to take his first vows in that same monastery; how in due course he had been promoted to the holy orders and ordained priest; how he had sung his first Mass at the convent of San Bartolomeo in Campagna, a town in the lands of the Kingdom but quite far from Naples; and how he had worn the habit of the order, saying Mass and the divine offices and remaining obedient to his superiors and the priors of any other monasteries he had visited, until the year 1576, which was the one after the Jubilee.

"What happened then?" asked Saluzzo.

"I ended up in Rome in the monastery of Santa Maria sopra Minerva, which at that time was under the priorship of Sisto Fabri da Lucca, the Procurator of the Order."

"Why did you go there?"

"I decided to go there because two disciplinary proceedings had been brought against me in Naples."

"What were the charges?"

"The first one was to have given away certain figures and images of saints and to have only kept a crucifix." He smiled. "I was accused of showing a lack of respect to the images of saints. The second one was to have reproached a novice who was reading the *History of the Seven Joys of the Virgin*."

"What did you tell him?"

"I told him: 'What are you doing with that book? Throw it away and read some other book instead, for example *The Life of the Holy Fathers*.'" He chuckled.

"Is that all? Are these the only reasons you decided to abandon your monastery?"

"Well, at the time I went to Rome, I heard these old proceedings were being renewed against me, together with some other allegations – I don't know which ones – so I left the order, gave up my habit and went to Noli, in the Genoese district." There was a short pause. "There I stayed four or five months, teaching grammar to small children and—"

"Very well," interrupted the Patriarch. "It is getting dark, and our honourable clerk must be finding it hard to write without a candle. If Your Excellencies agree, the questioning can be resumed on another date."

Saluzzo nodded and said that the defendant could be taken back to his cell. The clerk concluded the session reading out the usual statutory formulas and warnings, and Bruno was led away.

"It seems a very weak case to me," the Patriarch muttered as he shuffled away with Foscari to attend to another duty.

"It is still early in the trial," said Saluzzo. "Many other elements may emerge."

"Will you favour us with your company at dinner?" said Taverna.

"I'm afraid I have another engagement," said the Patriarch. "Please keep me informed if there are any developments in the coming days, will you?"

"Of course," said Saluzzo.

The prelates bowed and the Patriarch left the room, followed by Foscari and the clerk.

"The Patriarch is right," said Taverna. "There seems to be little substance in your informer's claims: neither witness has confirmed any of Mocenigo's allegations of heresy. The case will be dismissed by the Doge and the Senate."

"Leave it with me," said Saluzzo, resting his hand on Taverna's arm. "I'll have another word with Mocenigo – and I'll write to Cardinal Santoro in Rome for advice. One thing's for sure: now that he's in our clutches, I won't turn that man loose again so easily."

13

Peter stepped out of the Tower at eight o'clock the following morning for his meeting with Mr Al-Rafai. He walked, coffee in hand, towards the black Mercedes waiting for him outside the lobby. Two burly men in suits with thick moustaches were waiting for him.

"Majed having a day off?"

"Yes, Mr Simms. Day off with family and children."

He sat in the back, poring over the logs that he had extracted from the IT department. Late last night he had spent a couple of hours familiarizing himself with the data, and now he was building up a picture of Marini's movements. He could trace Marini's daily arrival in the building, his check-in at the library and his departure in the evening – but there were other recurring trips, to and from a location on the same level as one of the scanning rooms, which seemed curious. Did the Jesuit go there to make copies of some of the documents? Or to hide away the papers?

"Time to take a sniff around," Peter thought to himself.

The car sped down the highway and then through the streets of Amman – Peter had not appreciated, until now, how careful a driver Majed was. Soon they were again out of the city and on an empty straight road going north or north-east, judging from the position of the sun in the sky. After a while he thought he recognized a building on a scrubby hill that was looming up.

"Mr Al-Rafai's house, right?"

The driver turned with a smile. "Yes, yes."

They went past the exit that led to the top of the hill.

"Weren't we supposed to take that one to the right?"

"No, no. We go other way, Mr Simms."

"Other route," said his companion.

"OK."

But they left more exits behind, and the hill receded into the distance.

"Guys, are you sure we're going in the right direction?"

"Yes, yes," said the driver.

"How far are we?"

"Not far, Mr Simms, not far. Shall I put music for you?"

"No, I don't want music. I want to know when we are going to get to our destination."

"Five minute."

"Right." He reached for his phone to call Al-Rafai, but there was no network coverage. "Great." Peter looked around – they were in the middle of the desert. "Will you at least let me know when we cross the border to Iraq?"

This time the driver turned with an unsmiling face and gave no reply.

Twenty minutes later the traffic began to intensify again, and they took a turn to their right to enter a long stretch of road flanked by trees and vegetation. At the end of it, they joined a queue of vehicles – mostly pick-ups and lorries – waiting to get past a gate. When their turn arrived, the driver flashed his documents. They went through a second checkpoint and beyond a wire fence.

As the car moved forward at a slow walking pace, Peter glanced around: tents – endless rows of tents – and shacks, makeshift shops, water tanks, Portakabins and squat prefab buildings. Abject-looking figures straggled about or sat in the shade, while scraggy kids played in the dirt or ran towards the car to peer into the back windows.

"Where are we?" he asked.

They advanced through that vast, unreal city which seemed to sprawl for miles in every direction. Wherever he turned his gaze, Peter saw signs of precariousness and deprivation – and children, children everywhere: a boy ferrying his little sister in a rusty wheelbarrow; another pushing a broken wheelchair around, tilting it on its back wheels as if it were a bike; a girl beating on a plastic bottle with a stick.

They stopped in front of a large tent, over which flew the flag of Syria.

"Jesus..."

The driver opened the back door and nodded towards the entrance to the tent.

"OK."

The interior was Bedouin-style, with low sofas and brightly coloured cushions. Two men were sitting at the far corner: a cleric, older, with a turban and a long beard sweeping down his robes, and a young man.

The younger man stood up and stretched out an arm.

"Please Mr Simms, take a seat. Thank you. I am Kamal, and this is Sheikh Mahfuz." The cleric gave a gentle nod of acknowledgement. "I'll be your interpreter today."

"Where is Mr Al-Rafai?"

Kamal smiled. "Mr Al-Rafai is busy in Neverland."

"Does he know I'm here?"

"He will know tonight or tomorrow."

"Oh Christ."

Kamal shook his head, amused. "Don't worry – you'll be back at your hotel later."

"I'll believe that when I am."

"Would you like some tea?"

"No."

Kamal poured tea in a small glass anyway and handed it to him. The cleric nodded again, then began to speak, breaking off at the end of each sentence to allow Kamal to translate.

"This is a very strange country, Mr Simms. There are cities that have existed for millennia, and others that have sprung up in less than a year, like this one. The westerners visit Petra or Amman, but no one knows about Za'atari or Azraq: it's like they are not on the map. A lot of people suffer in these places – people without a life, without a future – but the West is blind, indifferent. All it cares about is selling Coca-Cola to every person on the planet, and infecting the mind of young people with false dreams. They come here, to a country that is not their own, and build their towers, as tall as the sky. Why do they do it? What do they want to achieve? They want to control, to influence. They waste billions on their towers when a small part of that money could improve the life of the people in this city."

Peter opened his mouth to respond, then clamped it shut again: he knew better than to contradict a mullah in his own tent.

"Mr Al-Rafai doesn't know and doesn't care about the suffering in this country. He is a pampered child. He studied abroad, and his mind is poisoned. His religious beliefs prevent him from joining in the struggle on the path to God. He has embraced evil values: money, greed, lust, excess. He prefers dead things to the simple duty of living as God commands. And he is happy to get into bed with the Devil so long as he can satisfy his animal needs. But he will be punished. Hell will be filled to the brim with people like him." Sheikh Mahfuz raised his index finger and Kamal's tone went up a register: "The men who built their tower in our lands, they are not acting in good faith. They say their aim is to spread learning, but they are only interested in lucre. They work in the service of the last of the thirty false prophets. And Al-Rafai, he should not have listened to the whispers of the Deceiver. He should not have consorted with the enemies of truth and Islam. So he is warned – and you are warned too, Mr Simms. You are both treading close to the edge. You are tempting the wrath of God."

Peter, trying not to appear intimidated, waited as the cleric paused and the interpreter turned a blank stare on him.

"Amman was already a flourishing city thirteen hundred years before the birth of Isa, the Messiah," Mahfuz resumed. "At that time, when we were building marble temples and studying the course of the stars, your people were in the Bronze Age, and America still in its prehistory. For centuries we were the heart of civilization. For centuries we have practised art, literature and science. So don't think you can teach us anything. You should come here with a humble heart, to learn from a culture which is deeper and more ancient than yours. If you have killed God in your soul to replace it with your own image, it doesn't mean that the whole of mankind should follow your example. This is the last warning, and there will be no more warnings. *Allāhu Akbar* – God is great."

There was a long, uncomfortable silence.

"Is that it?" Peter ventured after a while. "Can I go?"

Mahfuz gestured and mumbled.

"The sheikh asks if you will take more tea."

"I don't want more tea."

"He would like to tell you a story before you go," Kamal said, pouring another glass.

"Right."

"It is the story of Nimrod, who made men rebellious against God. After defeating his enemies, Nimrod was made king over all the people on earth. Before that time, he had lived in fear of God; now he became an idolater and only worshipped power and gold. He hated the good man Abraham, who respected God, and tried to kill him. He gave orders to throw him into a heated furnace, but Abraham came out unscathed. Nimrod decided to build a high tower so that he could ascend into the heavens and strike down God for protecting Abraham. But when the tower was completed and he climbed up to the top, he realized that the skies were not any closer. So he descended in a rage and tried to think of other ways to reach the heavens and defeat God. But the following day the tower collapsed, and all his stonemasons and architects were dispersed into the world, babbling with terror at the might of the Lord in an unintelligible language." The cleric raised his finger again. "All the houses erected by Nimrod are built on sand. The time of a great tumult, the tumult of the Deceiver, will come soon, before the advent of the true Messiah. The Deceiver will arrive on the earth and call out in a loud voice, and some people will respond to him and believe in him. He will order the sky to rain, the dry land to yield grain and the cattle to return to their barns in the evening with their udders full of milk. Then he will go to another people and repeat his call, but they will refuse to listen to him. So he'll go away, and that people will be stricken with famine and lose all their wealth. He will pass by the ruins and say, 'Show me all your treasures now. You have ignored my call. You have rejected me as your king and saviour. I've brought you heaven on earth, but you have chosen to seek protection from your god. Now ask him to help you.' These will be the words of the Deceiver, the last of the thirty false prophets, masquerading hell as heaven and heaven as hell." The cleric stood and put his hand to his chest, bowing his head. "*Fī amān Allāh*."

Peter got to his feet. "*Fī amān Allāh*."

"What would you like to say to Sheikh Mahfuz?" asked Kamal.

Peter studied the floor at his feet, pondering. "Please tell him that his words will not be taken lightly."

Kamal translated and the cleric gave a slight nod.

The drive back took them through more misery and wretchedness – old men bearing heavy sacks on their backs, women carrying thin babies in the fierce sun, clutches of gaunt teenagers kicking at a red ball among clouds of dust, children holding sticks and stones, threatening to use them – until they reached the rear gate and joined the ring road around the refugee camp. Soon they were back on the highway, speeding across long stretches of desert back to Amman.

"Shall I put music, Mr Simms?" asked the driver.

"Yes, put on some music."

As the notes of an Arabic song drifted over to him, Peter took out his wallet and looked at the message given to him in the restaurant last night. He couldn't believe he had fallen into such an easy trap. He shook his head – "Idiot!" he hissed – and put a hand over his eyes, recalling Mahfuz's warnings, the raised finger, the reedy voice telling him that he was "tempting the wrath of God"… The dead worm and rat were games compared to this clear and real threat by a zealot who held life to be worthless.

14

Venice, 2nd June 1592

Monsignor Saluzzo, the papal nuncio Taverna, the Patriarch of
Venice and the Wise Man Sebastiano Barbarigo were assembled
for the third session of the trial. Since all the judges, apart
from Saluzzo, had been absent during the previous session,
the clerk was asked to read a summary of the proceedings
on 30th May.

"Before I do that," said the clerk, "perhaps I should bring to
the attention of this court that Signor Giovanni Mocenigo has
presented further evidence in support of his accusations. Here-
with is a copy of his letter of 29th May last." He passed a sheet
to the Patriarch and to Barbarigo. They scanned the document
and conferred between them for a few moments.

The clerk then went on to recapitulate Bruno's statement
from the last sitting of the tribunal. "The defendant told this
Court that after leaving Rome he led a wandering life, first
through northern Italy and then Europe. For a time he claims
to have worn the habit again, before taking it off for good
when he went to Geneva, where he was helped by the Mar-
quis del Vico and his Italian friends, who gave him a sword, a
hat, a cape and other items of clothing, and helped him find
a job as a" – he adjusted his spectacles – "as a proofreader.
Although he often resided among heretics, he claims he always
refused to embrace their religion and continued to live as a

good Catholic. Yet" – he raised his eyes and looked at the inquisitor – "yet, he admits attending, during his short stay in Switzerland, the heretical sermons of French and Italian theologians such as Niccolò Balbani of Lucca, who preached on the Gospel and lectured on St Paul's epistles." He cleared his throat. "In France he claims to have made a name for himself as a lecturer on philosophy. In Paris he gave thirty lessons on thirty attributes of God, taken from the first part of Aquinas's *Summa*. He claims to have acquired such fame in that city that one day King Henry III summoned him to court and asked him to give a demonstration of his memory skills, and he showed that they had been obtained through science, not by magic." Again, he looked up to the inquisitor. "The defendant insisted on this point. He had several books printed over the years, on the art of memory and other philosophical subjects – and the reason he wanted to go to Frankfurt now was to have some other works published – one in particular, called *On the Seven Liberal Arts*."

"Is that all?" asked Barbarigo, getting impatient.

"The accused also declared," the clerk continued, "to have communicated his intentions to Signor Mocenigo and some Dominican friars who are here in Venice for the general chapter of their order, in particular to Father Domenico da Nocera, rector of the college of San Domenico in Naples."

"Has Father Domenico been summoned as a witness?" asked Barbarigo.

"There will be no need," said Saluzzo. "He has produced a written statement."

"And what does it say?"

"It confirms the deposition given by the defendant."

The clerk handed copies of the friar's statement to the judges.

CHAPTER 14

"If my honourable colleagues agree," said Saluzzo, "we can now proceed to the cross-examination of the accused."

Bruno was shown into the room by two soldiers. In his hands he was holding a few books and a bundle of papers, which he was asked to place on the clerk's table.

"Will the defendant tell this tribunal," said Saluzzo, after Bruno had been sworn in, "if he has any recollection of all the books he has written and sent to the printing press, and if he remembers what subjects and ideas were professed in them?"

"I've made a list of all the books I've had printed, as well as those I've written and not published yet, which I was revising with a view to having them printed as soon as it was practical, either in Frankfurt or some other city."

"Could the clerk confirm that the list in question is written in the defendant's hand?"

The clerk examined it. "I can confirm it is written in his hand."

"Would you please add this document to the minutes of the trial?"

The clerk nodded.

"Will the defendant tell this tribunal," Saluzzo continued, "if all the books published under his name or still in manuscript form that are included in this list have been written by him and express his own ideas?"

"Yes, they have all been written by me and express my ideas – with the exception of the last one in the list of those still unpublished, *De sigillis Hermetis, Ptolomæi et aliorum.* That's not one of my books. I had it transcribed from another manuscript."

"And where is that manuscript?"

"It's with one of my students, Hieronymus Besler."

"Where is that gentleman from?"

"From Nuremberg in Germany. He was in Padua until not long ago, and he worked for me as a copyist for about two months."

"Were the books printed in the cities and places that are stated on their title pages or elsewhere?"

"All those that say 'Venice' on their title page were printed in England."

"Why?"

"It was the printer's idea to do that, so that they could be sold more easily and have a better chance of success. He claimed that if their title pages said they were printed in England, he would have struggled to sell them in that country."

"What about the other books?"

"Nearly all of them were printed in England too, even though the title pages say 'Paris' or some other city."

"Would the defendant tell this tribunal what the subject matter of these books is?"

"Broadly speaking, all these books have a philosophical subject. They are obviously very different, as can be seen from their titles. In all of them I have argued my points philosophically, according to the principles of natural reason: my main concern was not what ought to be believed according to faith. And I don't think you'll find in them anything that shows I'd rather challenge religion than exalt philosophy. Although I grant you," he added, smiling, "that I may have expressed many impious ideas based on my natural reason."

Saluzzo gazed at him with a grave look. "Have you ever taught, professed or debated, in any of the public or private lessons you have held in various cities, as mentioned in your previous depositions, any opinions that are contrary or offensive to the Catholic faith and what is sanctioned by the Holy Roman Church?"

"I have taught nothing *directly* against the Catholic religion. But indirectly yes, I may have done so, as some people thought in Paris." He gave a soft chuckle. "But even there I was allowed to engage in certain disputes – for example when I published *One Hundred and Twenty Articles against the Peripatetics and Other Vulgar Philosophers*, which was printed with the permission of the superiors – because it was deemed fair to do that following the principles of natural reason, without prejudice to the truth according to the light of faith. Aristotle's and Plato's works may be read and taught in that way too. And they are, in a similar way, *indirectly* contrary to faith – indeed much more so than the opinions I've put forward and defended philosophically. And if you would like to know my views, you'll be able to find all of them in my latest Latin books printed in Frankfurt, called *De minimo*, *De monade*, *De immenso et innumerabilibus* and, in part, in *De compositione imaginum*."

"What are your views, then?" asked Saluzzo. "We don't have time to read all your books."

"I believe the universe to be infinite – the effect of God's infinite power – and to be filled with infinite worlds similar to the earth and an infinite number of other celestial bodies and stars. A universal providence governs all things: thanks to it, everything lives, grows, moves and exists in its perfection."

"How do you see this providence?"

"In two ways: first, in the way the soul is inherent in the body, both in its entirety and in any part of it – which I call 'nature', the shadow and trace of the divinity – and secondly, in the way the Godhead, by essence, presence and power, is in all things and above all things – not as part, not as soul, but in a manner that cannot be described."

"So you don't believe it's one of the attributes of God?"

"I believe, together with the theologians and the greatest philosophers, that all the attributes of God are one and the same thing. The three divine attributes of power, wisdom and goodness – that is mind, intelligence and love – are in everything and above everything."

"But what about your ideas in relation to faith?"

"You mean, not philosophically speaking?"

"Yes."

"Well…" Bruno hesitated and flicked his eyes to the floor. "Regarding, in particular, the three persons of the Godhead, the divine wisdom and the son of the divine intelligence, which philosophers call 'intellect' and theologians the 'Word', and which is said to have taken upon itself a human body…"

"Yes?"

"Well, from a strictly philosophical point of view, I have had doubts about it and believed in it with inconstant faith."

"Have you?" Saluzzo aimed a knowing look at the other judges.

"Though I don't remember showing signs of it in any of my writings or speeches." His lips twitched. "Unless someone, as for the other things, may have *indirectly* gathered it from the ideas and opinions I've expressed on what can be proved by logic or deduced through reason." There was a short pause. "And the same applies to the third person's divine spirit: I was not able to believe in accordance with faith, but regarded it as the attendant soul of the universe, in line with Pythagorean thought and also with what Solomon says in his Book of Wisdom: 'The Spirit of the Lord filleth the world – and that which containeth all things…' This seems in perfect agreement with the Pythagorean doctrine as expressed by Virgil in the sixth book of the *Aeneid*:

"Know that the heavens and the earth, the watery plains,
the bright orb of the moon and the Titanian stars are sustained
by a soul within them: a mind infused through every limb
stirs their whole mass, etc. etc.

"And according to my philosophy, it is from this spirit, called
'life of the universe', that the life and soul of every living thing
derives – including that of the bodies. And I believe it to be
immortal. As far as their substance is concerned, all bodies are
immortal, since death is nothing but separation and reaggregation. And this doctrine seems to be expressed in Ecclesiastes,
where it says: 'There is no new thing under the sun. *Quid est
quod est? Ipsum quod fuit*', etc. etc."

"Will the defendant tell this tribunal if he, in actual fact,
has always believed and still believes and holds true that the
Trinity – Father, Son and Holy Spirit – are one in essence but
distinct in person, as is taught and accepted by the Catholic
Church?"

Bruno confirmed that he had had doubts about the concept
of "person" as applied to the Son and the Holy Spirit. He had,
however, read in St Augustine that it was a new concept even
for him at that time.

"This has been my opinion," he added with a smile, "since
I was eighteen years of age, but I have never, *in actual fact*,
expressed it in my lectures or in my writings. As I said before,
I only doubted in my own mind."

"And will the defendant tell this tribunal if he has always believed and still believes in everything the Holy Mother Catholic
Church teaches, believes and holds true about the first person
– and whether he has ever had doubts of any kind about the
first person?"

"I have always, and without any doubts, believed and held true what every faithful Christian ought to believe and hold true regarding the first person. As to the second person, I should say that, really, I've always considered it one in essence with the first – and so the third – because being indistinct in essence, they cannot be susceptible of any inequality: all the attributes belonging to the Father must also belong to the Son and the Holy Spirit. My only doubts, as I said before, were about how this second person could be made flesh and suffer. But I have never expressed this in word or teaching. And if I ever said anything about this second person, it was only to quote the opinion of other thinkers, such as Arius, Sabellius or one of their followers." He shook his head and snorted. "I'll tell you what I might have said that caused so much scandal – I suspect this was noted down in the first proceedings against me in Naples, as I said in my initial deposition."

"Tell us, then."

"One day, I was talking about Arius's doctrine and I argued that it was less pernicious than it was commonly thought and believed. I said that Arius never claimed that the Word was the first thing created by the Father: I said that for him the Word was neither creator nor creature, but a *medium* between them, just like between the speaker and the thing spoken."

"That's all you said?"

"Well, perhaps I pushed my arguments too far, and this must be one of the reasons I was held in suspicion and disciplined. But I told you what I really thought about this. And even here in Venice," he added, "I remember arguing this point: that Arius never meant to say that Christ, the Word, was a creature, but rather a *mediator*, as I explained before."

"Where in Venice?" asked Saluzzo.

"I don't remember where, exactly – whether it was at an apothecary's or a bookseller's – but I know I said this in one of these shops. I was having a conversation with some priests who claimed to be theologians."

"Do you have their names?"

"No, I don't. And I wouldn't recognize them if I saw them again. But all I was doing was expressing my own interpretation of Arius's doctrine."

"Very well," said Barbarigo, who was tired of all those theological disquisitions and looking forward to his lunch. "It is past noon, so I suggest that we adjourn until this afternoon at three o'clock."

Giordano was led away by the soldiers, and the judges left the room soon after.

Over lunch, Saluzzo and Taverna continued to talk about the trial, in particular about Bruno.

"He is a very shrewd man," said the nuncio.

"As shrewd as the Devil," said Saluzzo, knitting his brows. "He only mentions people who are dead, unavailable or untraceable. And have you seen with what impudence and brazenness he plays about with the dogma of the Trinity? Ah!" He shook his head and placed his fork on the table. "But he is mistaken if he thinks that striking a philosopher's pose will protect him. He won't be able to hide much longer behind that cloak of irony and sophistry. Next time he'll hear my voice he'll tremble, because I am going to shatter him to pieces."

15

The day after his forced trip to Za'atari, Peter woke up late and with a groggy head. Without shaving or having breakfast, he went to see Jim, but his office was closed. Through the glass wall he could see his ultra-flat screens turned to face the door, with the words "BACK IN 20 MINUTES" appearing across their length and getting chomped up at regular intervals by a giant Pac-Man.

From the main reception desk on the ground floor, he tried to call Chad, but he wasn't in either, so he walked off to Starbucks to get himself a coffee. The entrance hall was deserted, and no one appeared to be entering or leaving the building. Now that he thought of it, he had not even seen the guard outside his room that morning. Where was everyone?

After ordering a black Americano, he said to the girl at the till: "Not many people around today, uh? I thought the Tower was open on Saturdays."

The girl smiled and gave him a puzzled look. "Of course it's open. They're all outside to see the world-record attempt. It's even on TV." She pointed at one of the flat screens hanging on the wall, which showed helicopter images of the building and news headlines in Arabic. He collected his coffee and decided to go and see for himself.

Outside, he found tens of thousands of people gathered around the base of the Tower and looking up, many of them holding up phones and tablets, as two helicopters circled overhead.

"What's happening?" Peter said to the tubby man beside him, joining in the direction of the collective stare, but seeing nothing other than the dazzling flank of the building.

The man glanced at him, then raised his chin again. "Oh, he's on the thirtieth floor or thereabouts. It'll take him at least seven hours to get to the top."

"Who's he?"

"German guy, I think."

"Is he wearing a harness?"

"No, just free-climbing."

"Crazy." Peter shook his head and returned inside.

Jim wasn't back in his office yet, so he looked into the room next door and saw Boris sitting at his desk with his eyes glued to the screen of his laptop. Peter gave a gentle knock on the glass door as he went in.

"How are you, Boris?"

"Not a good day," he said. "Not a good day." His eyes were red-rimmed and circled by dark rings. "Take a seat," he said, waving towards a sitting ball.

"Is anything wrong?"

"Didn't sleep at all last night."

"What's the matter?"

He took off his glasses and massaged his eyes. "The system crashed and we're all trying to fix it. The Internet's dead too. Thank God it happened yesterday, which wasn't a working day."

"That's why my connection isn't working. What caused the crash?"

"Not sure — we're still investigating. Hackers, probably, a DDoS attack or something like that."

"What are they trying to do? Break into the system?"

"Just create disruption, I suppose."

"Then why did they do it on a Friday, when everyone's off work?"

"Maybe it's a dry run for a bigger assault."

"What makes you think it's not a technical glitch?"

"These." He handed Peter two sheets of papers. "Shutdown threats. We've received a lot of them recently."

"Handwritten?"

"Uh-huh."

"Bookworm…" Peter mused, frowning as he looked up. "Does Chris Dale know about this?"

"Of course he does. He sent circulars over the last few weeks. He asked the staff to be vigilant. Everyone's nervous about these Bookworm people."

"Why?"

"Because we know they're planning an act of sabotage."

"Are the threats sent by post?"

"No, they're left all over the building: in the main hall, in the library, in the middle of corridors."

Peter glanced at the letters. "This seems very low-tech for someone who's just launched a cyber attack."

"This is how they usually operate. Paper is less traceable than an IP address."

Peter drummed his fingers on his thigh. "Who are they?"

"Who? Bookworm? I don't know. Maybe they're a splinter group of Anonymous or LulzSec."

"How can they be opposed to new technology if they're using it themselves?"

"Well, they are not against computers or technology per se. They're against the mass digitization of printed works – that's different." He put on his glasses again and yawned. "They see it as the expropriation of knowledge by the big

Internet companies – the content of books reduced to a form of property serving the interest of the few rather than the common good."

"Free flow of information, no governmental or corporate control, that sort of thing."

"Yes, free access to information, free distribution of content. No filtering and censoring."

"No capital-driven exploitation of human knowledge."

"Yes."

"Boris, do you mind if I take these shutdown threats with me?"

"Sure."

"Thanks. Look, I know you're busy, so I won't take more of your time. But I need to know the location that corresponds to this code. It's from one of the sheets you gave me on Thursday."

"Right. Let me see," he said, typing. He craned his head forward and narrowed his eyes. "It's at the back of Scanning 2. Oh, it's one of the new rooms of the Hive."

"The Hive?"

"It's a large business centre – hundreds of suites we're leasing out to local and international businesses."

"Could you look up who has been using that room?"

"The system's down, so I can't check."

"Do you think I could go there and have a quick look around?"

"Sure, but I don't think I can take you there myself at the moment."

"Of course."

"But what I can do is ask someone from reception to escort you. I'll give them a buzz now."

"Cheers. I hope you can sort out your system – and get some sleep."

"That would be good."

In the lift Peter examined the shutdown threats. They were written in a neat, regular hand: "The mind of the great beast will go dark soon: prepare for the digital Apocalypse." "Long live human memory: death to the memory of machines." Peter pulled a puzzled face. Chris Dale, VP of Biblia, had kept this information from him, lying to him by saying that the group was not active in that country. What game was he playing?

A young Arabic woman from reception took him down to the Hive, not before giving Peter a full update on the world-record attempt.

"He's on the forty-sixth floor now."

"Not even a quarter of the way up."

"He should reach the top at around four thirty."

They meandered through a series of white corridors and hallways in the deep entrails of the Tower. Left and right, straight ahead, right and left, with door following door in regular succession, and not a single person in sight.

"Ninety per cent of the units are still empty," the girl explained, "but we expect full occupancy by the time we open later in the year."

"When will that be?"

"I'm not sure. They keep postponing the opening date."

They came to a large glass partition frosted with the Biblia logo.

"This is the section you're interested in," the woman said, swiping her card and opening the glass door.

Peter stepped inside: a long corridor with countless doors off it stretched ahead.

"I thought the code would take me to a particular room."

"You don't know which unit?"

"No, that's all I have."

"Then the person was probably visiting someone who had the key to one of the suites."

"You mean someone who came with him or was already in one of these rooms and let him in?"

"Exactly."

"How many suites are there?"

"Five hundred."

Peter gave a sigh. "The proverbial needle in a haystack. Do you have a universal key?"

"Yes."

"How fast can you knock?"

They checked the suites one by one. Most of them were still vacant, with cables dangling from the ceiling and a pungent odour of new plastic. Others were full of cardboard boxes and stacks of furniture and folders. A few were furnished but empty. In one of them there was a snooker table with the overhead lights still on; in another, a desk stood in the middle of the room, surrounded by aquariums and vivaria with menacing little creatures inside.

As soon as they opened the door to Unit 72, the smell of old paper wafted out. They switched on the lights: the walls were lined with floor-to-ceiling shelves filled with printed matter. Peter ran his fingers along a shelf: manuscript bundles tied with string and ancient books bound in morocco, vellum or light calf.

He examined the titles of the volumes: *De le tre vite* by Ficino, *De hominis dignitate* and *De animæ immortalitate* by Ioann. Picus Mir., *Sphæra Mundi* by Ioann. de Sacr., *Scholæ* by Ramus.

"Mm…"

The next bookcase contained the *Encyclopædia Britannica*, the *Enciclopedia Italiana Treccani* and other multi-volumed works of reference. He continued to scan the spines and came to another section: tomes by Romberch, Cornelius Agrippa, Lully and Thomas Aquinas – and then, with a blazing feeling of discovery, he saw rows and rows of books by and on Giordano Bruno.

"I think I've found what I was looking for," said Peter, stroking his chin. "I'll have to come back with my colleague."

"OK."

He had a final look round and stopped by the desk. Neatly arranged on its wooden top were a Latin dictionary, a history textbook, some pencils, a pair of compasses and a paperweight in the shape of a skull – which he lifted, revealing a yellow sticky note with five concentric circles drawn on it.

The computer was off: a business card was taped to the screen. Peter leant over to have a better look at it.

"Mmm. Such a small world."

On the card were printed the contact details of Dr Abdul-Basir Al-Rafai – the same Al-Rafai who had made him travel over seven thousand miles to investigate the disappearance of papers which could very well be tucked away in a corner of that room. That made no sense at all. What was going on?

"Good," Peter said, clearing his throat from the dust. "We can go."

They locked the door and made their way back towards the main reception. The TV screens were no longer showing pictures of the world-record attempt, but were filled with talking heads.

"How's Spider-Man doing?" Peter asked a man in green uniform who was passing by. The man stopped and stared at him with a blinking expression. "The German climber, you know?"

The man smiled and waved his hand. "Oh. Embarrassing, sir. Very embarrassing. He give up."

"He gave up?"

"Yes. He give up." The man laughed and continued to wave his hand. "He get scared on sigsty-three floor. Banick attack. *Yani*, he don't want to go up or down any more... Helicopters has to bring him down. Very bad. Very bad. All world watching."

16

Venice, 2nd June 1592

The trial resumed after the three-hour intermission. The Patriarch and the nuncio did not return for the afternoon session, but asked their deputies to attend in their stead. Barbarigo ordered that the defendant be brought before the judges. Once Bruno was sworn in, Saluzzo continued his cross-examination.

The inquisitor asked him again if he had ever expressed in word or writing anything else which was contrary to the teachings of the Holy Church – in particular about the Incarnation of the second person – and Giordano repeated what he had declared in the morning, admitting that he had had doubts about this point, but saying he had taken comfort from the words of St Augustine, who wrote: "It is with awe that, when we speak of matters divine, we pronounce the word 'person', and we use it only out of necessity."

"And I don't think I have ever come across this term or figure of speech," Bruno added, "in the Old or in the New Testament."

Saluzzo examined his notes and took his time before continuing the interrogation. "Since you had doubts about the Incarnation of the Word," he finally said, "what were your beliefs about Christ?"

Bruno was taken aback by the bluntness of that question.

"I… well, my understanding…"

"Your understanding?"

153

"My understanding is that... the divinity of the Word and the humanity of Christ met in one... individual being. I don't see how the two natures can coexist in the same way as body and soul in a man."

"Why?"

"Because there can be no relation between the infinite divine substance and the finite human nature. But I've only doubted the ineffable character of this union, without denying the authority of the Scriptures."

"Give a precise answer to my question," Saluzzo pressed on. "What were and are your beliefs about Christ? Now you're saying that you've had doubts about *how* the two natures coexist – earlier on, you said you've long questioned the *possibility* of the Word being made flesh."

"My only doubt about the Incarnation of the Word," said Bruno, retaining his composure, "was that it didn't seem to make sense from a theological point of view: the divine nature can only coexist with the human by way of *assistentia*, a kind of 'presence', as I explained before. But from this I didn't infer anything contrary to the divinity of Christ, or of the *suppositum divinum* that is called Christ."

Saluzzo lowered his eyes and paused, reading through his notes. That fiend was slipping away from him again. He kept changing his story and equivocating, resorting to the subtleties of rhetoric and the dazzling terms of Thomism. The inquisitor glanced up, and the look on Bruno's face was one of haughty determination, of defiance. Gone was his sarcasm, gone were his angry manners and, more worryingly, gone was any trace of fear or dejection. Saluzzo realized that standing in front of him was one of the best minds of his age, fully in control of himself and resolved to fend off any attack.

"Very well," he said. "What are your beliefs about the actions, the miracles and the death of Christ? Have you ever said anything contrary to what is sanctioned by the Catholic Church?"

"No."

"Have you ever talked about the sacrifice of the Holy Mass and the ineffable transubstantiation of Christ's flesh and blood into bread and wine then taking place? What were your beliefs about this?"

"I believed according to the dictates of the Holy Church."

"Why didn't you attend Mass then?"

"Because I knew I was excommunicated. But I never doubted or disbelieved transubstantiation – even when I was among Calvinists, Lutherans and men of other religions. I've already confessed what my doubts about faith were – and of my own accord. When I lived among heretics, I only dealt in philosophical matters – and the reason I wasn't persecuted by them is that I didn't meddle or interfere with their doctrines. In fact, I'd rather let them believe I was a man of no religion, so that I did not have to take on their beliefs."

"Have you not," asked Saluzzo, "contrary to what you're saying, affirmed that Christ" – he glanced at his notes – "was not God but a wicked person, and that because of his wicked actions he should have expected to be put to death – although he then proved himself unwilling to die?"

Bruno widened his eyes in surprise and agitation. "Why are you asking me this? I never believed, said or thought anything about Christ other than what I have just said – which is this: that I believe what the Holy Mother Church believes." His voice trailed off. He covered his face with his hands, and his emaciated frame was shaken by a series of sobs and little gasps. "I… I don't know how… how I can be accused of these things," he managed to say through the tears.

Barbarigo exchanged some whispered words with the Patriarch's deputy, and for a moment Saluzzo feared that the Wise Man might call the entire trial off on the grounds of unfair treatment of the accused. But he soon realized that his worries were unfounded, as he saw the deputy nod and smile.

Once Bruno managed to collect himself, the inquisitor continued to question him on other points of faith – about the immaculate conception, the sacrament of penitence, the immortality of the soul – and the Nolan's replies betrayed no sign of unorthodoxy.

"Are you well versed," asked Saluzzo, "in theological studies and fully conversant with the precepts of Catholicism?"

"No, not really," Giordano said. "My main area of interest has always been philosophy, since that was my profession."

"Is it true that you despise theologians and claim that all theological studies are vain?"

"I never said anything other than good things about theologians – at least those who are not regarded as heretics."

"And which ones do you consider heretics?" Saluzzo insisted.

"All those who profess to be theologians but who are not in agreement with the Church of Rome."

"Have you read any books by any of these heretical theologians?"

"Yes."

"Which ones?"

"I've read books by Melanchthon, Luther, Calvin and other foreign heretics."

"Why did you read them? To learn their doctrines and use them in your works?"

"No," he said, laughing, "I believe they are more ignorant than myself."

"Why then?"

"Just out of curiosity."

"Have you ever kept any of these books with you?"

Bruno shook his head. "I would never do that."

"Why?"

"Because I know they deal with subjects that are contrary and repugnant to the Catholic faith – but I did keep some books by other banned authors."

"Such as?"

"Ramon Llull and other thinkers, but only covering philosophical matters."

"And what is your opinion about the heretics you mentioned before?"

"I despise both them and their doctrines, because they do not deserve the name of theologians, but of pedants. On the other hand, I duly admire the doctors of the Catholic Church – especially St Thomas. As I said before, I've always loved him and revered him as my own soul. And to prove I'm telling you the truth," he said, turning towards the clerk's desk and grabbing one of the books he had placed there at the beginning of the morning session, "you will see here on page 89 of this book of mine, entitled *De monade, numero et figura*, what I say of him."

He showed the passage to the clerk, who read it out to the judges.

"Very well, very well," said Saluzzo, gesturing with his hand to stop. "If what you say is true, then how do you dare to describe the Catholic faith as" – he looked at his notes – "'full of blasphemy and worthless before the Lord?'"

"I never said anything like that," was Bruno's firm reply. "Neither in writing, nor in word, nor in thought."

"What is necessary for salvation?"

"Faith, hope and charity."

"Are good works also necessary, or will it be enough to live righteously and not to do to others what we wouldn't want them to do to us?"

"I have always believed that good works are necessary for salvation. As a proof of this, you can read another book of mine called *On Cause, Principle and Unity*, or" – he lowered his head and brought a hand to his brow, then looked up – "or *On the Infinite Universe and Worlds*, first dialogue, page 19, where you can see that I say in particular, among many other things demonstrating that good works are necessary to salvation in addition to faith—"

"Yes?"

Bruno thought for a moment and decided to give an adapted version of the passage he intended to quote. "What I say there is: 'These so-called religious men who teach that salvation can be achieved without good works – which should be the aim of all religions – deserve to be eradicated from the earth more than snakes, dragons and any other animal harmful to man, because thanks to this belief a barbaric people will become even more barbaric, and a naturally good one will become evil.'" There was a short pause, then he smiled. "What I meant, when I said 'religious men', were those who give themselves that name in their reformed – or rather, *deformed* – religion."

"And did you ever say anything against the religious men of *our* faith, in particular those who have some form of income?"

"No, no, no. I never said anything against religious people – and certainly not for having some income. On the contrary, I deplored the fact that some of them, having no revenues at all, were forced to go begging – and I was shocked, when I was in France, to see some priests going around the streets asking for money with their missals open."

"Did you ever say that the life of our religious people fails to imitate that of the Apostles?"

"I've never said or believed anything like that!" Bruno shouted, raising his hands and throwing wild glances around in disbelief. "Oh, Lord! Go on, ask more preposterous questions about this and other similar things!"

"Please control yourself," said Barbarigo, "and show respect for this court."

Bruno heaved a deep breath and bowed his head.

"Please continue, Father," the Wise Man added, turning to the inquisitor.

"Did you ever say," Saluzzo went on, pleased to have rattled his opponent, "that because of the wicked ways of religious people, the world could not go on like this for much longer – that no religion was good and each was in need of stricter rules, in particular the Catholic one, suggesting that soon there would be a general reform?"

Giordano relaxed his puckered lips and said: "I've never said or believed anything regarding this matter."

The inquisitor pressed him with more questions and requests for clarifications, but Bruno replied without much conviction and became evasive. The truth was that he was exhausted: he wanted to see an end to all this – he wanted to go out, breathe clean air, walk across fields under a gentle sun, like the one that now filtered through the windows and came to warm up his numb feet.

"Will you favour us with an answer?" said Saluzzo.

"What?" Bruno roused himself. "I am sorry, I have not heard what you asked."

"Will the honourable clerk repeat my question, please?"

The clerk adjusted his eyeglasses and brought his face close to his minutes book. "Would the defendant tell the judges if he ever said that the miracles performed by Jesus Christ and the Apostles were only illusory, done by magic arts and not real – that if it took his fancy he could have done the same or even greater ones, and that he wished, ultimately, to have the whole world following him?"

"What is this?" Bruno cried, lifting his hands. "Who has come up with these diabolical accusations? I never said such a thing – and it never crossed my mind! Oh, Lord, what is this? I'd rather be dead than be confronted with such allegations!"

"Really?" said Saluzzo. "Then please answer this too. Did you ever say, while talking of the doctrine of the Apostles and the Doctors of the Church, and of the beliefs of our faith: 'You'll see how much you'll profit by believing all these things! Just wait until the Final Judgement: then you shall all have your deserts!'"

"I never said these things, Your Excellency. Please, please look in my books. It's true I threw off my habit, but I never said or thought anything like that – you can see proof of that in my books, as I say."

"Will the defendant tell this tribunal what his opinion is concerning the sin of the flesh outside the sacrament of matrimony?"

Bruno frowned in puzzlement.

"Have you ever talked about this?" prodded the inquisitor.

"Yes, sometimes."

"What did you say?"

"I said that, generally speaking, it was a lesser sin than the others, but that adultery was the greatest carnal sin, after the one against nature. My point was that the simple sin of fornication was trivial and almost venial."

"You said this?"

"Yes, I did say this sometimes. And I know and admit I was mistaken, because I can remember the words of St Paul, who said that 'fornicators shall not inherit the kingdom of God'." There was a short pause. "But it was only frivolous talk: I was among others having a conversation about mundane things of little importance."

"And did you ever say that the Church made a great mistake in condemning the sin of the flesh, which provides such a good service to nature – and that you very much approve consorting with women, or words to this effect?"

After Giordano refuted these last allegations, Barbarigo signalled that the proceedings should be brought to an end for the day.

"Will my honourable colleague allow me to add a few words of caution for the accused?" said Saluzzo.

Barbarigo nodded.

"You should not be surprised," said the inquisitor, directing a scornful smile at Bruno, "that you're being asked all these questions. The Holy Office has received clear information about these charges, and since you have lived among heretics of so many cities and nations, it can only be expected that some of these accusations may be true."

As Saluzzo went on to recapitulate the alleged indictments against him, Bruno studied his face with care. Who was this hideous man, this intellectual pygmy who showed such single-minded determination to destroy him? Where did he come from? Who was his family, where did he study, which books did he read? What did he look like when he was a child or a boy with no beard? What food had gone through his bowels to make him the man he was? Who had put him in office? He had heard from other prisoners that he had been appointed only in August the previous year. That must be why he was filled with such zeal and anger: maybe he wanted to look good with one of the inquisitors-general in Rome – an old friend perhaps. Still, this man, this nobody, was now the master of his destiny on earth and, if he wasn't careful, had the power to crush him and annihilate him in the name of his Christ and his God.

Meanwhile, going through the usual hackneyed expressions, the inquisitor was appealing to him and entreating him with all his heart to mend his ways. Since Bruno had shown himself willing to acknowledge some of his errors, he invited him to continue to unburden his conscience and say the whole truth: he could rest assured that the Tribunal would exert the utmost care required for the salvation of his soul.

"However," concluded Saluzzo, "if you persist stubbornly in denying anything for which you will later be convicted that concerns the Catholic faith and is against the precepts of the Holy Church, then you should not be surprised if the Holy Office were to inflict on you the punishment usually reserved for those who fail to repent, to accept God's mercy and to see how this Holy Office, through Christian pity and charity, strives to bring those who live in the dark back into the light, and those who are walking astray back to the path to eternal life."

Giordano bowed his head and brought a hand to his chest. "So may God pardon all my sins as I said the truth about everything I was asked and I could remember. But to be more satisfied and at ease with myself, I will give further thought to the events of my life. And if anything I said or did against the Christian and Catholic faith should come to my mind, I'll admit it freely. And I declare once more that I said the whole truth and intend to do the same in future. And I trust I won't be found guilty of anything else."

With glaring eyes, Saluzzo followed each word as it left Bruno's lips. There it went again, that brazen assurance, that tone of defiance, that hint of irony! He had won a few points, there had been partial admissions, but he felt that he had been foiled – and that the trial was going nowhere.

Bruno was escorted back to his cell by the soldiers, and this time, having barely nodded goodbye to the other judges, Saluzzo was the first to storm out of the room in his wake.

17

"So, who wants to begin?" said Peter.

He let his gaze roam anticlockwise around the table and only met sullen, tired and bored expressions in response to his question. Al-Rafai, who was sitting to his right, was annoyed with the latest developments and angry that he had to come all the way to the Biblia Tower on a Sunday evening, when they could have met just as easily in central Amman. Helen was resentful at having to work overtime for the second day in a row. Jim was on the brink of dozing off, having slept less than five hours over the last seventy-two. Chad was not sure how relevant his presence was and what value he could add to the meeting. Chris Dale was in a complete state, as the system was still down and the Internet working only on and off: he kept checking his tablet for signs of life every other minute, and his fancy eyepiece sat inert on the table. Giulia felt she was wasting precious time that she could use poring over the Bruno collection.

"OK, since everyone's brimming with enthusiasm, I suppose I'll have to do the honours." Peter looked at his notepad, then continued: "Thanks for coming. I thought it might be easier to get together and discuss in person rather than by email. Giulia, can you tell us about your latest findings?"

"Yes." She brushed her hair back. "I think I know what the missing documents are." Al-Rafai straightened on his chair and Dale glanced up from his tablet. "I can say with a certain degree of confidence that the papers that have disappeared are an unpublished work by Giordano Bruno called *Clavis magna*." There was silent blinking around the table. "But it's not clear why this particular work has been stolen. We know it's a treatise on mnemonics, but maybe it also has some religious or magical interest."

"My investigation into Marini's movements adds more detail to the bigger picture," Peter said, "and we can't be sure whether he was responsible for the theft and acted alone or was merely a scapegoat."

"Could you elaborate on this?" said Dale.

"During the ten days he spent in the Tower, Father Marini visited the same location in the Hive over thirty times – nearly four times a day on average – and twice last Saturday, the day he disappeared."

"That would be my suite, Unit 72," said Al-Rafai. "It's used by my librarian, Father Andreoli. He is the curator of my early printed books and manuscripts."

"The room contains many useful resources for a scholar," continued Peter, "so it is possible that Marini went there to consult some of the reference books or ask his colleague for advice. Of course, the other possibility is—"

"That the two were conniving," said Dale.

"Exactly."

"And that the Vatican may have a hand in it."

"That would be highly speculative at this stage."

"But if they were, then why was Marini killed – or why did he kill himself?"

"This we don't know yet." Peter stroked his chin. "Clearly, it's not implausible that Mr Al-Rafai's librarian might be implicated in some way in all this." He turned to Jim. "I'm going to be coming to you right after this meeting to get the data on the movements of Andreoli's swipe card." Jim didn't nod in reply.

"Where is Father Andreoli now?" asked Helen. "I haven't seen him in the library for a few days."

"He left on Tuesday, the day Mr Simms and Miss Ripetti arrived." said Al-Rafai. "A short spiritual retreat with a group of friends, he said. He should be back at the end of next week."

"Did he ask for permission before leaving?" asked Peter.

"He left a note in the morning with my personal assistant."

"A sudden departure."

Al-Rafai nodded.

"But you didn't make a connection?"

Al-Rafai shrugged. "No."

"Did he tell you anything about Marini?"

"He never mentioned seeing him."

"Have you tried contacting him?" Dale asked.

"I did, yesterday and today, but I can't get through to him."

"How long have you known him?" asked Peter.

"Only about six months or so."

"What was he doing before you employed him?"

"He studied for a doctorate at the École Biblique in Jerusalem. This is his first job, I think."

"Do you have any reason to believe that he might have escaped with the manuscript?"

Al-Rafai raised and lowered his eyebrows. "I suppose everything is possible, but Father Andreoli... I don't think he could ever do anything bad or dishonest. He's the typical bookish sort: quiet, studious, diligent. I can't imagine him to be a criminal. He came to me with excellent references."

"Have you checked if the missing papers are inside the suite?" asked Chad.

"Helen, Giulia and I," said Peter, "spent the best part of yesterday and the whole of today going through the shelves and searching every proverbial nook and cranny, but nothing came up."

"Is Father Andreoli also a Jesuit?" asked Giulia.

Al-Rafai thought for a moment, then said: "No, I think he is a Dominican."

"A Dominican? Really?"

"Yes, I think so."

Peter gave a perplexed look at Giulia, then turned to Dale. "Now, moving on – about this Bookworm business—"

"Yes, I'm sorry," Dale cut in, raising his hand in a mea-culpa gesture. "The reason I didn't bring it up is that I'm convinced this is the act of an isolated individual, not the concerted strategy of a global group of activists or hacktivists."

"What makes you think so?"

"A number of things. First of all, the tone of the shutdown threats: they are written in the language of a religious zealot. Then their vagueness and the lack of any pattern or coherence. But more importantly, a discrepancy between the usual style of Bookworm's attacks and the methods used by the author of these messages."

This seemed to contradict what Boris had told him. Peter glanced at Jim, but the IT director looked on in silence. Was Dale lying? Was he trying to cover something up?

"So you think it's just one religious nutcase?" Peter asked.

"Religion is everywhere," Dale said. "Religion is often a smokescreen for other material interests."

"What do you mean?"

"I mean that religion is the age-old instrument of temporal powers. Even today, in the recent wars in Afghanistan, Syria and Iraq, you wonder whether it's about religion or more practical and less ideological reasons. The world's oil reserves are destined to dry up soon. The centres of wealth and economic influence are shifting. Data is the new oil, Mr Simms – data and content. The old order of supremacy is being challenged. This causes upheaval and unrest. Didn't someone say that religion is the tyrants' protest against change?"

"So you don't think the motivation is entirely religious."

"I think that someone may be trying to hide behind a larger, impersonal organization." Dale smiled. "Of course I may be wrong and there may be some powerful forces behind this – that's why we should remain vigilant and not underestimate these threats. But I don't think we should let ourselves be scared by a few scribblings on a piece of paper."

"Well," said Peter, leaning back in his chair. "I've done some… research over the past few days" – the image of Mahfuz raising the finger in his tent appeared in his mind – "and I believe the acts of intimidation at the Grand Hyatt may be the work of Islamist militants. I think that there may be a link between the Bookworm threats – including these letters – and religious extremism."

"Right."

"Anyway, what is clear is that your presence and your activities in this country are upsetting a few sensitive souls. Has Biblia attempted to engage with local communities and establish a conversation – involve them a bit more in what you are doing, because—"

"Involve them?" said Dale, shaking his head. "They don't *want* to be involved. Not even in a hundred years would they understand what we are trying to do – bring knowledge to the masses, freedom from ignorance, emancipation from despotism. This is what access to content grants. We embody change, transformation – and, as such, we are dangerous to the religious authorities. We are their enemies." He gave a strange smile. "But history moves only in one direction, Mr Simms: forward. You can't turn the clock back. They can try to disrupt and delay our work, but nothing can stop progress, and…"

The lights in the meeting room dimmed for a moment and then went out, plunging them into total darkness.

"Uh-oh."

A deep rumble, a sort of mechanical growl, was heard in the distance, and a light tremor shook the walls and the table.

"What was that?" said Peter.

"The nearest back-up generator, I think," said Dale. "I hope. But if so, I don't understand why the lights aren't back on." Far away, on one of the lower floors, a siren began to wail. "Let's get out of here."

They were all fumbling with their phones to get light. Chad walked towards the door. "Does anyone have signal?"

Six bluish glows appeared around the table.

"Nah."

"No."

"Nope."

"The internal phone system is down too."

"Do you think it's sensible to go around the building in the dark?" Al-Rafai asked.

"The emergency lighting will guide us out," said Chad.

"What if it's not a power cut?"

"How do you mean?" Dale said.

"What if it's a terrorist attack, like the one at the shopping mall in Nairobi?"

"Come on," said Dale, "let's keep our cool be and rational. It's just a temporary blackout. We had some in the past. The Jordanian national grid gets easily overloaded."

"The trouble is, it can last for hours," said Chad.

"Just stay calm and we'll get you out of here in one piece," continued Dale. "There's nothing to worry about. No one's going to harm you. I'm sure there's no threat out there."

"Is there a panic room?" asked Al-Rafai.

Dale flickered his tablet's light on to see if the question had been asked in earnest. "The nearest one is more than a hundred floors away. We might as well try to get out of the building."

"It depends," said Peter. "What floor are we on now?"

"Seventy," said Chad's silhouette near the door.

"Do you know a way out from here?"

"More or less."

"Great," said Peter. "I suppose we don't have much choice – unless we want to stay here all night waiting for the power to come back. Do you think the lifts will be working?"

"I guess so," said Dale. "At least some of them. But I'm not sure how safe it is to use an elevator during a power outage."

"Let's go and find out, before the mujahidin storm in," said Peter. There was a long silence, filled by the distant whine of the siren.

"English humour," Giulia's voice said in the near-darkness.

They filed out of the meeting room into a long hallway. Still using their phones as torches, they reached the nearest lifts, which were unlit and out of service.

"Damn," said Dale. "The fast elevator line is that way." He pointed ahead of him. "Maybe it's working."

They followed him through more passageways and glass doors, until they came to a large open-plan office, with rows of empty desks and pitch-black computer screens. Beyond it opened a maze of corridors branching off in every direction. After wandering about for a quarter of an hour, they found themselves back where they had started.

"I've lost my bearings," said Dale.

"Perhaps it's not here," said Jim, "but on the other side."

"Take your time," Peter said. "Take your time to decide: we're in no rush. For all we know, the building may be going up in flames."

"Please…" Mr Al-Rafai was trying to suppress a tremor in his voice. "Get us out of this place."

"Look, Mr Simms," Dale said, "it's not exactly my fault if we are stuck in this situation, OK? Under the circumstances, with poor light, no map, no compass, no electricity, no phone and no Internet, it's hard to find one's way in this place: it's so huge."

"That's what happens when you rely too much on technology," Giulia piped up. "We can't use our heads and legs any more."

They set off again, advancing slowly and staying close together. They had only taken a few steps when Chad pointed to the emergency-exit sign above the doorway on their left. They hurried towards it and reached a faintly lit stairway landing. Strange noises could be heard above the siren's distant moan – perhaps the echo of people shouting, or the groans of the blinded steel giant itself.

They started their descent and made a short pause after three flights of stairs.

"You all still there?" said Dale, who was leading the group.

"Only one thousand three hundred and sixty steps remaining," said Jim, looking over his shoulder.

They proceeded in silence down the stairs, stopping every now and then to catch breath, until their way was barred by a metal door with a red sign in Arabic on it.

"It's locked," said Dale.

"Unauthorized persons not permitted beyond this point," said Al-Rafai, reading the notice.

"What? Let me try," said Peter. He yanked at the handle and pushed with his shoulder, but the door would not budge. "This is absurd."

"We'll have to go back."

"Where?"

"A few floors up," said Dale. "We'll go through the thirtieth floor. There are restaurants and shops on that level. Even if we can't find a working lift or another exit, I'm sure someone will help us out."

They dragged themselves up seven flights of stairs and entered a long passageway that led them to a room full of stacked boxes. They walked on and went through a series of dark, deserted halls and corridors. The siren's noise continued to get louder, but they still could see no way out.

"I think we're lost," admitted Dale.

"My cell phone's battery is running low," said Chad.

"Mine too."

"We'll be in the dark soon: there seems to be no emergency lighting on this floor."

"And no signs at all. Where are all the restaurants and shops?"

"OK," said Peter. "What do we do now?"

"We can sit down and wait until the power's back on or try to get out via one of the upper floors."

"I'm happy to stay here," said Helen.

"No more stairs, please," said Giulia.

"Please, take us out of this place," said Al-Rafai.

"What's that noise?" said Chad.

"You mean the fire alarm?" said Peter.

"No. Isn't that a whirring sound?"

"Generators?"

"Lifts."

They stood listening in silence for a few moments.

"It's coming from over there," said Chad, pointing his finger to the corridor on his right.

They made a few hopeful steps in that direction and soon saw a green gleam in the distance.

"Thank Goodness," Helen cried.

The lift that took them down was empty. When they emerged into the main hall and saw people shouting in various languages and running around, they made an instinctive dash for the exit. They gathered again outside, where a crowd was assembled around the blue-and-red lights of police cars, as two helicopters chugged overhead, sweeping their searchlights over the dark mass of the building.

Al-Rafai went over to one of the policemen and had a long conversation with him. When he came back he was shaking his head.

"They still aren't sure what's happened," he said. "Some people claim they heard an explosion. Others say they could smell smoke inside. And then there are rumours."

"What rumours?" asked Peter.

"That the German climber was an Al-Qaeda agent who planted a device to guide an unmanned aircraft to crash explosives into the Tower."

Peter burst out laughing. "That takes some creative thinking."

"Well," said Al-Rafai, looking at his phone, "my driver's waiting for me." He turned to Giulia and Peter. "Would you like to stay here or would you rather spend the night in Amman? I can get Majed to come and pick up your stuff later."

Peter darted a glance sideways at Giulia. "We're coming with you."

"Very well. Let's go."

18

Venice, 30th July 1592

Saluzzo let his glance roam over the crammed pages of notes in front of him. He brushed his beard with his hand, mulling over what to ask next, but he could not think of anything. He felt a shudder of anger run through his body when he looked up and saw a smile on the friar's lips.

The cross-examination had been completed. He had moved Bruno to a cell with other prisoners in the hope he might let something slip, exchanged letters with Cardinal Santoro, met a few times with the Master of the Dominicans, Ippolito Maria Beccaria, looked for more informers. Nothing seemed to help. He had been trumped, bamboozled. Surely there must be something he could do to bring that hateful little man to justice...

"You claim," Saluzzo said in the end, making a show of looking through his papers, "that you never taught any heretical dogmas or doctrines here in Venice, and that you only took part in philosophical conversations with a number of gentlemen." He fixed an icy stare on Bruno. "According to the deposition of some witnesses, you have done exactly the opposite."

Giordano laughed. "With the exception of my accuser – who I believe is Signor Giovanni Mocenigo, son of the esteemed Signor Antonio – I don't think you'll find anyone who can say that. And I am sure no one else can say anything against me in matters of holy faith."

"So where and with whom did you have these learned conversations?"

"At an academy held in the house of the esteemed Signor Andrea Morosini. It's in San Luca, on the Grand Canal, I think. It was frequented by many gentlemen and men of letters. And also in some bookshops."

"With whom?"

"I don't remember with whom in particular, because I didn't know those people, as I said before."

"You don't remember." Saluzzo shook his head. "Well, I hope you will at least remember your situation and decide to unburden your conscience."

"It may well be that in the course of so many years I erred and strayed from our Holy Church in other ways than I've declared, and that I find myself enmeshed in more accusations, but I can't recall any instances of it, even though I thought long and hard about it. I have already admitted and readily admit again my errors. I put myself in the hands of Your Excellencies in the hope of being offered a remedy for my salvation. I wish I could say – I wish I could properly express how remorseful I am for my misdeeds."

He knelt down.

"What's this?" Saluzzo called.

"I humbly beg forgiveness from the Lord and from Your Excellencies for all the errors I have committed. I am prepared to do whatever you, in your wisdom, will order for the benefit of my soul. And I entreat you that you'd rather give me a harsh punishment – that you'd rather exceed in the severity of the punishment – than make a public display of it, as it would bring dishonour to the holy religious habit that I used to wear. And if through the mercy of God and of Your Excellencies my life shall be granted to me, I promise I will reform my ways completely: I will make amends for the scandal I have caused with a commensurate number of edifying actions."

He bent his head and fell silent.

"You may stand up now," said the inquisitor. "There's no need of such *public displays* in front of this tribunal. Will you stand up?" Bruno did not move. "Stand up! I said stand up! Guards! Help him to his feet!"

The guards lifted Bruno by the arms and forced him to stand.

"Is there anything else you would like to add?" asked Saluzzo, with as much spite as he could muster.

"I have nothing else to say," was Giordano's reply.

Saluzzo watched as Giordano was led away to his cell, brooding over the prisoner's declaration. He caught the eye of the clerk, who was tidying up his writing materials.

"Would you please make a copy of the entire proceedings and send them to Rome as soon as possible?"

"You mean the usual summary, Your Excellency?"

"No, the entire trial." The clerk blanched. "Please do as I say. I have cleared it with the nuncio and Cardinal Santoro. Because of its gravity, this is going to be treated as a special case."

"I will need a few days, Your Excellency."

"I want the documents dispatched by tomorrow night. Get some help if necessary."

* * *

Eight weeks later, on the morning of 28th September, Saluzzo, the Wise Man Tommaso Morosini and the Patriarch's deputy marched into the Doge's Palace and requested an immediate audience with the Council of Ten.

"But the Council is in session, Your Excellency," explained a flustered ducal counsellor.

"That is why we are here," murmured the Patriarch's deputy.

"But—"

"They will want to see us – and they will want to see us now!" Saluzzo barked.

The counsellor tried to remonstrate again, but to no avail. The three prelates were escorted down a long corridor and ushered into the presence of the Ten.

"Apologies for disturbing the Council," the Patriarch's deputy said, addressing the Doge Pasquale Cicogna, while Saluzzo watched with a smile playing at the corners of his lips, "but we are here for a matter of extreme urgency on the orders of His Excellency the Patriarch."

"Very well," said the Doge, gesturing to his secretary to take notes. "What is it?"

"I've come to inform Your Serene Highness and these esteemed lords about a man called Giordano Bruno of Nola. He has been detained over the past few weeks in the prison of the Holy Office on charges of being a heretic and a heresiarch. He has written several books in which he gives high praise to the Queen of England and other heretical princes and expresses some pernicious ideas in connection with religion – though he claims he's only talking about philosophical things. He renounced his faith and left the Dominican order, then he lived in Geneva and in England for many years and was investigated in Naples and other cities for the same allegations."

"What has any of this to do with us?" said Cicogna.

"His Excellency the Archbishop of Santa Severina, Secretary of the Holy Office and Major Penitentiary, has been informed that Bruno is in custody here in Venice and has written to

Monsignor Saluzzo giving instructions to send him to Rome. May I read you the relevant passage in his letter?"

"Proceed."

"Now, where is it? Oh, yes. 'I therefore command that this criminal be dispatched, at the first opportunity of a safe and secure passage, to the city of Ancona, whence its governor will have care to send him on to Rome.'" The Patriarch's deputy folded the letter and added with a smile: "Of course we didn't want to go ahead with this without first advising Your Serene Highness and these esteemed lords, who will order as they deem more appropriate."

The Doge exchanged a look with the other members of the Council. Saluzzo waited – but no one was responding.

"Well," the Patriarch's deputy said at length, "we shall look forward to hearing how we should reply to Rome, then." He glanced at Saluzzo, who was staring at him with burning eyes, inviting him to continue. "But I hope you'll give your consent," he hastened to add, "because there is an opportunity to send him off securely."

"Very well," said Cicogna, "very well. We have heard what you had to say. Our esteemed lords will give the matter due consideration and let you know. You may leave now."

Saluzzo stormed out of the Doge's Palace ahead of Morosini and the Patriarch's deputy.

"'I *hope* you'll give your consent'!" he said, with an acrid grimace stamped on his face. "That was tame, sir. You were too timid, too deferential. The situation is grave, and one needs to be resolute."

"I was afraid I'd upset the Doge and the Council even more, Your Excellency. It was clear they were irritated by our request – and we need their authorization in order to proceed."

"Tut," the inquisitor said, waving his arm. "From now on I'll have to take the matter entirely into my own hands. Goodbye." And he strode off to his gondola.

He returned home and had something to eat, though he had very little appetite. The food was insipid, the wine tasted sour. His manservant was scolded and the cook was sent word of his displeasure.

After lunch he asked his gondoliere to take him back to St Mark's. A menacing storm was gathering over the lagoon, but he insisted they should sail all the same. Just as he was stepping off the boat, he was met by gusts of wind and rain. He ran under a portico and waited until the downpour eased a little, then walked towards a large vessel moored along the Riva degli Schiavoni, just after the Rio di Palazzo.

"Captain! Captain!" he called out.

An old bearded man with a blind eye and a scarred face appeared on deck.

"When are you sailing off?" shouted Saluzzo.

"Not now," said the man, pointing at the sky.

"When, then?"

"Maybe tomorrow or Saturday."

Saluzzo shook his head and turned back in a fury. This time he was caught in heavy rain as he was crossing the Ponte della Paglia, and was drenched by the time he reached the Doge's Palace.

The guards and the ducal counsellor followed him down the corridor.

"I'm sorry, Your Excellency—"

"You will be, if you don't let me through."

"The Doge gave strict orders—"

"I have an important affair of state to discuss. The security of the whole Republic depends on it. Let me in!"

One of the three Capi of the Council, hearing the shouting outside the room, opened the door and allowed Saluzzo in.

"Again?" said the Doge with a slight grin, studying the fraught expression, dishevelled beard and soaked dress of the inquisitor.

Saluzzo made a few small steps forwards and bowed his head. "Sir," he said, raising his gaze to meet Cicogna's eyes, "I've come... I've come to hear what you have decided on the matter we talked about this morning... about sending off that man to Rome." There was a pause. "You see, we have a vessel that is about to leave, and..."

A broad smile appeared on the Doge's face. "And?"

"Forgive me, Your Serene Highness – but it is a matter of pressing urgency."

"It's urgent?"

"Yes."

"When did you receive your letter of instructions from Rome, Father?" asked the Capo who had let him in.

"Well, it must be about two weeks now, but—"

"Was it sent through a special ambassador or the ordinary one?"

The Doge raised his eyebrows as Saluzzo hesitated.

"The ordinary one."

"Was it the last one that arrived in Venice?"

"The one before."

"The one before. So it wasn't so urgent after all," the Capo remarked, making the Doge smile.

"Oh, it is *very* urgent. It's an issue of the greatest moment, and it requires due consideration."

"Then," said the Doge, "if the issue is of the greatest moment and requires due consideration, we shall need more time to examine it. This state has many other serious matters on hand to deal with first, and we haven't had a chance to deliberate on your very... urgent... request."

"So what shall I do now?" Saluzzo almost pleaded.

"What do you mean?"

"With the vessel, I mean."

"Oh, the vessel. You can let it go, Reverend Father."

"Let it go?"

"Yes."

There was a long pause.

"Well then," Saluzzo nodded, "I shall let it go, as Your Excellencies wish."

He stepped out of the room seething with rage, and winced to hear laughter once the door was closed behind him. He was not surprised when, five days later, the senate voted against transferring Bruno to Rome with an overwhelming majority.

A few weeks passed, and he was having supper at Mocenigo's palace in San Samuele with the papal nuncio Taverna and the nobleman Federico Contarini who, as well as being one of the richest men in Venice and the owner of a famed collection of Greek antiquities, was a pious man who never spared any efforts in trying to help the cause of the Church. He had been Procurator of St Mark's for over twenty years, and had since held a number of public positions and political offices for the Republic, serving many times in the Council of Ten. His name had now been put forward for the post of Wise Man on Matters of Heresy, and he hoped he could work at the service of the Holy Office in the new year.

"They can't find a shred of evidence against him in the Holy Office's archives," Saluzzo said. "It's as if this man never existed. Cardinal Santoro insists we should try again to get him sent off to Rome. He can't understand why this is being refused now after being approved several times in the past, as in the case of Spadafora, the Sicilian."

"He's right," Contarini said, scratching his bald pate, "even though that was a long time ago, and things have changed since then. Your mistake was to barge in on the Council and try to force a swift decision. Seeing how keen you were made them even more determined to thwart you. They'd never rule on anything without the show of a debate in the senate, anyway. They're very jealous of the Republic's independence, and they won't bend to the will of the Pope that easily. You need to bide your time and let politics take its natural course."

"What would you recommend?" asked Saluzzo.

Contarini looked at the rings on his fingers. "I would leave the matter to rest for a little while. Then I'd request an audience with the Council for some other question. At that point the issue of Bruno could be mentioned again, almost by the by, without making it sound so urgent. And perhaps it could be suggested that an impartial official of the Republic of Venice" – here he brought his hands to his chest to indicate himself – "could put together an unbiased report on the situation so that the senate could take, in its own time, a well-informed decision."

"That sounds like an excellent plan," the inquisitor said, becoming animated. "Who do you think we should send to the senate? Barbarigo? Foscari? Morosini?"

Contarini sipped from his chalice and shook his head. "I think you'll find that none of them are exactly burning with religious zeal."

"Who, then?"

"I was thinking that perhaps His Excellency..." he said, turning towards the nuncio.

Taverna nodded. "Very well."

"All you have to do, then, is to inform Santoro in Rome, see if he approves of our strategy and await instructions. Leave the rest to me. I have a great many friends in the senate – and some in the Council too."

"This brings new hope of success," said Saluzzo, drawing a sigh of relief. "Rest assured that we'll know how to reward you for your services."

Contarini nodded and smiled.

* * *

Months went by. Autumn gave way to winter, and spring was almost at the door. Giordano raised his eyes and saw the Doge's Palace and St Mark's bell tower emerge from the dusk through the grated window of his prison cell. After a troubled night he had woken up and felt a sudden urge to pray. He didn't know to whom or what he would offer his silent words, but he knelt down in a corner and yielded to that old comforting habit.

His cellmates were still asleep on their beds of straw. Enduring the presence of these vulgar companions – listening to their superstitious talk, resisting their constant provocations – added to his torment and vexation. If only he were allowed his own cell, where he could be alone with his thoughts – then he would not begrudge so much the loss of his freedom. His great work was almost finished: he only needed a few more years – perhaps just a few months – of lucid thinking.

But would he ever be released? His tormentors seemed to have forgotten about him. Why was the sentence being delayed? Was it to wear him down in body and spirit, knowing that they would have to set him free soon? Or were they still trying to find informers to have him convicted and executed? He was not afraid of death or physical pain, but the notion that he might not be able to complete his great system… that, at times, kept him awake at night.

Whenever they saw him wrapped in thought, gazing into his inner world, his cellmates found every excuse to distract him or taunt him. There was the cripple Francesco Graziano, a madman from Udine who claimed to be a great lord and to own several cities, baiting him in dog Latin, trying to engage him in theological disputations and arguments about Christ and the Bible. And worse than Graziano, there was Celestino, a Capuchin friar from Verona, who kept goading him with abstruse philosophical questions and often attacked him unprovoked.

"Why are you sitting there in silence all the time?" he had asked him once. "Are you thinking up some slanderous accusations against me?"

Bruno did not deign to reply.

"Or are you thinking about your death – how painful it will be?"

Again Bruno ignored him, but his silence only seemed to fuel Celestino's attacks.

"You can think as much as you like, but you'll end up like your fellow townsman – what was his name? Pomponio. The Serenissima sent him from Padua to Rome to have him cooked in boiling oil, pitch and trupentine."

"Turpentine, you fool."

"Well, whatever. I hope I can come and see you scream your heart out before you go up in smoke to one of your infinite worlds and come back as a swan or an ass." The other prisoners laughed.

"You'll die before me, Celestino."

"Then you'll have to tell me what it's like to be burnt alive when we meet again in hell. First you'll burn for a while on earth and then you'll burn for ever among the devils."

"You won't be waiting for me there."

"Why?"

"Because hell does not exist."

"Hell does not exist?" Celestino looked around at the other prisoners. "And what authority can you quote to support that?"

"*Esse aliquos manes et subterranea regna nec pueri credunt.*"

"Ha! So not even kids believe in hell and gods any more? Where did you get that?"

"Juvenal, you ignoramus."

"Well, you see, I studied the Holy Scriptures, not some heathen's poetry. Where does it say in the Bible that hell does not exist?"

"The Prophet says in the Psalms: '*Non in perpetuum irascetur, neque in æternum comminabitur Deus.*' God will not always chide – neither will he keep his anger for ever."

"Does he really? Well, my word, I'll look this up when they give me back my Bible." He gave a nervous laugh.

"So there is no hell and no purgatory?" continued Graziano, waving the stump of his arm.

Bruno exhaled. "No hell, just a long purgatory – which is in fact what we call hell. The pains of hell are not eternal: they will end one day. We'll all be saved in due course."

"Everyone? Even the devils?"

"Everyone. 'O Lord, thou preservest man and beast,' says the Prophet. So there's hope for you, Graziano, since you're stupid as a goat, ignorant as a goatherd and lame as the Devil."

CHAPTER 18

A clang of keys interrupted Giordano's prayer. The cell's door was unbolted and opened with a creak, rousing most of the prisoners. Three figures appeared in the doorway: the chief warder, the papal nuncio and a grim-looking man wearing a Dominican habit. His face was familiar.

"Iordanus Bruni!" shouted the warder.

Bruno got to his feet.

"Come with us," said Taverna.

He followed them out, not daring to ask the reason for that early visit. They went through a maze of corridors, and as they reached the hallway leading to the main staircase of the building, Bruno caught a glimpse, through a half-open door, of the inquisitor's pale face glaring at him.

And then they were outside. He drew a long breath of fresh air and raised his eyes to the clear sky. Were they setting him free? Was this a new spring, the beginning of another new life for him, after these long months of confinement and anxiety?

"Soldiers, proceed," said the warder.

The guards stepped from behind Bruno with shackles and heavy chains.

"What—"

He watched in disbelief as the soldiers began shackling his arms and legs.

"In the name of the Most Serene Republic of Venice," said the warder, "and on the orders of His Holiness Pope Clement, you are hereby handed over to the authority of the Holy Office in Rome as an apostate and a heretic."

Bruno collapsed to the floor and broke into silent, shaking weeping.

"You will be taken by boat to Ancona," said the nuncio. "From there you'll be sent to the prison of the Holy Inquisition in Rome, where you will await trial on charges of apostasy and heresy."

"No! No!" Bruno shouted, trying to raise his arms, but succeeding only in rattling his chains. "No! Let me free! I am innocent! Why are you doing this to me? I've never harmed any creature of God! Please! Please! Let me go... let me go..." He started crying again.

"You should rejoice, my son," said the Dominican friar. "I'd call you 'brother'," he said, smiling, "if you had not decided to leave our order and lead a life of sin and evil for so many years, poisoning the minds of your fellow Christians. I say you should rejoice because you are being given the opportunity to repent and reform. You should rejoice because you can entrust your soul to the cares of your Holy Mother Church. You should rejoice because you can reject your ungodly ways and find again the path to salvation."

"Who are you?" Bruno shouted.

Taverna opened his mouth to answer, but the Dominican stopped him.

"Who are you? Tell me," said Bruno. "I know your face. I have seen you before. Are you one of my secret enemies?"

The soldiers lifted Bruno to his feet and dragged him towards the gondola that would take him to the vessel leaving for Ancona.

Pushed down into the hull, Giordano raised his head as the gondoliere started to scull: "Whoever you are, you can rejoice now! You can rejoice both for yourself and on behalf of the entire Holy Mother Church! But don't worry, the rejoicing won't last long! The Devil knows how to take his revenge!"

The Dominican gave the nuncio a tense look as the gondola pushed off.

From his room on the first floor, Saluzzo observed the whole scene with a strange grimace – a mixture of triumph and pride. This had been his most difficult case – and the most testing period of his entire life – but also his greatest victory. The honour and glory of the Catholic Church had been safeguarded – and although he spurned the allurements of earthly fame, he basked in the notion that once his mortal body would be reduced to ashes, and through the centuries to come, his name would be remembered as that of the man who brought to justice and consigned to his rightful fate the infamous Giordano Bruno of Nola.

19

There was hard knocking on the door. Peter jerked up and listened. Silence: perhaps he had been dreaming that noise. As he was about to lay his head on the pillow, there again came a loud rapping – and he jumped out of bed, still in the previous day's clothes.

He opened the door and peered out at the young hotel attendant standing in front of him with an embarrassed smile.

"Sorree, sir," the boy said. "Wake-up call."

Peter scratched his cheek. "Are you sure? I didn't ask for a wake-up call."

The boy looked at a sheet of paper he was holding. "Yes, sir. Room 341. Driver waiting for you outside, sir. We call your room but no answer."

"I unplugged the phone. I unplugged it because I didn't want to be disturbed. What time is it?"

"Seven fifteen, sir. Sorree, sir."

"All right," Peter said. "Tell the driver, whoever he is, that I'll be down in five minutes."

"OK, sir."

The boy turned and made to leave.

"Hey," Peter called him back. "Take this." He rummaged in his pocket and fished a crumpled one-dinar note.

"Thank you, sir."

"You'd better be right about the wake-up call and the driver outside, or I'll come and take this back from you, OK?"

"Yes, sir."

Peter washed his face, picked up his mobile phone from the bedside table and was out of the room.

In the hall downstairs he met Giulia, as spruce as ever. "Had a bad night, Mr Simms?" she said.

"I was knackered but couldn't sleep. What's up?"

"You haven't received the message from Mr Al-Rafai?"

"No. My phone's dead and I left the charger in my room at the Tower. What's happening?"

"We're going to Jerusalem."

"Jerusalem? What? Why?"

"The Dominican friar, Andreoli, was seen there on Friday, at the École Biblique."

"Oh, right." He scratched his cheek. "And why do you need to come along?"

"Because if we find the manuscript we need to make sure it's the right one, and I can check. I don't think you'd recognize it from the Dead Sea Scrolls."

"Very funny. What about our luggage?"

"Majed took it this morning: it's in the car."

"Where are we flying to, Tel Aviv?"

"Flying?" Giulia smiled. "We are not flying. We're going over the bridge."

"Are you joking? The Allenby Bridge?"

"Mr Al-Rafai says there is no problem if we use the VIP service. It's much quicker. Majed has some cash for us."

"All right."

In the car, he read Al-Rafai's message on Giulia's phone, then asked Majed if he'd heard any news about yesterday's blackout at the Tower when he went there to pick up their stuff, and whether everything was now back to normal.

"Still big poblem, Mr Peter," he said, shaking his head. "Police was there, fire beople was there, engineers was there, but still no electricity. They say maybe rats eat cables. Everyone outside Al-Burj and nobody can work. Big, big poblem."

An hour later they were queuing up behind a long column of taxis, buses and coaches on the approach to the Allenby crossing.

"Very busy today," said Majed.

Twenty minutes later they still had not moved an inch. Seeing that people were getting out of their taxis and walking towards the terminal building, Peter and Giulia decided to do the same. Majed opened the boot and handed Giulia her three pieces of luggage and Peter his scarred suitcase and an envelope containing ten thousand dollars and five hundred dinars.

"Should be enough," Peter said.

"If there is poblem, please call me, Mr Peter," said Majed. "Good luck."

They walked for almost a mile under a merciless sun, enveloped in the exhaust fumes of old diesel vehicles. In the end they reached the terminal area, full of buses with their engines running, piles of luggage and people milling about. A cigarette-smoking border agent asked them to put their luggage through a security scanner before entering the terminal building. Once they were in, they collected their bags, wrote their name, passport number and nationality on two small forms and made their way towards passport control. There was a long, chaotic line leading to three counters and a small queue in front of a window marked VIP.

"Doesn't look too bad," said Peter, taking his place behind a woman reading an Arabic newspaper. "Only three people ahead of us."

Ten minutes passed, then twenty, then half an hour, and no one was ushered through.

"Excuse me. Is there anyone behind that window?" Peter said aloud. The other people in the queue turned to look at him but did not answer.

When, after another fifteen minutes, there was still no sign of progress, he went over to the window and noticed that a small piece of paper in Arabic script was taped to the glass.

"What does it say?" Peter asked, but the elderly man who was heading the line didn't speak any English and just shook his head. He turned to the others: "Do you know what it says?"

The second in the queue, a young man in a business suit, said: "This desk temporarily closed."

"What? How long have you been waiting here?"

"An hour and a half." The young businessman didn't seem to be annoyed at the delay or in any rush. "They say they go and check, and then come back."

Peter returned to his place and tried to remain calm as he observed the line to his right advance at a regular pace.

The best part of another hour had gone when someone finally appeared behind the window. There was a short altercation between the elderly man and whoever was sitting on the other side of the VIP desk, then the queue broke up and the three people in front of Peter and Giulia moved off to join the longer line.

"What's happening?" shouted Peter.

"No VIP service today," said the young businessman.

"Oh, great."

Peter lifted three of the suitcases and stepped behind the woman with the newspaper; Giulia followed with her trolley. After a long wait they reached the front of the line and handed in their passports and forms.

The border agent examined their passports, stamped the forms and passed everything on to his colleague at Desk 2, who said: "Very good, now you pay exit tax at Desk 3 and come back here."

"And then?"

"And then you go to bus outside."

"What about the passports?"

"Later," said the agent.

They did as instructed and got onto an empty bus, which took almost an hour to fill up. There were some Australian backpackers travelling with tents and mountain bikes, and a family of six trying to carry a kitchen sink across the border. Once the bus was fully boarded, the driver came down the aisle to collect the fare, followed by one of the border agents, who returned the passports to their owners.

The bus moved off, but was immediately stopped at a checkpoint, where a Jordanian officer inspected the passengers' exit stamps. It then proceeded onto the bridge over the River Jordan – nothing more than a sickly, muddy stream trickling through parched rocks – and went through a series of barriers and iron gates, pausing before each one, until it arrived at the Israeli terminal. The entire journey must have been only about three miles.

Half of the passengers got off the bus, while the others – including Peter and Giulia, who were sitting towards the back – had to wait another twenty minutes before they were allowed to disembark.

"This is turning into a real mission," Peter said.

"You wait until you get to Israeli customs," said an American man behind them. "That's where the fun begins."

"We're definitely going back by plane," said Giulia.

"You can't," said the American. "Once you exit through the Bridge, you can only re-enter Jordan the same way."

"Great," said Peter, shaking his head.

When they climbed off the bus, the temperature was close to thirty-five degrees. They joined a shapeless, motley queue of people carrying backpacks, pushing prams and dragging heavy suitcases, luggage carts and boxes. Men, women and children jostled their way through as soldiers carrying rifles shouted orders in English, Hebrew and Arabic.

Having reached the front of the line, Peter and Giulia dropped their bags on a conveyor belt to have them scanned again, got a receipt and advanced to the first passport control. The officer had a cursory look, placed a sticker on the back of their passports and invited them to proceed towards the terminal building. There they showed their passports to a girl standing behind a desk, joined a short queue and walked through an X-ray machine. At that point they entered a large hall and found themselves at the back of another seemingly endless line. They began to feel dispirited.

"We'll never get out of here," said Giulia.

"Let's remain positive," Peter said. "There's always an end to purgatory."

"There's a man staring at us," Giulia said.

"Where?"

"Over there."

Peter turned and caught the man's eye just before he could look away. A young Arab. Maybe one of Mahfuz's friends following them?

"Perhaps he finds you attractive," he said, laughing it off.

Giulia smiled. "So, what do you think? Andreoli has the manuscript?"

"We'll find out soon, I hope. By the way, why were you surprised yesterday when Al-Rafai said he was a Dominican?"

"Because Marini was a Jesuit."

"So?"

"Well, usually Dominicans go with Dominicans and Jesuits go with Jesuits. They don't mix together, they are kind of rivals."

"Why?"

"Oh, it's an old story. It started as a controversy about divine grace and free will at the time of Giordano Bruno. The Dominicans believed in predetermination, the Jesuits defended human freedom. There were endless theological disputes between the two orders, then the Pope had to intervene and put an end to all that."

"What did he do?"

"Nothing. He said that the Dominicans and the Jesuits could continue to profess their ideas until the Holy See decided who was right and who was wrong. But the decision never came."

"The controversy was never resolved?"

"No, and the two orders kept bickering and fighting until today, for one reason or the other."

Step by step, to the rhythmic thump of passport-stamping, they advanced towards their designated counter, where a dour-looking red-haired officer was awaiting them. Every so often, Peter shot a glance behind his shoulders, but the young Arab now seemed more interested in the architectural qualities and neon lighting of the drab building they were in than in the two of them.

When it was their turn, they stepped forward together and handed over their documents. The officer, a woman, studied their passports and asked: "What is the reason for your trip?"

"Holiday."

"Study."

The woman raised one of her eyebrows. "Holiday or study?"

"Both," said Giulia.

"Study where?"

"École Biblique."

"What kind of study?"

"I am writing a book about the influence of Mesopotamian cuneiform literature on the Old Testament."

"Which hotel are you staying at?"

"Not far from Damascus Gate."

"Where is it?"

"It is in Jerusalem."

The officer scowled, but stamped the passports and motioned them to proceed.

"Are you mad to joke with these people?" Peter whispered. "Do you want to spend the rest of the day here having every cavity of your body searched?"

"It's OK. You need to show them who's in charge, otherwise they walk all over you."

"Well, let me handle things from now on, all right?"

Giulia smiled. "All right."

They were photographed, fingerprinted, then joined another queue for further checks. Once they got to the front of the line, they gave their passports to the girl behind the counter and waited to be questioned. The girl checked every page of their passport twice, then typed something on her computer and stared at the screen. She shook her head and called for a more senior colleague.

"See what you did?" Peter grumbled, wondering what incriminating information might have emerged from the depths of the Israelis' database.

"Relax…"

The two officers took their time, exchanging looks and quick words in Hebrew.

CHAPTER 19

"What's reason of your trip?" asked the senior agent in the end.

"Holiday," said Peter.

"How long you going to be here?"

"Two or three days at the most."

"You going to the West Bank?"

"No, Jerusalem."

"You married?"

"No." Peter and Giulia answered in unison.

"Do you sleep together?"

"Not at the moment." Peter went red and cleared his throat. "I didn't mean that we're not sleeping together *now* but we did *in the past*."

"Or that we're not sleeping together *now* but we will *in the future*," pointed out Giulia.

"What did you mean, then?"

"We're just friends on holiday."

"OK, OK." The agent and the girl were trying not to smile. "Just friends on holiday. I understand. Welcome to Israel."

"You handled it very well," said Giulia, as they walked through the barrier to pick up their bags. "Bravo, Peter. You even managed to make them laugh."

Peter pressed on without replying, following the signs to the taxi rank, eager to get out into the scorching sun.

20

Rome, 12th April 1593

He was often woken at night by the sound of crying or crazed laughter, by the rattle of chains or distant screams of agony. He had been in a solitary cell before, but never in one so dark, cold and desolate as this. The only light and air came from a grated window high up on the wall, which allowed but a restricted view of the infinite spaces his intellect had been trying to probe for most of his life.

Not far from that grate, less than an arrow's flight away, rose the greatest temple of Christendom. He had glimpsed its majestic dome the day he arrived from Ancona, before being hurried into the dungeons of the Palazzo del Sant'Uffizio. The House of the Lord was now finished and stood in all its glory: its marble glowed under the sun and gleamed in the moonlight. But the work of the Holy Mother Church was far from over, and would not be complete until every land on earth was brought to the obedience of the faith and all evil uprooted from the heart and mind of every child of man.

It was six weeks since his latest incarceration. He had seen no one but the prison guards, who brought him food at the appointed times and never spoke. He knew his mental faculties were as sharp as ever, but although powerful images whirled in front of his eyes, they were often disjointed, and their combinations ineffectual, leading to nothing – no discovery, no revelation, no insight. Sometimes he even forgot the premises or the objective of his inquiry, and he was left with a painful, baffling sense of emptiness, of memory loss. It was as if his mind, confined in the gloom of that cell, was losing its intellectual light and, with it, the confidence in its ability to grasp the cloudy emblems of a higher reality.

He was gripped, at times, by a strange sense of fear. He wasn't so much afraid to leave his great work unfinished now as to witness a decline of his powers of understanding or, even worse, a gradual descent into stupor or madness. He began to lose sleep: he would stare for hours into the darkness, unable to think of anything, only feeling restless and dejected. There were times when he doubted whether he was still alive at all.

As the soft glow of dawn lightened the walls of his cell, one of the jailers unlocked the door and stepped in.

"Come," he said.

Giordano joined a long file of convicts outside, none of them wearing chains around their ankles or their wrists. They advanced down the corridor at a slow, shambling pace, stopping along the way to collect more prisoners. Whenever a door was opened, a stench of damp and human waste filled the air, and out came some contorted figure with a besmirched face and a look of terror in his eyes.

They were shown into a large wash house and arranged into two lines leading to steaming bathtubs in which hot water was being poured from big copper buckets. Towards the back of his line, Bruno watched as, one by one, the prisoners took off their garments, climbed into the tub and washed themselves with soap, while an attendant tipped more warm water over them. After being towelled dry by two prison guards, they put on their clothes again and joined another queue to have their hair cut and their beards trimmed or shaved.

"Why are they giving us a wash?" Giordano whispered to his neighbour.

"Next Sunday is Easter," said the man. "You'll receive this special treatment twice a year."

"You mean now and before Christmas?"

The man nodded. "That's when we get *visited*."

"By whom?"

A soldier's cane landed heavily on the man's shoulder, and the exchange was over.

Later that morning they were served a hot soup – the first proper meal Giordano had had in months. He was disgusted with himself for the joy this gave him, but wolfed it down nonetheless, like the rest. In the afternoon they were assembled in a large hallway on the first floor in front of a tall wooden door. When this opened, a name was called out and a prisoner was led in by two soldiers. After a while, the door opened again, and the prisoner was escorted out and taken away by two other guards.

It was Bruno's turn to be summoned inside. As he walked in, the first thing that struck him was the contrast between the bleakness of his cell and the opulent decoration of that room. He let his gaze roam around him and took in the frescoed walls and ceiling, the rich furnishings, the shiny upholstery, the glittering mouldings and candelabra, then his eyes focused on the prelates in front of him, about twenty of them, sitting behind a long table, some dressed in the habit of the Dominican order, others cloaked in a wealthy cardinal's garb.

"Iordanus Bruni," said Santoro, one of the six cardinals who occupied the central seats at the table. "Come closer."

Bruno advanced a few steps and looked into those deep-set eyes above the venerable white beard.

"Will you tell this Congregation," Santoro asked, "the reason you are detained in the prison of the Holy Office?"

"Because of slanderous accusations against my name."

"I meant on what charges."

"Of being a heretic – which is untrue."

"That will be left to this Congregation to ascertain. To that end, you will be subjected to strict interrogation, and you are hereby admonished to say nothing but the truth, as you will be deposing under oath."

Bruno drew a long breath and remained silent.

"In your depositions," the cardinal continued, looking at some papers in front of him, "for example in the third, fourth and fifth hearings, you mentioned some of your books and claimed that they contain no heretical opinions. You produced a list of the works you've had printed, as well as others that are still unpublished. Since these may yield important evidence in your favour or against you, this Congregation orders that all your writings be handed over to His Excellency Cardinal Bernieri" – the man to Santoro's right nodded his head – "so that they can be thoroughly examined." There was a pause, then he added: "Both printed works and manuscripts."

"All my books and manuscripts have been seized by the Holy Office in Venice."

"Very well."

Santoro raised a hand and signalled to the notary Flaminio Adriani, who was writing the minutes of the Congregation's prison visit, to put down his pen.

"During your trial you declared," the cardinal went on, "that just before being arrested you were working on a book on the seven liberal arts and seven other inventive arts which was to be presented to His Holiness. If that is so, why is there no mention of it in the list you drew up? And why can't the manuscript be found among your papers?"

"Because there is no manuscript," said Bruno.

"What do you mean?"

"I haven't written it on paper: it's all in my mind."

"I see." Santoro pressed his lips together. "And what is the content of this book?"

"It's a treatise on memory."

"Be more specific."

"It describes a new system, a new language that allows the human intellect to memorize an infinite number of words and notions."

"Why do you think His Holiness might be interested in such a thing?"

"I've heard he is a lover of true learning," said Bruno, "and I am sure he will recognize the importance of my work. It will change for ever the way we think, acquire knowledge and look at the world. It will give men of every science a powerful new tool of inquiry and understanding."

As Giordano continued to talk about the merits of his revolutionary technique, which he claimed would unify all the fields of human endeavour, the inquisitors-general and the other prelates along the table exchanged worried looks and whispered among themselves.

"This... this new system of yours," said the oldest of the cardinals, Pedro de Deza, "does it pose any danger to our holy faith?"

"On the contrary, Your Excellency," Bruno said, with an ambiguous smile. "I believe that it could be used to defeat all the enemies of God on earth." He gave a soft chuckle. "I gave a small demonstration of it to Pope Pius over twenty-five years ago, and later to the King of France, and they were both greatly impressed. But now I've almost perfected it. This is why I am confident that His Holiness would welcome my labours with open arms."

"Have you communicated your discoveries to others?" asked Santoro. "Taught anyone your methods?"

"Not in their current form. The books I wrote on this subject are flawed. They are just fragments, pale shadows of my great design."

"What is the title of your work?"

"*Clavis magna.*"

"If we were to give you a pen and enough paper," intervened Cardinal Bernieri, "would you be prepared to write it down so that it can be examined with the rest of your books and manuscripts?"

Giordano remained silent.

"Will you give His Excellency an answer?" said Santoro.

"I will consider this," said Bruno, "if the defamatory allegations against me are withdrawn and I am allowed to live religiously outside the cloisters."

Santoro banged his bony fist on the table. "How do you dare to come before us and dictate conditions? How do you presume to escape judgement for your misdeeds?"

"I am innocent, Father."

"That will be determined by this Congregation after a proper examination of all the evidence against you – which is manifold."

"Then I'll need no pen, Father, and no writing paper."

"We shall see if you change your mind. Soldiers!"

Giordano was led away and taken back to his cell.

In the evening a Dominican friar and a priest came to see him. The friar was holding a candle, the priest carrying a bundle of documents.

"Good day to you, Brother Giordano," said the priest in a Spanish accent. "I've brought something for you, eh."

"Who are you?" said Bruno.

"My name is Serafino. And this is Francesco, a brother of your order."

"My former order," Bruno said.

"Eh. Anyway, this is your paper, brother. You can write on it."

"Write what?"

"Whatever you like. Your book, for example."

"Which book?"

"The one you discussed with Their Excellencies this morning, eh. The one about memory. Cardinal Bernieri is very interested in it. Very interested. He wants to read it. As soon as possible."

"Will they consider my request?"

"Oh, yes, yes. Of course, brother. They will consider your request as soon as you show them your book, eh. First they'll examine your book, and then they'll decide on it."

"I'll write it only if they let me out of here immediately."

"Eh. That will not be possible, brother. There is a trial awaiting you. A trial for heresy. Not a trifling matter."

"Then tell Cardinal Bernieri he can find another use for that paper."

"But, brother," intervened the friar. "Try to be reasonable. You cannot challenge the authority of the Holy Office. It's simply impossible."

"Then I won't write a single word for them."

Serafino darted a quick glance at his companion, then said: "I'll tell you what we'll do, brother. We'll leave the paper here with you, eh. Just in case you want to start writing. Then Brother Francesco and I will go and talk with the father inquisitors, and we'll see if we can give you some written assurance that the Holy Office will consider your request once you have finished your book. What do you think?"

"I don't want written assurances. I want to be taken out of here at once."

"Very well, brother, very well," said Serafino. "Here's the paper for you, eh. I'll put it on this table. Just in case. Give it some thought, brother. Give it some thought. I know you need time. We'll be back, eh."

The priest and the friar walked out of the cell, and once the door was locked and bolted behind them, Bruno was left in total darkness.

It was the first of many unannounced visits by the two clerics. They would come at any hour of the day, sometimes accompanied by a Jesuit friar and often bringing some bread or fruit as a gift. But despite their coaxing ways and obsequious entreaties, they were unable to convince Bruno to put pen to paper.

One night at the beginning of June, Giordano was sitting on his bed, staring at the flame of a candle that threw flickering shadows around the room. Images coursed and combined in his mind's eye: a horned woman astride a dolphin holding lilies in one hand and a chameleon in the other, two servants carrying silver vases full of gems and gold – and then a pale-faced man wearing dirty clothes and brandishing a stick as he lay on the ground, while a pig rooted around mounds of earth. Suddenly the light around the wick turned purple. He jumped back and, looking up, said:

"Are you... the Devil?"

A gaunt hand was riffling through the reams of paper. "You haven't written a word yet, Bruno."

"No."

"You are stubborn man."

"Maybe. But a stubborn man who can still distinguish truth from falsehood and good from evil."

"His Holiness wants to read it."

"Then he knows what he has to do."

"The Holy Office has enough evidence to convict you."

"I'll know how to defend myself."

"Very well. I bid you good night."

The darkling figure of Cardinal Santoro retreated into the shadows and disappeared.

Serafino and Francesco stopped visiting him. He was moved into a larger and brighter cell occupied by two other prisoners. The first one was Pier Francesco Trevani, an elderly man from Como with an extremely long white beard, a pointed nose and foul breath. It was not clear why he had been locked in that prison, but he kept pestering him and rambling about Adam and Eve, Cain and Abel and God knows what other fable from the Old Testament. The other inmate was, by his own account, a nobleman from an ancient family and an accomplished poet and man of letters. His name was Francesco Maria Vialardi, and he hailed from Vercelli. He claimed to have led an adventurous life across Europe, travelling more than Columbus and seeing more cities and countries than Ulysses. He counted several powerful people among his friends. He was on familiar terms with many famous men of letters, such as Chiabrera and Guarini. How could Bruno not have heard of them? Every *bell'ingegno* had read their works. Vialardi never stopped talking, and his occasional curses and blasphemies were so ingenious, his elegant clothes so worn out and shabby, as to make him sound and look amusing. If Giordano wished at times he'd been left in solitary confinement, he also thanked his good fortune not to have been put in the same cell as David Wendelius, a lunatic from Bahn in Pomerania, whose constant banging and wolflike howling kept him awake most nights.

One hot September morning he was led before the Congregation of the Holy Office and asked to swear on the Bible. The six inquisitors-general questioned him for hours on the same matters and charges for which he had been tried in Venice. At the end of the hearing, he felt he had acquitted himself in the best possible way under the circumstances, remaining steadfast in his views and coherent in his statements. But it was clear that the examination had only just started.

A few weeks later he was dragged again in front of the assembled tribunal of the Inquisition – and from the moment he stepped into the room and saw the faces of the inquisitors, he knew that something was afoot.

"You declared under oath," said Cardinal Santoro, "that no one, with the exception of Signor Giovanni Mocenigo, could claim that you have professed heretical doctrines or accuse you of any wrongdoing in matters of faith."

"Yes."

"Well, we are in receipt of a whole set of fresh accusations from a number of other sources." There was a long pause. "Do you have anything to say to this? Have you been struck dumb, Bruno?"

"They can't be from honourable people."

"Very well. Perhaps our esteemed notary can start reading some of the depositions."

During the rest of the day and over the course of that week, Giordano was forced to listen to and defend himself against the most vicious allegations. He was accused of saying that Jesus was an evil man, a necromancer, a charlatan who deserved to be punished, of despising the cult of saints and relics, of wanting to set up a new sect, called the Giordanists, of being often blasphemous and pouring scorn on Christ, Moses, the prophets and the Catholic theologians. These and many other serious charges were levelled at him – and not from one source only, but from several.

"This is absurd! I never said anything like this! Never!"

But who were the informers? Were they his cellmates in Venice – perhaps Francesco Graziano or Celestino – who bore a grudge against him or had been suborned by Saluzzo? Were they some mercenary friends of Mocenigo? Were they his fellow prisoners in Rome – Vialardi and the old man from Como? Or had the new charges been fabricated by one of the devils in purple sitting in front of him to see how he would react and whether he would admit to any guilt? One thing was sure: his situation was now much more serious and precarious, and he could not afford any mistake. He had no friends, but only enemies in the world.

After eight tense hearings, the prosecution case was completed. Bruno was returned to his solitary cell and kept under strict confinement. As the cold season advanced, the dampness, the gloom and the sense of isolation, mixed with a strong feeling of frustration and injustice, became almost unbearable for him.

Just before Christmas, on 22nd December, there was a new visit by the Congregation.

"Are you happy with your current accommodation?" asked Cardinal Deza.

"Yes," Bruno said.

"And with the food?"

"Yes."

"Do you have any grievances, my son?"

"I'm cold."

"You're cold?"

"I'm very cold, Father."

The Holy Office commissioner, Alberto Tragagliolo, whispered in the ear of the friar sitting next to him, Giovan Vincenzo of Astorga, Vicar of the Dominicans, who nodded.

"Very well, my son," said Cardinal Deza, "the brethren of your old order will provide you with a mantle and a cap."

"I would also like to make another request, Father."

"What is it, my son?"

"A copy of St Thomas's *Summa*."

"The entire *Summa*?"

"Yes, Father."

"What do you need it for, my son?"

"Just for my comfort, Father. And also to prepare my defence."

"I am sure the Congregation will have no objection to this," Deza said, looking around and receiving sparse nods of approval.

Bruno bowed his head in acknowledgement.

Before the end of the visit, the public prosecutor Marcello Filonardi asked him if he still rejected all the charges laid against him and whether he agreed to have the witnesses re-examined, as it was customary in order to protect the defendant against the possibility of false statements and calumnies.

"What would happen if I were to refuse, Father?"

"Their depositions will be taken as they are."

"Then I would like to have the witnesses re-examined."

"Do you wish to avail yourself of counsel for their re-examination?"

"I will need no counsel, Father."

"Very well. Here is a list of the articles for the reinterrogation. They have been extracted from the minutes of the trial and certified by our notary." Adriani, who was sitting next to him, nodded. "And here's some paper and a pen. You can write down your questions, which will then be submitted to the witnesses."

"May I know who they are?"

"They must remain unnamed, my son."

Bruno took the pen and the papers and bowed his head. As he did so, Cardinal Santoro gestured to the notary to stop taking notes and said: "Do you still refuse to obey the order of this Congregation?"

"Which order?"

"To hand over your unpublished manuscript – your book about this supposed new system of knowledge?"

"I can't hand over a manuscript that doesn't exist, Your Eminence."

"You said you could write it down."

"I can barely think, let alone write, in this dismal place."

"Once we've examined your work, or part of it," said Cardinal Bernieri, shifting in his chair and glancing at the other inquisitors, "we may consider keeping you as a prisoner at large within the confines of this building, pending your sentence."

"I can't, Father, I can't. I need light, air, space. I need my freedom."

"Enough with this, Bruno," cried Santoro. "Will you surrender your book or not?"

"No," Giordano shouted back.

"Then you'll die in your cell – if you're fortunate."

"Then my book will die with me."

"We shall see about that," said Santoro, and waved at the soldiers to take him away.

21

Giulia was sitting in the hotel lobby reading a newspaper when Peter arrived.

"Sorry I'm late," he said. "I was checking my email."

"Don't worry: they make decent coffee here. Any news from Jordan?"

"I'll tell you everything on the way."

The École Biblique, housed in the Dominican monastery of St Stephen, was a twenty-minute walk away, so they decided to take a stroll rather than get a taxi. The late-afternoon sun was still strong as they advanced through the busy streets outside the walls of the old city.

"Al-Rafai says that someone is coming to see us at the hotel this evening," Peter said. "Someone who can give us a hand."

"We need a miracle more than help."

"And the police confirmed that Marini didn't commit suicide."

"I told you it wasn't plausible."

"Someone staged his hanging. He'd already been dead for hours when he was left to swing from the bridge."

"Do they know how he died?"

"That may take a few more days to find out. The other thing Al-Rafai mentioned is that he is worried Biblia might not compensate him for the loss of his manuscript."

"Why?"

"Because they are under some financial pressure at present."

"How can that be?"

"Well, they've been spending huge amounts, and their profits are lower than expected, so their shares have been tumbling in the last few weeks. This may explain why Dale was keeping quiet about the Bookworm threats."

"He didn't want more bad news to get out in the open."

"Exactly. And if the markets were to get wind of the recent theft and Marini's killing, that wouldn't make their stock soar, would it? The last thing Dale wants is to spread panic among Biblia's shareholders. I think they are in a very vulnerable situation at the moment."

Leaving Damascus Gate behind, they turned into Nablus Road and walked past the stalls of street traders selling breads, fruit, drinks and all sorts of bric-a-brac. A little farther on, to their right, they saw a crowd of tourists queuing by the entrance to the Garden Tomb. They crossed the street and, following a stone perimeter wall, came to a solid steel gate that blocked the view of what lay beyond.

"This is it," said Peter. "Let's see if they'll let us in."

Just as he was about to press the buzzer, the gate swung open. A car came out, and before the gate closed again they were able to sneak inside. They found themselves in a peaceful courtyard surrounded by trees and bushes. In front of them, beyond an arched entrance, rose a white-stone church built in Romanesque style, looking out onto a porched atrium with the statue of a kneeling man atop a column in the centre.

"St Stephen," said Giulia, "the patron saint of the monastery. His relics are supposed to be preserved here."

A wide lane on the left led them to the entrance of the monastery. Beyond a locked glass door, they saw a flat arch with painted decorations and the words "CONVENTVS SANCTI STEPHANI" written along the top. A friar in a white habit emerged from a basement staircase and, seeing them, came to the door.

"*Je suis désolé*," he said. "*La bibliothèque est fermée.*"

"Would it be possible to see the prior?" asked Peter.

The friar turned a blank stare on him.

"*Est-ce qu'il est possible de parler avec Monsieur le Prieur?*" said Giulia.

"*Attendez, s'il vous plaît.*"

The friar disappeared under the arch and returned five minutes later in the company of an elderly man in lay clothes with thick spectacles and a white beard, who opened the door a little and said: "I'm afraid the Prior is not available. How can I help you?"

"Sorry to bother you," said Peter through the crack. "We are here to visit—"

"Visits are not allowed at this time," the elderly man interrupted. "Please come back tomorrow morning."

"We'd like to talk for a moment to one of your ex-students, who is apparently staying here."

"And you are?"

"I'm a relative," said Giulia. "He has something for me. Something very important."

The man exchanged a quick look with the friar. "I'm afraid we can't allow any visitors now. Please return—"

"Couldn't you make an exception?" Peter said. "We travelled all day to be here."

"I trust you know the exit, sir. Goodnight."

The glass door was locked and the two men disappeared through the arch, murmuring and shaking their heads.

"Very friendly," Giulia said, as they headed back to the hotel.

"Do you always lie that much?" asked Peter.

"Only when it's easier than telling the truth."

They joined the main thoroughfare again, and they were walking towards the path that runs along the city walls when they looked at each other.

"Do you see what I see?" said Giulia.

"I do."

On the other side of the road, a young Arab turned and disappeared down the steps leading to Damascus Gate.

"So we're being followed."

"Probably."

"Why?"

"I don't know."

"Are we in danger?"

Peter took a deep breath.

"I hope not," he said.

Twenty minutes later they were back at the King David Hotel. As they made their way towards the lifts, a concierge informed them that a gentleman was waiting for them in the lobby.

"Must be our miracle-worker," Peter whispered to Giulia, trying to cheer her up.

They approached a small round table where a middle-aged man in a white-collared religious habit was reading a book.

The priest saw them advance and stood to greet them. "Mr Simms? Miss Ripetti? How do you do?" he said, with a slight Spanish accent. "My name is Ángel – Father Ángel."

They shook hands and sat down.

"Did you have a good journey into Jerusalem?" the priest asked.

"Super," Peter said. "Super. Have you travelled a long way to come and see us?"

"Me? No." Father Ángel said. "I'm staying at the Pontifical Biblical Institute. Literally around the corner." He turned to Giulia. "So you're Italian, Miss Ripetti?"

"Yes, from Rome."

"Oh, Rome…"

As the priest described the countless beauties of the Italian capital and the many happy years he had spent there, Peter studied Father Ángel's remarkable face – his long, thinning grey hair crowned by an unmonastic tonsure, his pockmarked skin, his bushy eyebrows and sunken eyes, and then the full lips under a red bulbous nose that took some time getting used to. When was the man going to explain what he was there for?

"Have you been out to visit old Jerusalem?" the priest asked, turning to Peter.

"Actually, we've just come back from the monastery of St Stephen. We tried to speak to Father Andreoli, but they wouldn't let us see him."

Father Ángel looked worried. "Whom did you talk to?"

"A French friar and another man we met at the door."

"You told them you wanted to see Andreoli?"

"I don't think we mentioned his name, no."

"Good." Father Ángel nodded. "Good. If he were to know that someone is after him, he may try to make himself unavailable."

"I'd only have used his name if we'd managed to get into the place."

"One must be careful with Dominicans." The priest chuckled. "Sly foxes – difficult to ensnare. Now, about Father Andreoli…" He slid a photo over the table for them to look at. "He was born near Naples in 1978. Received a baccalaureate in Philosophy at the Angelicum in 2002, one in Theology three years later, a licence in Biblical Theology in 2007 and a doctorate in 2009. Then he took some interest in medieval and Renaissance paleography, did research at Cambridge and later at the Sorbonne. Finally, this year, he obtained another doctorate in Biblical Studies here in Jerusalem. He's written several books and articles, mostly in the field of philosophy." The priest looked up and smiled. "Clever young man."

"Indeed." Peter put the photo in the pocket of his jacket. "How should we go about talking to him?"

"Don't go asking the prior or the hosteller. Try to speak to him directly." Father Ángel scratched his cheek.

"Can you approach him for us?"

"It's complicated." Ángel scratched his cheek again. "Jesuits, Dominicans – you see, some old wounds never heal. Do you know anything about the history of the École Biblique?"

"I don't," Peter said.

"Well, it was founded at the end of the nineteenth century by a Dominican friar, Marie-Joseph Lagrange. Have you heard of him? No?"

"I think I've come across his name," said Giulia.

"He was a great scholar, a great mind," the priest continued, "and he was one of the first to apply historical criticism to the study of the Bible. Unfortunately, this provoked the censure of the Holy Office, who accused him of modernism and rationalism. His school was closed for a period of time and he was banned from publishing his work. Meanwhile, the Jesuits opened a rival school, the Pontifical Biblical Institute – first in Rome and then here – to fight his methods and ideas."

"So there's a long-standing animosity between the École and the PBI?"

"Well, things have improved with the years, and we fully co-operate now – but yes, there is still a certain friction, a certain mistrust. The École and the Dominicans are very jealous of their own autonomy – I am not sure how they would react to a request made on behalf of the Holy See or the Jesuit order."

"Yes, but I'm not working for the Vatican, and we're not asking them to hand over Andreoli. We just want to have a quick chat with him. For all we know, he may be innocent of any wrongdoing."

"Sure, sure. But they may get protective and over-defensive. I am only warning you to tread very lightly, that's all. It's difficult for people outside our world to understand religious politics and the psychological subtleties at work within the walls of the cloisters."

"What should we do then?"

"Well…" The priest scratched his cheek again, and Peter felt an itch on his own face. "It might be easier to talk to him at the end of the morning service or the conventual Mass. The Mass is at noon in the Basilica of St Stephen, in the monastery compound."

"OK, then. Perfect. Thank you."

"Not at all. It was very nice talking to you." Father Ángel stood up and stretched out his arm to shake hands. If you need anything at any time, please let me know." He handed Peter his card. "Remember, we are just round the corner from here. We're only too happy to help. And we're anxious to see this matter resolved."

Father Ángel picked up his book from the table, gave a gentle bow and left.

22

Rome, 10th September 1599

Giordano let his gaze roam over the desk where he had been working all night. He saw his muddled papers, the pen, the inkwell, a breviary and the volumes of Aquinas's *Summa* – his closest companions for many years now – and drew a pained sigh. Sitting down, he put on his spectacles and read once more a letter to the Pope he had written the day before.

"He must save me," he murmured. "He must save me."

Shaking his head, he took off the glasses and exhaled. His eyes drifted over the colophon on the title page of the book open in front of him. It depicted a naked woman astride a dolphin, holding a sail in her right hand and resting her other arm on her hip, at an angle. The sea on which she was floating was calm and, behind her, in the background, the sun shot its rays into a clear sky. On the elaborate oval frame surrounding the image ran the words "BONA FORTUNÆ".

"The benefits of Fortune!" thought Bruno, closing the volume and pushing it away. But not for him. His was the fate of a man buried alive. Seven years now he had been locked in a prison, mostly by himself, summoned in front of the inquisitors only at Easter and Christmas, brutally interrogated from time to time, forced to defend himself from more villainous accusations, urged to recant and abjure his heresies, threatened with fitting retribution if he still refused to deliver his work on memory to the Holy Office.

Seven springs, seven summers had followed one another in soundless succession, only punctuated by the crying and shrieking of his fellow prisoners and by the clank of their chains. So many of the old inmates he had seen go. Many, no doubt, were dead. Wendelius, the mad Pomeranian, was no longer seen or heard. Trevani and Vialardi had also been freed and granted back their lives. Not him, though.

An endless supply of newcomers replaced those who disappeared – priests, friars, noblemen, philosophers, witches, papal-bull forgers, adulterers – as if the god served by the Holy Tribunal were a greedy beast with a monstrous appetite that needed constant appeasing. Giordano shuddered. The darkness of that prison and the horrors perpetrated in the deep entrails of that building were enough to eclipse the light diffused by all the past and present torchbearers of faith.

"Even that of Jesus and the Apostles," he mumbled to himself, not scared by the blasphemy of his thought.

But why was he being kept in that prison so long? Was it because they didn't have enough proof to convict him? Was it to torment and humiliate him before the inevitable sentence of guilt? His mind went over the lengthy phases of the trial once again.

After the witnesses had been re-examined, he had been given a copy of their declarations. There were no names on them, but from their cloddish style and the ludicrous allegations they contained, he could see the faces of his accusers: Francesco Graziano, Celestino, Brother Giulio of Salò, Matteo de Silvestris, Francesco Vaia – his cellmates in Venice – and of course that cur, Giovanni Mocenigo, who must have bribed them with the promise of money, lenience from the Holy Office or even freedom.

He had argued his defence with success – of that he was proud. Standing by his previous statements, he had shown the inquisitors that the delators were discreditable individuals, motivated by malice or revenge. In the absence of further proof against him, the Congregation had ordered the examination of all his published and unpublished works. In some cases he had to supply the whole text, or a summary of it, from memory. It took the censors over two years to review his works.

Then, when a list of the unorthodox ideas contained in them was compiled, he was subjected again to ferocious questioning and presented with eight heretical opinions to reject. He was given only six days to decide. He appealed to the Pope, declaring he was willing to abjure the heresies, subject to certain conditions, but Clement showed no mercy and threatened to hand him to the secular authorities if he didn't recant in full.

"What is your final decision, Bruno?" Santoro had asked.

"I will recant," Giordano had said, his voice trembling, his face pale, his body shaking.

"Do you repudiate all your errors?"

"All of them."

"All of them?"

"Yes. Everything. Anything."

But as the time of his public abjuration at the Church of La Minerva approached, he had started to have misgivings. The thought of being dragged among curious crowds like a strange beast from the New World, of being forced to make a show of submission in front of a throng of sneering prelates, of having to wear the penitential garment and being pointed at wherever he went, and possibly having to spend many more years in prison, was loathsome, unacceptable.

So, just before the Easter visit by the Congregation, he prepared a new letter of appeal to the Pope. He was willing to accept the eight counts of heresy, but only in order to be reconciled with the Church, because from a philosophical point of view he remained unconvinced about some of them. To show his goodwill, he would give a sample of his great treatise on memory to His Holiness, if he could be granted pens, ink and paper, as well as a knife, a pair of compasses and eyeglasses, because his sight was failing.

But when the time of the visit arrived and he entered the inquisitors' room, he regretted bringing the letter with him – because sitting next to a grim-faced new cardinal, he recognized the Dominican friar who years before had seen him off in chains from the Venetian prison. His eyes clouded over.

"Are you happy with your cell and the food, my son?"

Bruno felt a chill down his spine.

"Will you give an answer to Father Beccaria, the General of your order?" said the stern-looking cardinal, Roberto Bellarmino.

Giordano raised his gaze to meet the eyes of his superior. That face, so familiar... that's who he was... With an enemy like that plotting all the time behind his back – an enemy with almost as much power and influence as the Pope – no wonder he had been unable to escape the Inquisition and rotting in jail for so many years.

"Yes, I'm happy, Father," Bruno said at length.

"Do you have any grievances?"

"I have no grievances, Father."

"Do you need anything?"

"I need nothing, Father."

Then all he remembered was placing his papers into the bony hands of his other tormentor, Cardinal Santoro, and being escorted back to his cell as if to a place of execution.

Towards the end of August, the grated door to his cell was pushed open and the familiar figure of Father Serafino appeared, in the company of a young, blond Franciscan friar.

"How are you, brother, eh?" Serafino said. "I've brought you the material you requested. Not the knife or the compasses, eh. They're not allowed in a cell. This is Brother Kaspar," he said, noticing Giordano's suspicious looks. "From Germany. Speaks Latin." He put paper, ink, pens and glasses on Bruno's desk. "The *Clavis magna*, eh. Kaspar can help you with Latin better than I can. You can dictate the book to him, eh."

"This is not a book I can dictate," Bruno said. "I need no help."

"As you wish, brother. As you wish, eh."

"I may decide not to write it, after all."

"Oh, but you must, brother, you must, eh. The inquisitors will lose their patience."

"I'm not afraid of torture."

"Don't say that, brother, don't say that. Torture is painful, eh. It can leave you a cripple, eh. They'll hang you from the ceiling with your hands tied at the back. They'll let you drop down. They'll put weights on your feet. They'll burn you with torches, eh. You can die from it."

"I'm not afraid of death."

"Oh brother, brother. Please. There is death and death, eh. There is a peaceful death when you die with a clear conscience, and there's a horrible death when you die in sin. And then you have the torments of hell – devils, damnation. If they torture you and you confess your crimes, you're sentenced to a terrible death. Burnt alive, eh. The most painful way to go out of this world. If they torture you and you don't confess, you're forced to abjure in public *de vehementi*. You should have seen what they did to that poor friar from Verona the other day."

"Which friar?"

"I think his name is Celestino, eh."

"Celestino…"

"Given a good dose of the strappado, as I've heard, eh. And did he profit from it? No. He's still impenitent – and he will probably be handed over soon to secular justice."

"I told him he'd die before me."

"But you mustn't die, eh. Not now. You must write your book first, your great book. We'll leave you in peace now. But take my advice, brother. Avoid torture, avoid death."

"Your great book"… Bruno turned the phrase over in his mind. Day and night he had sat at this desk, trying to put down on paper the whirl of ideas that had accumulated over more than two decades. All he could jot down were disconnected fragments and diagrams: there was no intellectual light left to link up the dark spaces that separated them – no *Clavis magna*, but only a scattering of insoluble questions.

Opening the volume, he looked again at the small engraving on the title page. It looked like one of the images that had crowded his imagination for years, but Mnemosyne did not whisper in his ear any more, and his mind was dark – dark as his cell, dark as the night sky, dark as the soul of his tormentors – teeming with petty preoccupations, cavils, regrets, maddened by fear of failure and dreams of vengeance.

A clang of keys made him turn towards the door, where he saw one of the warders.

"Come, Bruno," the warder said.

"Where?"

"The inquisitors want you."

"What, now?"

"Come."

He took the letter he had written for the Pope and followed the warder out of the cell. He was led upstairs and made to wait outside the room used for the visits to the prisoners. He gazed at the tall wooden door in front of him with an empty stare. Was this the moment he was going to learn his fate after so many years?

When he entered the room, he saw the entire Congregation – the notary, the referendary, the commissary, the assessor, the public procurator, the consultors and the inquisitors-general – gathered behind the table. This time it was Santoro who was the first to speak.

"Iordanus Bruni," the cardinal said, "we have been informed by the Holy Office of Vercelli of new accusations against you."

"New accusations?"

"That you lived as an atheist in England. That while you were there you wrote a book called *The Triumphant Beast*, which is not included in the list you gave us."

"I did not live as an atheist in England or anywhere else."

"Did you or did you not publish that book?"

"I did."

"Why did you not inform the tribunal of the Holy Office in Venice or this Congregation?"

"Because I forgot."

"You forgot?"

"Yes."

"You, a man who has written several works on the art of memory, who claims to have developed a system allowing one to remember all human knowledge, have forgotten the writing

231

and publishing of a book?" Santoro stroked his beard. "Did you not forget this book because in the 'triumphant beast' you ridicule the Catholic Church and, in particular, His Holiness?"

"This is absurd. I… Please… Please… I can't take this any more…"

"Our esteemed notary will now read out this Congregation's final resolutions on your case."

Old Adriani stood up, holding a sheet of paper. "As to the first part of the trial against the accused," he said, "our reverend consultors could not reach a unanimous verdict of conviction, but they were in total agreement that he should be subjected to torture."

Bruno fell to his knees. It was all over now – his battle had been lost.

"However," Adriani went on, "His Holiness Pope Clement VIII, in his mercy, has decided to grant the accused one last opportunity to recant his errors."

Giordano brought his hands to his face and began to sob and laugh at the same time.

"Stand up, Bruno," Santoro said, "stand up."

He was lifted to his feet by the guards.

"Do you have anything to say?"

"I'm…" He wiped his eyes and cheeks. He was still shaking uncontrollably. "I'm grateful, Your Excellency. I… I intend to own up to all my mistakes and do whatever the Holy Catholic Church of Rome instructs me to do."

"Good. I hope you mean it this time. What are those papers in your hand?"

"A letter, Your Excellency. It's for His Holiness."

"Give it to us."

"It should be read only by him."

CHAPTER 22

"Very well," said Cardinal Bellarmino, "we'll pass it on."

With a tentative gesture, under the fierce look of Beccaria and the other prelates, Bruno handed it over to the cardinal.

"Is there anything else?" asked Santoro.

"No, Your Excellency."

"Then you may leave."

Giordano turned and made to go, but Santoro's voice forced him to stop.

"And Bruno… You know what is expected of you: you should hasten to finish your work, your *Clavis magna*."

* * *

He was taken to a new cell – the cleanest and brightest, in fact, of all his many confinements. Father Serafino and Brother Kaspar were waiting for him there, sitting by the desk, with all his books, papers and pens neatly laid out on it.

"Beautiful room," the priest said, getting to his feet. "Fit for a prince, eh."

"I'll need fewer candles here."

"Eh. I've heard the Congregation has granted you a reprieve. I'm delighted."

"Well, if the consultors had got their way I'd be swinging from the ceiling by now."

Serafino lowered his voice to a whisper. "The Father General wanted you to be tortured not just once or twice, I'm told, but until you were ready to depose."

"To depose my blood and soul, perhaps," Bruno said through his teeth. "I have only to thank Pope Clement for saving me from that. Perhaps, with the Jubilee starting soon, he'll be prepared to grant me a pardon."

Father Serafino knitted his brows. "Don't count on that, brother. His Holiness is not in a forgiving mood. Did you hear what happened this morning at dawn?"

"What happened?"

"That beautiful young girl. From a noble family, eh. Beatrice Cenci. With her brother and stepmother. They were killed at Castel Sant'Angelo, in front of a crowd. Screaming their innocence to the high heavens. Priests and cardinals asking for them to be pardoned. Didn't help, eh. First they beheaded Lucrezia, the stepmother, then they cut off Beatrice's head. She looked like an angel, eh. It didn't save her, though. Then it was the turn of the boy, Giacomo. They pinched him with red-hot pincers and gave him the hammer. They slaughtered and quartered him like a bullock, eh. And his younger brother was tied to a chair and forced to see all the executions. Don't look for mercy where you can't find it, brother."

"I'll bear that in mind, Father."

Serafino put a hand on Giordano's arm and gave a gentle squeeze. "Listen to me: write that book. Finish it soon, eh. Don't risk His Holiness's displeasure. Or that of the Congregation, eh. Remember – for any help you need, Brother Kaspar and I will be here."

The priest and the friars bowed their heads. As they left, the young German peered behind him to give Bruno an ambiguous smile.

23

"That's him, isn't it?"

"Which one?" Peter whispered.

"The one at the back, walking on his own."

"I can't see him."

"Look, he's about to go into the church now."

Peter had a brief look at the photo Father Ángel had given him.

"Yes, it's him." He looked up. "Let's wait until the service is over."

The bells rang the hour, and Peter and Giulia continued to pace about the courtyard in front of the church in silence, casting watchful glances over their shoulders from time to time. It was half-past noon when they saw two friars emerge from St Stephen's and disappear through a wooden door that opened on the right-hand side of the cloister.

They waited some more, expecting Andreoli to appear any moment, but ten minutes passed, then twenty, and no one came out. They approached the church entrance and tried to listen in: they could hear no music or voices.

"Let's go in," said Peter.

They stepped inside with caution, and were surprised to find the nave of the church completely deserted. They looked at each other in puzzlement, then advanced up the right aisle, cut across the choir and came down the left aisle. They had another good look around, in case they had missed some tucked-away chapel, but there was no other person to be seen in the church, and no noise to be heard other than the echo of their own steps.

"Where have they gone?" Peter said.

"They've vanished."

Just then, an elderly friar came out of a door on the left and, seeing them, walked over to them.

"Are you all right there?" he said.

"Was there Mass today at twelve, Father?" Peter asked.

"Yes, it finished a while ago."

"We saw the brothers go in, but not out."

"They must have left that way." He pointed at the door through which he had come. "There's a corridor that leads back to the library and the monastery."

"I see."

They returned outside and considered what to do next.

"Perhaps we should give Father Ángel a call," Giulia said, "see what he suggests."

"Leave Father Ángel out of this," Peter said. "I don't like that man. Come with me: let's try something else."

They again followed the wide lane to the entrance of the monastery. The glass door was open and unattended. They were about to walk in when a friar appeared from under the flat arch in front of them and proceeded down the staircase leading to the basement.

"Father Andreoli?" Peter called.

Without stopping, the friar glanced at them sideways and disappeared down the stairs.

"Shall we follow him?"

They cast a nervous look beyond the arch. The monastery's reception desk stood momentarily empty. With a light step, they reached a narrow landing with wooden lockers, a small table and a red office chair. A glass door opened on the left, and a crude sign on the wall warned against the use of mobile phones.

"The library," Peter said.

Inside it was as gloomy and deserted as in the church. An eerie silence enveloped the place, as did a smell of musty old paper. The tables were empty, and no one could be seen walking around or browsing the shelves.

They advanced through the main corridor and looked into the alleys opening to their left and right. Still, there was no trace of Andreoli or of any other student or researcher.

They continued to roam around the library, exploring the length and breadth of the entire floor without seeing anything but shelves full of books, journals and bundled papers. As they walked back towards the exit, they thought they saw a figure cross the main corridor in front of them, blending into the shadows to their right. They took a few wary steps forward and noticed a staircase going down to another floor.

The lower level of the library was just as big as the upper floor, but the ceilings were not so high, the shelves not so full, and the atmosphere was darker. They looked everywhere, but they still couldn't find the elusive friar. They came to a glass door with a wooden frame and a crucifix hanging on the arched top above: beyond, a long corridor stretched ahead and, to the left, stairs could be seen going up. They exchanged a dispirited look.

"This is the end of the road," Peter said. "Unless…"

He pointed at two wooden doors, one on the left and one on the right. He gave a gentle rap on the one nearest to him. There was no answer. Giulia knocked on the second one. No answer. She knocked again, loudly – and this time, after a few moments, the door was opened and the young friar appeared behind it.

"Padre Andreoli?" asked Giulia.

"*Sì?*"

"I'm Giulia Ripetti, from La Sapienza. Latin Philology. Can we have a quick word with you?"

"I'm sorry, but I'm busy."

Peter pushed the door open and forced Andreoli to take a step back.

"What do you want from me?"

"You know what we want," said Peter. "Where's the manuscript?"

"Which manuscript?"

"Bruno's manuscript. The one that you stole in Jordan."

"Who are you?"

"My name's Simms – Peter Simms. I'm working for Mr Al-Rafai."

"How do I know you're telling the truth?"

"Here's my letter of engagement," Peter said, taking a folded sheet out of his pocket and pushing it into Andreoli's hands.

"OK, OK. There's no need to raise your voice or get physical. Who told you I was here? One of our friends at the Holy Office? Some Black Angel from the Pontifical Biblical Institute?"

"Where is Bruno's manuscript?"

Andreoli stared at him, stone-faced.

"Where is it?"

"Upstairs, in my room."

"Let's go and see it, then."

"You can't come inside the monastery."

"Then go and fetch it."

Andreoli nodded his head, unruffled. As he stepped towards the door, Peter stopped him.

"Don't try to escape, or you'll regret it."

24

Rome, 16th September 1599

Bruno worked at his treatise night after night. The inhuman shrieks coming from the chamber next door in the daytime – sobs, entreaties, rising to groans and howling, until the victim's screams were pushed to the highest pitches that physical pain can produce – made it impossible for him to write or rest. Now it was clear why he had been moved here: not to enjoy a more spacious room and better light, but to be reminded what would be in store for him if he refused to deliver his book to the Inquisition.

He put his pen down for a moment, placing his hand over his ears. The worst thing was not knowing whom those shouts and cries belonged to. It was as if they were detached from a human body: they came back to haunt him again and again, echoing in his mind, disturbing his inner vision. His *Clavis magna*, however – or at least the scattered leaves he was able to collect from the cave of his imagination – was somehow proceeding: he had written over two hundred pages and drawn some of the most complex memory wheels that illustrated the system.

That evening, he received a surprise visit in his cell from Santoro, accompanied by Father Serafino and Brother Kaspar.

"This is the letter you wrote to Pope Clement," he said, handing the sheets back to Bruno.

"Did His Holiness read it?" asked Giordano.

"Yes, he did, at yesterday's congregation. Part of it, at least."

"What did he say?"

Santoro began pacing around the room with his arms behind his back. "He commends your intention to recant, after so much wavering and procrastinating. And he looks forward to seeing your book on universal memory." He stopped and looked Giordano in the eye. "This is your chance to prove that you are the great virtuoso you claim to be, Bruno, and that your invention can be used in the service of our Holy Catholic Church. I am told you are making good progress with your work."

"Yes, Your Excellency. It will be completed soon."

"How soon?"

"I cannot say. By the beginning of the Jubilee year in January, perhaps."

"Try to finish it by the next visit of the Congregation in December. It will be an excellent Christmas present for His Holiness."

"I will do my best, Your Excellency."

"Your best won't be enough if you fail in your task, Bruno. Have you prepared the sample that you promised to show to His Holiness?"

"No, not yet. I'm sorry, I've been—"

"Then perhaps Brother Kaspar can copy a few pages."

"The text is very intricate, Your Excellency, and my notes need to be tidied up. I would prefer to do it myself. I will have something ready for you by tomorrow morning at the latest."

"As you wish, Bruno. As you wish. As long as you don't disappoint us again. Brother Kaspar will come and collect the papers after terce."

Serafino stayed behind after the cardinal and the Franciscan left, taking a seat near the desk and opening the breviary with an absent-minded gesture.

240

"What is it, Serafino? Why do you look so dejected?"

"Eh." He wiped his watery eyes with the back of his hand. "It's just that sometimes… You see, brother, the sun, the sun always shines on high, eh, it's always there – but sometimes, sometimes there is smoke, eh, or clouds, and the sun doesn't seem so bright any more."

"I know exactly what you mean, Father."

"But I'm not worried about the sun losing any of its brightness. No, my son: what I worry about is how people are blinded, eh, how their sight is clouded and obfuscated most of their lives – how human history looks like a long journey in the dark." He began sobbing.

"You're a good man, Serafino," Bruno said, putting an arm on his shoulder. "A very good man. But you need not fret about the inhabitants of this earth. Their allotted fate is to grope for that perfect glow – which they can attain only when they die. Nothing changes in this world. *Nihil sub sole novum.* What matters is that your eyes never shy away from the unperturbed blaze, the light intellectual, the heroic fire."

"You are a good man too, Iordanus, and I wish I could help you. But I'm only a frail old man." He wiped his eyes again. "There are dangerous powers at work, eh. Vicious cogs in the machine. You should stay away from their teeth, my son, or they'll crush you."

"That's what I hope to do, Father."

Serafino shuffled towards the door. "Show humility. Do and say what you're told, even if you think otherwise, eh. Don't be unrepentant, like that poor friar from Verona."

"What happened to him?"

"They dragged him out of his cell before dawn, stripped him of his clothes, tied him to a pole and burned him alive. He's a heap of lukewarm ashes by now, eh. God have mercy on his soul, wherever it is. *Vale*, Iordanus, *vale*."

With that, Father Serafino signalled to the warder to open the door and left Giordano to the cold and deepening gloom of his cell.

* * *

Bruno, hunched over his desk, woke up with a start and groaned – his pen had traced his falling asleep with a thin line scarring the page. Mad, anguished writing, every night – it felt like months had passed since Santoro's visit. The blood-curdling noises from the room next door had ceased, and the violent disruption in his mind was replaced by potent images that he'd despaired of ever recapturing.

"Father," he said one day in early November to Serafino, who was visiting him with fruit and fresh water – and he pointed to his manuscript.

"Finished?"

Bruno nodded.

"Well, my son," the priest said, glancing through the pages crammed with small writing, "this is a great achievement. This can save you. I'll fetch you a ream of paper, eh, so that you can start making a fair copy."

Giordano began pacing around his room. A tear of joy rolled down his cheek. So he had made it: he had finished his *magnum opus*. It wasn't perfect, of course. Just as Dante had to reduce his lofty vision to inadequate human words, he too could only offer a pale rendering of his grand design – but his work would now outlive his mortal body, and he hoped it would bring a spark of intellectual light to the infinite legions of the unborn.

It was a relief not having to sit at his desk that night. He took the manuscript to his bed, reading sections and grunting in agreement with himself, taking notes as he went along. As the candle spread its dying light across the cell, his mind sank into one of those dreams between waking and sleeping. He had devised a universal system for human memory and knowledge – but what about dreams? Where did they come from? Did they have a meaning? Could they be controlled or predicted? Was there a way to make sense of that amorphous mass of images, ideas and feelings that flowed through our intellect when we were not awake? Yes – to grasp the connection between rational thought and irrational dream – to write an even more ambitious and comprehensive treatise than *Clavis magna*… He saw the structure of this new great work… the complex diagrams… But then a chilly, bony hand snatched the papers from him, thugs grabbed him from behind and hauled him off to the torture chamber – the grinning face of his torturer, the clang of his chains as he was lifted higher and higher, the physical torment…

"Aaah!" Drenched in sweat, he woke up, his heart pounding, his breathing short. He looked around and could only see darkness. What was that noise out in the corridor? Whispers? Someone running away? He jumped out of bed and fumbled his way to the door. He banged his fist on the grate and called out to the warder.

"Light! Light!"

The guard came shuffling up with his torch. His face was white and taut, as if he had seen a ghost.

"Are you mad, Bruno, to shout like that in the middle of the night?"

"I need light," said Giordano. "Now!"

"Calm down, calm down. Here is your light – but don't go shouting again like that, or I'll give your back as fine a texture as laid paper."

The guard lit a candle and passed it through the bars. "As if I were his valet." He tutted and shambled off.

Bruno looked around in his room. The papers on his desk – dozens of pages of notes and diagrams – gone. A few sheets were scattered on the floor by his chair. His eyes darted towards his bed – thank God, there was his manuscript, by the extinguished candle, next to the ream of paper Father Serafino had given him. That is what the night thief had been after.

He picked up the sheets from the floor and sat at his desk. Tears welled in his eyes – but then a loud laugh burst through his lips. He had been duped and betrayed. He had been given hope that he could save himself if he wrote his book, when in fact all they wanted was to snatch it from him and get rid of him. Who was the Judas – Brother Kaspar, good man Serafino? How could he have been such a fool, how could he have believed that there would be leniency or pardon? His fate had already been written long ago, and could not be changed. All his efforts, his struggles, his resistance had only served to delay the inevitable, which he should now embrace with dignity and without fear. Yes, he had been deceived, but nothing was lost yet: he still had enough courage for his last stand.

It was an hour before the warder's snores rumbled down the cold passageway. Bruno picked up his manuscript and the candle and sat by the grated window. A few sheets at a time, he fed his book to the flame. He'd rather see his magnificent system vanish up in smoke than hand it to an evil and despotic power who could find infinite ways to misuse it, now or in future.

The paper rushed from brown to black, chased by the scorching tide, and as he watched the big flakes of soot whirl in the air, it was as though all the ideas, dreams and memories contained in those pages were being released. "*Sic transit gloria mundi,*" he said to himself with a self-mocking smile, seeing in that blaze a prefiguration of his own final conflagration.

When his manuscript was reduced to ashes, he took some blank paper, went back to his desk and sat down to write. If they wanted his *Clavis magna*, he would give it to them. On the first sheet he scrawled "CM". Then, with a strange joy and lightness of hand, he filled page after page, until the birds began singing outside and the light of dawn replaced the candle flame.

"To be opened and read by His Holiness Pope Clement" said the note placed on his new manuscript, wrapped in parchment and tied with white ribbon. He left it on his desk, then lay down and entered into deep sleep.

"Have you gone totally crazy, Bruno?" the warder shouted – only a moment later, it seemed. "Has the Devil got into you?" He poked the heap of ash with the toe of his shoe. "You're lucky I don't have my cane with me now, or I'd whip the skin off your back." Groaning and cursing, the guard kicked Bruno's chamber pot over on his way out to report to the fathers superior.

* * *

On the following Wednesday, 17th November, the cardinals voted for Bruno's case to be finalized at the next congregation in the presence of His Holiness Pope Clement. Bruno was moved to a dark dungeon cell and deprived of his desk, books, paper and pens. The visits from Father Serafino and Brother Kaspar stopped altogether, and he was kept in complete isolation.

After little more than a month, on 21st December, it was time again for the Congregation's Christmas visit to the prison of the Holy Office. Bruno was the first prisoner to be ushered into the room. Santoro asked him if he was happy about his accommodation and his food, and he replied in the affirmative.

"Do you have any grievances?"

"I have no grievances."

"Do you need anything?"

"I don't need anything, no."

"Good," said Santoro. "Your Excellency?"

Cardinal Bellarmino stood, bowed his head to the inquisitor and, turning to Bruno, said: "Brother Giordano, you were given a *terminus ad resipiscendum* by His Holiness Pope Clement on 9th September last. The forty-day term is now long expired, and despite your repeated pledges and promises that you would admit your errors and mend your ways, you have shown no real intention to recant."

Bruno laughed. "I'm sorry, Your Excellency, but I don't know what you are saying."

"What do you mean?"

"I don't have to recant. I don't want to recant. I have nothing to recant. I have no cause to recant."

"Bruno..." Santoro began.

"You heard me. These are my last and final words to this Holy Congregation."

"Take him away," said the inquisitor.

After Bruno was escorted out of the room, the inquisitors decreed, according to custom and procedure, that two friars of the Dominican order should visit the accused in his cell, show him his heretical opinions and try to persuade him to abjure his views and recant before the sentence was passed. It was decided that this task should be entrusted to the General of the Order, Ippolito Maria Beccaria, and the Vicar, Paolo Isaresi.

* * *

Ten days later, the holy doors of the four papal basilicas in Rome were opened, and the bells of every church pealed in celebration as salvos were fired from Castel Sant'Angelo. The Jubilee year had begun: multitudes of pilgrims, all dressed in the costumes of their countries, crowded the streets of the city, joining processions, singing psalms and offering vows.

In the Apostolic Palace near St Peter's, Pope Clement did not share in the festive spirit. Afflicted by a most painful recurrence of gout during the first meeting of the Congregation in the new year – the feast day of St Fabian and St Sebastian – he grumbled and muttered during the whole proceedings.

The first item on the agenda was the case of Giordano Bruno of Nola. Cardinal Bellarmino summarized the various phases of the trial and mentioned the new evidence that had emerged against the accused. Cardinal Santoro described Bruno's changeable and at times unpredictable behaviour in recent months, his peevish temper and his unprovoked outbursts.

Clement waved his hand to call an end to all those preambles.

"What are these?" he sighed, pointing at a sheaf of papers that had been placed before him.

"These are the notes for his book on memory," said Santoro.

"Ah. Did he not complete it, then?"

"He did, Your Holiness."

"Where is it?"

"He burned it."

"He burned it?" Clement flinched as he shifted position. "Why did he write it and then burn it?"

"We don't know."

He shrugged. "The man must be out of his mind. And what is that?"

"It's a document addressed to you."

"Another one?"

Clement turned the bundle of papers in his hands and untied the string. "CM," he said. Clemente Magno? Clemente Magnifico? He leafed to the next sheet. As he tried to make sense of the words, his eyes narrowed and his expression became puzzled. "What is…" He turned to another page, then another. "…This?" With a strange grimace, he threw the papers to the floor. "Abominable!" he shouted. "I've had enough of this. Has he been visited by friars of his order?"

"We went to see him yesterday, Your Holiness," said Beccaria.

"He won't recant?"

"He won't recant. He claims he's never said or written anything heretical."

"What about all the accusations against him?"

"He says they've all been maliciously extracted by the officers of the Holy Office."

"What else does he say?"

"That he was prepared to offer explanations and defend himself against any theologians."

"Will he submit to their decision?"

"No: he will only submit to a ruling by the Holy See or to the Holy Canons – even if this produces a verdict against him."

Clement waved his hand again. "We've spent enough time on this." He turned to Santoro: "Do what you have to do, and hand him over to the secular justice."

Santoro nodded.

"Now let's move on to more important things," the Pope said.

"Your Holiness," Bellarmino said. "What should we do with all his notes and diagrams?"

"Have them burnt too," was Clement's reply, "together with the rest of his writings."

25

Peter was drumming his fingers on the side of his thighs when Andreoli entered the room with a box folder and a red book in his arms. He walked round to his chair, placed the folders and the book on his desk and sat down.

"Is this the…" Giulia's voice trailed off.

"I'd like to explain a few things first," Andreoli said. "Around six months ago – I had just completed my doctorate here – I got the job as Mr Al-Rafai's librarian, because of my expertise in late-Renaissance Italian and Latin books. It took me a while to settle in. Mr Al-Rafai's library is huge, and he keeps buying all the time at auction or from private collectors. There are still many parts of his collections that I am not familiar with." He played with the corner of a block of sticky notes. "Then, a couple of months ago, Al-Rafai signed a deal with Biblia to have his entire library digitized, starting with rare books and manuscripts, which is what they are most interested in. So we moved part of his holdings to a unit in the Tower, and they began the 'scanning and ingestion' process, as they call it." He gave a soft chuckle. "When Helen Barnett examined the Bruno collection, which was one of Al-Rafai's latest acquisitions, she realized that it was special, so she sought expert advice."

"Father Marini," Peter said.

"Correct. One of the best specialists in the field, and a lovely man too, but—"

"But what?" Giulia asked.

"Well, perhaps, since this was part of a digitization project, they should have asked someone a bit younger and more au fait with new technology. Father Marini didn't like working in the Tower's library. He found it annoying. He was used to working on his own without being disturbed. He also needed to consult reference books all the time. Most of them were available in my room, and I could help him with the Internet. And I can speak Italian. So one day he waited until the librarian was away and took a whole chunk of the Bruniana to my room – without authorization!" He laughed. "Perhaps he thought he was in his faculty library in Italy and could do as he liked."

"Did he tell you what was in the collection?" asked Giulia. "I'm still only halfway through assembling a comprehensive list."

"He said it contained most of Bruno's known works, as well as some unpublished ones and a great quantity of lecture notes – similar to the *Prælectiones geometricæ* and the *Ars deformationum*. Marini thought they were dictated by Bruno to his disciple Besler when he was teaching in Padua. All the other writings are manuscript copies of books that were never published or are missing from the printed works in the collection. They are all in the same hand."

"Bruno's hand."

"No, not Bruno's. A similar hand. Father Marini was adamant about it."

"Oh." Giulia slunk back on her chair. "I thought that Bruno had been forced to write down from memory the books the Inquisition could not find. During the years of the trial, you know."

"It's an interesting possibility, but there's no evidence in the collection that this might be the case."

"Maybe he dictated them when he was in prison."

"Yes, maybe. One could come up with a hundred theories, all equally plausible, and I am sure that thousands of books and articles will be written about this." Andreoli glanced at his watch. "Anyway, going back to Father Marini... He was a quiet companion, and that suited my own work. In the evening, we'd have dinner together and talk about our research and other things. But three or four days after he arrived, he began to change. He looked tense and worried most of the time."

"Did he tell you what bothered him?" asked Peter.

"I don't know if he was being paranoid, but he seemed to believe that he was being followed, both inside and outside the Tower. Also, I think the content of these papers made him very uneasy." He tapped the folder in front of him. "He seemed to think that he could get into serious trouble because of them – that he was in some sort of danger, or under pressure to do something he didn't want to do."

"How do you know?"

"Well, I inferred it. He once said that if he were to disappear all of a sudden, I should look after these papers, show them to the academic board of the École Biblique, make sure they were published. It was all very vague, and I thought he was joking or exaggerating, but now that I have had a look at the papers and read some of his transcriptions, I can understand why he was so anxious." He gave an uncomfortable smile. "Then, of course, poor Father Marini did suddenly disappear. He didn't show up for dinner on Saturday evening. He didn't come to Mass on Sunday and didn't turn up at the Tower on Monday. Perhaps I overreacted, but I thought I'd follow his advice and took off with these papers to a safer place until it became clear what was going on."

Peter turned a suspicious look on Andreoli, trying to read in his eyes whether he knew anything about Marini's death. "Have you shown the manuscript to any of the scholars who teach here?"

"Yes, I have, and I've also done some work on it. I have had each sheet photographed, and I have been studying Father Marini's transcriptions. This lot," said Andreoli, opening the folder, "around four hundred sheets and scraps of various sizes, are miscellaneous notes and drawings. For example…" He passed three pages to Giulia. "As you can see they're just fragments – perhaps preparatory notes for his *De umbris idearum* or *Cantus circæus*. There are some complex wheels and diagrams that I could not find in any of his other memory books."

"Have you checked the *Corpus iconographicum*?"

"Of course. Nothing. It could also be an original work – a follow-up to his *De imaginum compositione*, perhaps. There are some very bold statements and images in these pages, as is usual with Bruno. I am sure that with a little more study and research one could make sense of these fragments. But this," he said, lifting a bundle of papers wrapped in parchment and tied with white ribbon, "this is the gem – or perhaps the bomb – of the entire collection. This is what made Father Marini think he had something dangerous in his hands."

"The *Clavis magna*!" Giulia blurted.

"The *Clavis magna*?" Andreoli looked at her in puzzlement.

"The letters CM…"

"Oh, no, no, it's definitely not the *Clavis magna*. That work was never written, was it?"

"I think it was," said Giulia. "I'm sure it was."

"Well, this has nothing to do with mnemonics. It's unclear when and why it was written – nor how it was allowed to survive – but its significance exceeds a hundred times that of the *Clavis magna*."

Giulia, smiling, swapped glances with Peter. "I hardly think, Father…"

Andreoli reached out and placed the bundle in her hands.

Untying the ribbon, unfolding the parchment wrapping, she removed the sheets inside: around three hundred pages, all the same size, not much larger than A4. She ran her fingertips over the ribbed texture of the paper, then held the first sheet up against the light to see the chain and wire lines. "No watermarks," she said, then lowered her gaze to scrutinize the second page.

Salomon et Pythagoras

Quid est quod est?
Ipsum quod fuit.
Quid est quod fuit?
Ipsum quod est.
Nihil sub sole novum.
Jordanus Brunus
Nolanus

"This is the same inscription Bruno wrote on the back of Jost Amman's woodcut *The Siege of Nola*," she said.

"And in Johannes von Warnsdorff's *album amicorum* during his stay in Wittenberg," Andreoli added.

"The whole manuscript – it's in his hand?"

"In his hand."

She lifted the second sheet and found a page crammed with text. It was evident that the words had been scrawled in a great hurry, and at first she struggled to decipher them. "*Evangelium secundum Iordanum*," she read tentatively. "'*In principio erat Anima – et Anima erat apud Deum – et Deus erat Anima. Hoc erat in principio apud Deum.*' Oh my God—"

Giulia looked up and gazed at Andreoli.

"'In the beginning was the Soul,'" the friar said, "and the Soul was with God, and the Soul was God...' Quite something, isn't it?"

The two scholars were locked into each other's gaze.

"But what is it?" Peter asked. "Giulia? Father?"

Giulia sank back into her chair, flushing. "I can't believe I have something like this in my hands. It is unreal."

"Giulia?" Peter urged.

She let out a long breath. "It's... it's a fifth Gospel. It's an apocryphal Gospel, by one of the most famous free spirits in history." She shook her head as if trying to convince herself she wasn't dreaming. "Giordano's Gospel," she said. "It's... it's a heresy of unthinkable proportions. He must have been *insane* to... to write this..."

"Insane?" Andreoli grinned. "I think he was as lucid as ever. He based the text on St John's Gospel from the Vulgata. In his version there is no Joannes, no St John – and instead of Jesus there's another prophet."

"Iordanus," Giulia breathed.

Andreoli chuckled. "The structure is the same as the older Gospel. It starts with a philosophical prologue, then he gives an idealized version of his life, which includes a mystical supper, talks about his 'miracles' – as when he restores the sight of a man born blind and feeds five thousand people with his heavenly bread – and finishes by describing his passion, his death on the cross and his resurrection. Who else would have dared writing something like this? My favourite part is Iordanus's meeting with Seraphinus, the Black Angel disguised as one of his disciples, who betrays him to the *congregatio*, as he calls the Sanhedrin."

"Fascinating," said Peter. "But... I still don't get it. Why do you think Father Marini was so worried about this book?"

"Why?" Andreoli smiled. "Because it's a dangerous text, Mr Simms – a monumental blasphemy, a powder keg. First, it implies that Christ was not divine but only a human being, like Iordanus. Second, it subverts not just the Holy Scripture but also the authority of Holy See, as it mocks the Vulgata published by Pope Clement in 1592. Third, it would force Rome to revisit one of the most inglorious moments of its history. And finally – it would reopen old disputes within the Catholic Church."

"What do you mean?"

"Bruno was a Dominican—"

"Right."

"—and in this text there are many references to 'black angels', like the traitor Seraphinus and a member of the *congregatio* who is called Baal Amin, the brother of Baal Zebub, the Devil. His name is very similar to that of Bellarmino, one of the most influential officers of the Inquisition, who was a Jesuit, a Black Robe, and who's been made a saint by the Church. When you read the book, it's impossible not to make these connections."

"So you think Bruno wrote this when he was in the prison of the Holy Office?" asked Giulia.

"It is possible. Bellarmino got involved in Bruno's trial only towards the end – from 1597 onwards, if I remember well. That was also the time when the controversy between Thomists and Molinists was raging."

"That's the theological dispute about grace and free will I was telling you about," Giulia said to Peter.

"Bellarmino and some of the other inquisitors were right at the forefront of this dispute. My guess is that Bruno assumed that the Jesuits were trying to score a political point against the Dominicans by using him and his conviction as a pawn…"

"Interesting theory."

"So you'll understand why Father Marini was so concerned about this book, especially now that we have our first Black Pope."

"Excuse me?"

"A Jesuit Pope." Andreoli laughed. "That's what some of us call Pope Francis."

"I see."

Giulia was shaking her head. "I know you'd like to shift your guilt onto the Society of Jesus, but it's the Dominicans who persecuted and did nothing to save a man of their order – and it's Beccaria, their General, who wanted him tortured and executed. I think it's more likely that the Black Devils in the text are the Black Friars, the brothers of the Order of Preachers."

"We're not going to have a fight, now, are we?" said Peter with a smile.

"Well," said Andreoli, "the truth is never black or white. The battle is never between darkness and light. There're a million shades in between. Historians say: 'Bruno was persecuted by the Church', 'Bruno was killed by the Inquisition', 'Bruno was a martyr for science'. But the Church and the Inquisition were made up of people of flesh and blood like him and ourselves – people with their own little brains, eyes, hearts and passions – and science barely existed at the time. I think that the Black Angels, the ones that got Bruno burnt at the stake, are probably hiding in the cracks of history. A man who didn't do something to help him, a friend who didn't have the courage to stand up for him, a woman who didn't show him enough love, an enemy who wasn't able to forgive an old grudge. It's all down to the individuals and their choices. In our small lives, we have a great responsibility. And we all abandoned and killed Giordano Bruno, in some way or other, whether we are Black Friars or White Friars."

Giulia stopped leafing through the manuscript. "It's only seventy pages of text," she said, looking up. "The rest of the sheets are blank."

"Yes," said Andreoli. "It seems his task was interrupted. We can guess why." He glimpsed at his watch again. "I'm afraid I have to go. It's been a real pleasure to meet you and talk to you." He pointed at the bundle on Giulia's lap. "May I?"

Giulia turned a wide-eyed stare at Peter.

"We are actually taking the manuscript back to Jordan," he said.

"I'm sorry, Mr Simms, but that's out of the question. The papers will have to stay here. I'll bring them back to Mr Al-Rafai next week."

"I don't think so. Mr Al-Rafai won't be happy about that."

"I've still got work to do on them. I'm comparing the text to that of St John's Gospel in the Jerusalem Bible" – he waved towards the red volume on his desk – "with the help of scholars from the École Biblique. I don't have the same reference books or the same resources in Jordan."

"You're lucky that Mr Al-Rafai sent *us* and not the police. What did you think you were doing, absconding with a priceless manuscript across borders?"

"What are you suggesting? I wasn't trying to steal it."

"I'm not sure many people would take that view. Anyway, the papers are going back to their owner now. And that is non-negotiable. Will you take us back outside, please?"

* * *

On their way back to the hotel, Peter and Giulia were in high spirits and in a playful mood.

"Miracle accomplished," she said, keeping a large padded envelope close to her chest.

"Not quite," said Peter. "We'll have to make the pilgrimage back to Jordan via the Allenby Bridge." He exhaled. "Not looking forward to that."

"I'm a bit scared travelling with such treasure in our bags." She looked out of the window of their cab. "Especially since we may be followed."

Peter thought for a moment. "Don't worry. I'll carry it to safety in my own hands. I won't let anyone take it away from us."

"Do you think Andreoli was lying? Do you think he wanted to steal the manuscript?"

"I am not sure that 'steal' is the right word. Perhaps he simply felt it belonged to the Dominicans, Bruno's order, and that it could be used one day against their arch-rivals, the Jesuits."

"The power of books."

"The power of words."

They got out of their cab and made their way to the entrance of the hotel to take their bags and check out.

26

Rome, 8th February 1600

They took him out of his cell after sext. They gave him fruit and fresh water. They washed him and trimmed his hair and beard. They made him wear a tunic of white cloth and a black scapular. They took him out into the open air and made him climb onto a horse-drawn cart.

The sky was pale blue, the sun dazzling bright. As the cart made its slow progress through crowds of pilgrims, Bruno took a deep breath of warm air. So these were the people of the new century, this was the world he was leaving behind. Occasional pieces of news had reached his ear from time to time – a famous death, the taking of a city, the flooding of the River Tiber – and he had been aware that life continued to go on outside the walls of his prison, but it was unsettling, and it felt strangely sad, to see the obtuseness with which the human herd went about their business of existing.

The spring season was not far away, but he would not live to watch the trees blossom again. The habit he was wearing was not to signal the start of a new life. The journey he was taking was not towards light, but darkness.

The cart emerged onto the wide expanse of Piazza Navona. Carriages, riders, clerics, beggars, farmers with their oxen, street sellers milled about the square or crowded around the two fountains, the central trough and the market stalls. Throngs of worshippers were flowing in and out of the Church of St Agnes, while a smaller cluster of bystanders pressed round the entrance of the adjacent building, the residence of the Inquisitor General Madruzzo.

The horses nudged their way into the cardinal's palace, coming to a halt in the central court. A soldier bundled him off the cart and prodded him towards the *scala nobile* of the building. As he mounted the stone steps, accompanied by two guards, people followed him from behind or watched him pass by, stepping back to the wall and the balustrade, exchanging low whispers.

"Why not in Santa Maria sopra Minerva? That's where the heretics normally get stitched up."

"This one they want to make a show of."

He entered a sumptuous room on the first floor, decorated for the occasion. In front of him sat, in a semicircle, the Governor of Rome Ferdinando Taverna – nephew of the papal nuncio Ludovico – eight inquisitors general, Cardinal Bellarmino, Ippolito Maria Beccaria, the notary Flaminio Adriani and six other high-ranking prelates. Bruno looked around him. Along the walls and by the doors, which were left open so that whoever did not make it inside could hear, were curious onlookers shifting and craning their necks to have a better view of the scene.

"Iordanus Bruni," boomed Adriani, producing a loud murmur in the room and then silence. "You may kneel."

Bruno obeyed and bowed his head.

The notary read a roll-call of the inquisitors who were there to represent the Holy Office and confirmed Giordano's name, family, place of birth and age. He went on to describe the main events of Bruno's life, the reasons he had been convicted, the heretical opinions he had refused to recant and the solicitous

CHAPTER 26

attempts by the officers of the Inquisition to bring him back to God. He said that Bruno had been tried in Naples and Rome but had escaped censure – that he had lived as an atheist in England, Switzerland and Germany – that he had professed that the transubstantiation of bread into flesh was a blasphemous belief. Giordano's countenance remained unmoved.

As Adriani moved on to summarize the latest phases of Bruno's trial – his promises to mend his ways and his repeated changes of mind, his defensive letters to the inquisitors and *Sua Santità* the Pope, which showed he was still persevering in his errors, the new accusations that had emerged from the Holy Office of Vercelli, his obstinate refusal to abjure his heresies and recant even when visited by the most reverend fathers Beccaria and Isaresi – Giordano raised his chin and let his gaze roam around him. On the left, behind a soldier, the frightened face of Father Serafino – good man Serafino. Their eyes met for a moment. Bruno gave a wan smile to him, but the priest stepped out of sight. On the right, the corpulent figure of Francesco Maria Vialardi, the nobleman of Vercelli – pompous, arrogant, conceited, glutted with food that would be less wasted if given to a dog. But who was that young blond man behind him, smiling and whispering into the ear of a Jesuit priest? Father Kaspar? Looking so cheerful and pleased… Why was he not wearing his Franciscan habit?

"Therefore," Adriani was saying, "invoking the name of Our Lord Jesus Christ and of His Most Glorious, Ever-Virgin Mother Mary, with regard to all the aforementioned cases brought before this Holy Office by the Reverend Father Giulio Monterenzi, Doctor of Law and Public Prosecutor for the said Holy Office on the one hand, against you, the aforesaid Brother Giordano Bruno – accused, tried and found guilty, impenitent, pertinacious and obstinate – on the other hand; in this, our

263

final sentence – which we set out in the present writ after taking counsel and advice of our reverend fathers the consultors, Masters in Sacred Theology and Doctors in both Laws – we proclaim, announce, adjudge and declare you, the aforesaid Brother Giordano Bruno, to be an impenitent, obstinate and pertinacious heretic, and therefore to have incurred all the ecclesiastical censures and sanctions that the Holy Canons, the laws and the constitutions – both general and particular – impose on such confessed, impenitent, obstinate and pertinacious heretics."

Friars were pulling him to his feet. The Bishop of Sidon, Leonardo Abela, began the ceremony of degradation.

"Wherefore," Adriani continued, "we verbally degrade you and declare that you must be degraded, and we hereby ordain and command that you should in actual fact be degraded from all the ecclesiastical orders, both major and minor, in which you were ordained, according to what is sanctioned by our Holy Canons – and that you should be expelled, as we proceed to do, from our ecclesiastical tribunal and from our holy and immaculate Church, whose mercy you have shown yourself unworthy of."

Bruno listened with a sad smile on his face.

"By the authority of the Almighty God," Bishop Abela intoned, "the Father, the Son and the Holy Spirit – and by the authority invested in us, we take from you this clerical habit, we depose and degrade you, and deprive you of every ecclesiastical order and benefit."

The friars stripped Giordano of his scapular and tunic and made him wear the heretic's coat.

"Look," whispered someone in the crowd. "Dragons, devils, flames!"

264

Bishop Abela proceeded to excommunicate Bruno.

"You may kneel again," said the notary. "Therefore, we order that you should be handed over to the secular authorities – and we hereby hand you over to the authority of His Excellency the Governor of Rome, here present, so that the appropriate punishment may be administered on you. We earnestly pray him, however, that he will mitigate the rigour of the law with regard to the pains inflicted on your person – and that these will not put you in danger of death or cause you the loss of any of your limbs."

The collective murmur of the onlookers subsided as Cardinal Madruzzo rose from his chair and stepped towards Giordano, who remained still and impassive, with his head bent down.

"Did you not hear? Do you not tremble at these words, Bruno?"

With a deliberate movement, Giordano raised his head and smiled, fixing his gaze on the inquisitor. "Perhaps," he said with a thundering voice, "you have more fear in pronouncing this sentence than I have in receiving it."

The uproar among the crowd of onlookers was deafening.

"What did you say?" shouted Madruzzo, restoring the quiet. "What is it that you said?"

Bruno, however, did not reply: he bent his head to the floor and remained silent. Madruzzo made a wild gesture of contempt with his arm and turned to Adriani.

"You may proceed," he said, then returned to his seat.

As the notary concluded the reading of the sentence, condemning all of Bruno's books and writings as heretical, and ordering that all of them – those currently in possession of the Holy Office and those which may come into their hands in future – should be publicly destroyed and burnt in St Peter's Square, in front of the stairs, and placed on the Index of Prohibited Books, Giordano withdrew within the shelter of his own mind.

"You can set my books on fire," he thought, "you can hunt down and tear all my writings into pieces, and you can sunder me limb from limb, but ideas don't burn, dreams don't die, the fruits of the imagination cannot be destroyed – and the time will come when the intellect will triumph, when the human soul will shake off its shackles and see the heavens opened and the Son of Man standing on the right hand of God."

27

The weather had changed, and a sharp wind was blowing, threatening rain. Peter and Giulia arrived at the Jordanian side of the Allenby Bridge just before seven o'clock, as the sky was beginning to turn dark and lights were coming on. Having collected their bags, they made their way towards the taxi stand to get a cab for Amman. Before they reached the queue, a strong hand landed on Peter's shoulder, forcing him to turn and look back.

"Mr Simms. Car waiting for you."

"What?"

"Sheikh Mahfuz waiting to see you."

Peter looked at Giulia, trying to appear reassuring.

"Now?"

"Blease."

"I don't think—"

"Check phone, blease. Mr Al-Rafai instruct you."

"What's going on?" Giulia hissed, glancing across at a black Mercedes and its unsmiling driver standing by the open back door.

"OK then..." Peter said, pocketing his phone.

"Who are these people?" Giulia whispered, as they took their seats in the back.

"It's all right," said Peter. "I've met them before. Whatever happens next, Giulia – believe me, I know what I'm doing. It will be all right."

A half-hour journey ended on a bumpy dirt road. No houses could be glimpsed around – rare lights broke the horizon. They came to an iron gate set in a stone fence and guarded by two Arabs wearing chequered keffiyehs across their faces, who pointed their torches towards the car, then swung the gate open.

"Oh my God," whispered Giulia, grabbing Peter's arm. "Where are they taking us?"

"It will be OK. Trust me."

Kamal was waiting for them in front of a large tent with the UNHCR logo on it.

"This way, please."

The tent was empty and dark, except for the scattered light of floating candles. Giulia hugged the padded envelope containing the manuscript to her chest.

"This is for you, Miss," Kamal said, handing her a veil.

"I'm fine, thank you," said Giulia. "I'm not cold."

"Miss, you don't understand. You must wear it. On your head."

"It's a hijab," said Peter.

"Ah, OK."

Through a flap, they were led to a yard at the back. A small table stood in the middle, surrounded by low cushioned seats, next to a brisk fire in a stone pit. Mahfuz, in his turban and white robe, sat on the right, looking at them without expression. Sitting opposite—

"Mr Al-Rafai!" Giulia cried.

"Miss Ripetti, Mr Simms." He reached out to shake their hands. The cleric acknowledged the guests' arrival with a nod.

"Please take a seat," said Kamal.

Giulia sat next to Al-Rafai, while Peter took his place beside the cleric.

"May I offer you some tea?" asked Kamal.

They didn't answer.

"I understand you've brought back the missing manuscript," said Al-Rafai. His face was tense, his voice hoarse.

"Yes," said Giulia. "I've got it here in this Jiffy bag."

"Did Father Andreoli make any problems for you?"

"He was not very happy," Peter said.

"I know," said Al-Rafai. "He called me and handed in his resignation."

Kamal served the tea and sat on a folding chair between the cleric and the fire.

"Sheikh Mahfuz," said Al-Rafai, "came to see me yesterday" – Peter looked into his employer's nervous eyes as Kamal translated for the cleric, trying to gauge what was behind them: fear, duplicity? – "and told me how worried he was about my collaboration with the Biblia Group. We… have reached an understanding." The cleric nodded. "Especially in light of today's developments."

"Sorry, what developments?" asked Peter.

"This afternoon Biblia announced that they are shutting down their Middle Eastern operation," said Kamal.

"You are joking…"

"Does this look like the kind of place to make jokes?" said Al-Rafai with a strained smile. "Biblia have run out of cash and they are moving out of the Middle East, in order to cut costs. Their shares plummeted in New York yesterday. It's emerged that their system has been hacked and their data is corrupted. They will have to redo most of the scanning. It will cost them hundreds of millions. There are rumours that Google may buy them out. In that line of business, it takes nothing to go up or down."

"Unbelievable," said Peter.

"Anyway," continued Al-Rafai, "as a result of this, I have cancelled my agreement with Biblia for the digitization of my library. All the books and manuscript collections I had given them on loan are being returned."

"And following Mr Al-Rafai's decision," said Kamal, "three major foundations and five other big institutions in the Gulf and the Middle East have withdrawn their support for the Biblia project."

"I have also agreed," said Al-Rafai, "to make a donation for the creation of a new library in the refugee camp of Za'atari."

The cleric straightened up on the seat. "God is all-merciful. God is great." He fixed his stare on Al-Rafai. "They thought there would be no punishment, so they became blind. But Allah turned to them in forgiveness, and they were enlightened by God." Al-Rafai lowered his gaze to the table. "They came and built a tower higher than Mount Nebo – but the tower of Nimrod has collapsed. His masons and architects are fleeing in terror. All his houses are built on sand." The cleric raised his finger. "He thought he could ascend to heaven and strike down God. His pride has been punished."

Al-Rafai cleared his throat. "It's come to Sheikh Mahfuz's knowledge that the manuscript you have just recovered contains many blasphemies against the prophet Isa – or Jesus as he's called by Christians."

Peter and Giulia locked gazes. How could the cleric know about the contents of Bruno's Gospel? Who could have told him?

"Well," Peter said, "it's something written over four hundred years ago. One should put it in its historical context, and—"

"There is no changing the words of God, says the Holy Koran," the cleric rasped in his reedy voice. "No man can change His words. A blasphemy is a blasphemy – today, yesterday or a thousand years ago."

"With respect," Peter said, "what appeared true and right to our ancestors can seem false and wrong to us, and—"

"Do you dare to defend a sacrilegious work? I've already warned you that you're treading very close to the edge and tempting the wrath of God. You said that you would not take my words lightly: why are you disputing what I say?"

"We're not here to quarrel or have a fight," Al-Rafai said. "Mr Simms, Miss Ripetti, I have already spoken to the sheikh, and as a gesture of conciliation and pacification, I have decided to give the manuscript to him as a gift."

"What?" cried Giulia, grasping the padded envelope with both hands. "No! It didn't escape the clutches of Catholic fanatics for centuries to fall in the hands of a—"

"Giulia!" Peter barked, leaning over and grabbing her arm.

"Miss Ripetti, please…" Al-Rafai held out the palm of his hand.

"Giulia…" said Peter.

"*No, no e poi no!*" Tears welled in her eyes. "It's an important historical document. Scholars must study it. You can't—"

"Giulia," Peter tried again. "Please. Mr Al-Rafai is the owner, and he can do what he likes with it. It's only a bunch of old papers."

"How can you say something like *that*?"

"I mean, compared to flesh and blood – such as ours…"

She held his gaze. The Jiffy bag slipped down her torso a few inches.

"Miss Ripetti," Al-Rafai repeated, his palm still suspended in mid-air. "Please…"

THE TOWER

She pushed the envelope into Al-Rafai's lap. "You're making a huge mistake. An irreversible mistake. I wish I'd never brought this back from Jerusalem! I wish I'd never come to Jordan at all!"

"The sheikh is very grateful," said Kamal, taking the envelope from Al-Rafai and passing it to Mahfuz, "and would like to invite you and your guests to share some food in his company around this table."

"You people make me sick. Let's go, Peter." She stood up. "Let's go back to the hotel."

The cleric laughed and muttered something.

"What did he say?" Giulia shouted. "Why was he laughing?"

Kamal cleared his throat. "He said: 'Why is that woman so angry? Her English boyfriend is right: it's just a bunch of old papers.'"

"Peter – let's go."

The cleric had removed the tied bundle from the folder and turned it in his hands as if it were pig hide.

"Why would anyone want to write anything other than thanks and praises to the Lord?" the cleric said. "Who was this unclean person who put his pen into the service of Shaytan?"

"A man of courage and integrity," said Giulia.

"Why did he challenge the word of God?"

"Giulia, I'm ready," Peter said, fixing her with wide eyes.

"He defied his representatives on earth, not God."

"Did he benefit from that?"

"No."

"Giulia!"

"What happened to him?"

"He was killed."

The cleric grunted. "How did he die?"

272

"He was burnt at the stake."

"Then," said Mahfuz, the light from the flames dancing on his lips, "it's only appropriate that his work should share his fate."

"Wait—"

The cleric dropped the bundle into the blaze with a dismissive wave.

Giulia, Peter and Al-Rafai looked into the fire engulfing the Gospel of Giordano Bruno.

"Why? Why?" She collapsed onto her seat and began to sob. "Why?" she kept saying. "Why?" Then she jumped to her feet with an icy stare and tore the hijab from her head, throwing it to the ground.

"You," she cried, pointing her finger at the cleric, "you are an evil man."

"Giulia, let's go."

"It is you and your fellow priests who are the sons of Satan. Not just those from your religion, but from any religion. You may wear a white robe, but you're one of the Black Angels – a wolf in sheep's skin."

"In the name of Allah most merciful," the cleric shouted, turning his fierce gaze away from Giulia, "pick up that hijab and put it on your head. There is no need to get so angry around my table."

"I am not going to wear that veil again. You're a wicked man, do you understand? A wicked man." She turned to Kamal. "Please translate this for me."

"*Halas*, sister, *halas*," the cleric bellowed, getting to his feet and still avoiding eye contact with Giulia. "I swear to God that I'm leaving right now."

"No," cried Giulia, "I'm the one who's leaving, not you."

As they travelled back to Amman in Majed's car, Peter tried to console and calm Giulia.

273

"Nothing's lost. The manuscript—"

"I don't want to hear another word from you... '*I won't let anyone take it away from us*' – '*Only a bunch of old papers*'... Tss."

"But Giulia," he said, smiling. "Listen, I—"

"Not – another – word."

Majed was also gloomy and unusually silent, a taut expression pulling at his face.

"Is something the matter, Majed?" Peter asked, as they entered the outskirts of the city.

"Bad, bad things happening, Mr Peter," he said. "Many bad beople in this country. First they attack Al-Burj, now they attack Mr Al-Rafai."

"Attack?"

"His wife, she get injured badly today. Car accident. Terrible bump. I take her son to hospital this evening."

"Is she all right?"

"Very scared." He turned to look at Peter with a grave look on his face. "Terrible, terrible beople."

By the time they reached Le Royal, the wind had fulfilled its threat, and it had started raining with violence. Majed escorted them into the lobby with his large umbrella.

"I'm going up to my room," Giulia said.

"Nothing to eat?"

"How can I eat?"

Standing behind the windows of her room, she looked out across the nightscape of the city of Amman. The rain was pouring down in torrents now, and the wind was lashing against the window panes. Rising above the flat horizon, the lights of the Tower glimmered in the distance among scattered flashes of lightning.

The flames licking round the dry parchment... the paper turning brown, red, black... She shook her head, trying to expel the image from her mind. It was as if part of her had been burnt in that fire.

Her unseeing gaze lingered on the electric sprawl of the city below as the rain slanted down and dashed at the window panes. A powerful lightning bolt cracked the black shell of the sky and rested for a moment on top of the Tower. The lights of Al-Burj flickered and went out, and the peal of thunder that followed a few seconds later had the ominous ring of an apocalypse.

28

If Bruno thought that nothing could be worse than the prison of the Holy Inquisition, he realized he was wrong when he was thrown into one of the darkest cells of the Tor di Nona jail. There was no light, no air – the stench was unbearable. The walls were crusted over with mould, the floor caked with human grime.

Yet, what vexed him most was not the harshness of the place, but the continuous visits, day and night, by friars, priests and theologians pleading for his repentance. He shouted at them, tried to push them out of his cell.

"Devils!" he called them. "Devils! I don't want to repent! I have no reason to repent!"

But they kept coming back at all hours, when all he wanted was silence – all he craved was death.

The date of the execution had been fixed for four days ago, but the time arrived and the Governor's soldiers didn't come to take him away. He was left there to wonder and fear the sound of approaching steps, having to endure more visits from importunate priests trying to convert him *in extremis*.

Then, late that night, the ninth he spent in that horrible jail, when the grated door was unlocked by the warders and three black-robed friars from the Confraternity of St John the Baptist walked into his cell armed with breviaries, candles and an icon of Christ, he knew that the moment had come.

They took him to a room on the ground floor, washed him and trimmed his hair and beard. They led him to the prison chapel, where three more brothers of the Confraternity, the chaplain, two sextons and other "comforters" were gathered.

"Kneel, brother."

"I'm not kneeling."

"Will you confess?"

He shook his head.

The chaplain advanced towards him with a bowl of ashes. He smudged a cross on Giordano's forehead. "Dust thou art," he said, "and unto dust shalt thou return."

Bruno wiped his forehead with a hand. "I don't need you devils to remind me." Now he understood why his execution had been postponed: it was Ash Wednesday, and they wanted to subject him to the final humiliation of one of their empty rituals. "Bring this farce to an end. Take me to my death," he said.

"But you're not ready, my son," the chaplain said. "You're not ready."

He was not ready. He had to endure more hours of mental torment before being dispatched from this world. During the long night, more friars were invited into the chapel, begging him to repent: two Dominicans, two Jesuits, two Oratorians from the Chiesa Nuova and one from the Church of San Girolamo. At first Bruno ignored them and remained locked in silence, but as time wore on, he began to feel tired and to show all his impatience and annoyance.

"Leave me alone! Leave me alone!"

"We are here to show you your errors, brother."

"You are the ones who are in error!"

"You must repent before it's too late."

"*You* should repent, not me! I'm happy to die. I *want* to die. I'm dying a martyr. If there is a paradise, then my soul will go up with the smoke of my burning pyre!"

The friars continued to press him and urge him to feel remorse.

"You must leave this earth in peace."

"Leave *me* in peace. *Via, via, carogne! Diavoli, diavoli!*"

He hit them and threw their breviaries and the icon of Christ to the floor. The soldiers were called in, and they restrained him. He was fettered and branked, so that his tongue could utter no more blasphemies. He could scarcely breathe, and the sharp pain produced by the metal gag made his eyes goggle and shed silent tears. He collapsed to the ground, growling and writhing like a wounded animal.

The soldiers hauled him up to his feet and dragged him outside, where a wooden pushcart was waiting for him. Bruno was beaten with a cane and forced to climb on. Three hooded brothers of the Confraternity formed a line behind the cart, while the other three positioned themselves in front, carrying a large veiled crucifix on their shoulders. The chaplain and two hooded men clambered onto the cart and stood next to Bruno.

"Rrghh, aaarh," he snarled in agony, trying to shout.

The other friars, with the rest of the clerics, some soldiers and other members of the Confraternity, took their place behind the cross-bearers or at the back, and the sad procession left the prison of Tor di Nona and advanced through the dark and silent streets of Rome, lighting its way with torches.

Dawn was still more than two hours away. The sky was clear, the new moon cast only a pale light. It was shivering cold.

The torment caused by the branks, the friars' gloomy litanies, the priest's constant shoving of Christ's icon into his face... It was impossible for him to think. Vague impressions broke into his mind, adding to his suffering: thoughts of failure, emptiness, isolation, exhaustion.

He had been defeated. His bold and fearless spirit had been vanquished. All his works, all his writings would be destroyed and put on the Index. Even if some of them survived, they were full of mistakes and they would be misinterpreted. He would be forgotten soon, as if he had never lived. No one would ever even know what he looked like.

"Aaarh," he growled, pushing air through his nose.

An infinite sense of sadness swept through his body as he tasted blood in his mouth. He was blinded by the darkness of man's heart, deafened by the scream of injustice, crushed by the weight of chains and prison bricks. What had he achieved on earth? Nothing. He left no wife, no offspring, no friends – only sneering enemies. He had burnt his own Great Work. The only testament to his life would be the few ashes scattered by the wind or thrown into a mass grave in unhallowed ground.

Just as the chanting procession left Ponte Sant'Angelo and started down Via Florea, something hit his brow. He jerked his neck left and right to shove the priest's icon off his face and find the culprit. A boy in ragged clothes, not much older than a child. He was laughing now, pointing at Bruno's branks, at the dragons on his heretic's coat, at the blood trickling down his temple and mouth. The man next to him, probably his father, gave him a rough shake and a slap, bringing tears to his face.

But if Bruno had not been branked, if his tongue had not been hampered by the curb plate, he would have smiled to the boy and said thank you, because that blow had brought him back to his senses – and looking up at the moon and the stars in the sky, he cast away the pall of gloom that had been hanging over his mind. The clouds had dissipated: his soul was able once again to reach out to the eternal gleam, the light intellectual. *Nil igitur mors est ad nos, neque pertinet hilum.* What was death? Nothing but separation and reaggregation. *Contemne mortem.* A heroic life calls for a heroic death. He remembered some lines of poetry he had written shortly before his arrest in Venice:

> I've fought – a fair achievement in itself.
> I might have won, but nature and bad luck
> thwarted my aspirations and my efforts.
> It's something to have come as far as this;
> for winning, I see now, is in Fate's hands.
> I had, though, the potential. Future ages
> will not deny that I'd one quality
> a winner should have had: no fear of death.
> In this no one has ever been my equal –
> that I preferred to die in bold endeavour
> than live in idle cowardice…

Now it was time to live up to his own words.

The procession reached the end of Via Florea and emerged into Campo de' Fiori. The square looked dark and deserted. The only noise to accompany the friars' litanies was the bark of a dog in the distance. As they passed the fountain in the centre of the square, a pungent stench assailed Giordano's nose – the stench of the living, which he would soon abandon.

The wooden faggots were amassed on the far corner on the right, in front of the Palazzo Orsini. A small crowd was awaiting the arrival of the condemned man. There were jeers, shouts, laughter as he descended the cart. He recognized Cardinal

Santoro among the public – and the young German, Kaspar, if that was his real name. The pain was unbearable, but he put on a brave face and turned a fierce look on them.

As the brothers of the Confraternity continued to psalmodize, and as the chaplain kept pushing the image of Christ onto his face and the other friars begged him to repent, Giordano was stripped of his heretic's coat and left to tremble in the cold February night. He was then handed over to the executioner by the Governor's deputy, Giovan Battista Gottarelli, so that he could be tied to the stake.

"Will they take his branks off?" Kaspar asked the man standing beside him.

"Oh, no." The man tilted his head towards the Palazzo Orsini, the residence of the French Ambassador. "Someone might kick up a real fuss, you know?" The man grinned under his moustaches. "And half the city would wake up."

"Were you here when they burned that friar from Verona last September?" Kaspar said. "No? It was a right spectacle. His mouth had not been bridled, so he cried for all he was worth: 'Lord, have mercy upon me! Let the fire come to me! I cannot burn! I cannot burn!' Heh heh heh."

Meanwhile, as he was being installed on top of the wooden faggots, Bruno gave an inward smile, knowing that death was in him, basking in the never-changing light of the moon, the stars and the sun, which would rise again that day to bring warmth and life to all the creatures on earth. He would soon join the happy dead, the heroes of history, who had drunk their lives to the lees and whose destiny was now fulfilled, perfect, immutable.

Just like twenty-five years before, he found himself alone in the world, naked like Bias and about to set off on a journey into the unknown. It was a harsh and painful passage, but he consoled himself with the thought that every child of Adam had to face this trial sooner or later. If life was a dream, then death was like stepping from a smaller dream into a bigger, boundless one – as infinite as the universe.

The brothers of the Confraternity did not stop singing as they collected offerings in a metal box with the picture of the Baptist's severed head. Kaspar gave half a *scudo* – Santoro waved the alms-seekers away.

With the help of a torch, the executioner lit the fire, starting from the brushwood piled under the faggots, in order to keep the flames down at first and make the torment last longer.

With his hands tied behind the pole, Bruno stood motionless, looking on unflinchingly. The crowd got excited and raised their voices, shouting abuse and mockery, pointing at the simmering blaze ready to flare up and engulf him. But Giordano was no longer listening to the noises of this world. His mind was turned inward, conjuring up some of the most potent images he had ever created. These in turn evoked visions from his own life, from the happy days of his childhood. He was running through the fields towards the top of Mount Cicala, screaming with joy. The sun was scorching hot, but he took shelter in the shade of the castle's ruins, his secret hiding place. Through a window in the crumbled wall, he could see the smouldering mass of Mount Vesuvius in the distance. He stretched his hand and thought he could touch it, but it remained unattainable, like the dreams and the ambitions of his older days. The volcano's smoke rose to cover the horizon. He was now walking through a thick fog, looking for a way out. A door was ahead of him, luminous, suffused with a halo of glory. It lay just a few steps away, but his body would not move. Then, with a superhuman effort and intolerable pain, he reached it. But just as he was about to cross its threshold, he died.

Kaspar and Santoro, who were studying Bruno's face for any signs of agony, were disappointed when they saw him hang his head so soon without so much as a grunt, enveloped by the liberating flames. There he lay, the great philosopher of Nola, *doctor theologiæ*, *hæreticus*, *magus*. He could no longer infect the souls and poison the minds of Christian believers. If there was one regret, it was that he didn't seem to have suffered much.

The crowd began to disperse, the excitement subsided. Only a few people remained to watch the final moments of the burning, in the company of the officers, the friars and the brothers of the Confraternity, who had the unpleasant task of having to dispose of the corpse.

"Well, that was fast," said the man next to Kaspar.

"Don't worry," said the German, "he'll continue to pay in hell for what he's done."

"Or in one of his innumerable worlds, if he was right."

The man laughed and left.

29

At breakfast Giulia sipped her coffee and winced.

"Bitter," she said. "They need another two hundred years before they learn how to make good coffee." She looked at her watch. "In another eight or nine hours I'll have a real espresso in Via Veneto and forget all about this nightmare. When do we leave for the airport?"

"Half an hour."

"Good."

Peter smiled. "You saw the news this morning?"

"No."

"It was all about Biblia." Peter wiped his mouth with a napkin. "Closing down the Middle East branch and selling the Tower to a big Arabic investment company. Brought down by the way the NICK system was hacked and the data corrupted."

"I don't care."

"They said it was the work of someone with an intimate knowledge of how the system operates. They think it was their IT Director."

"Jim?" Her cup clinked in the saucer.

"He's disappeared. Gone into hiding. He's suspected of opening up the system to hacking attacks and having found ways to scramble up the information – not just live data but also the back-ups. Pages of one book were mixed up with those of another. Words replaced in files and scanned images deleted randomly. He planted some sort of self-feeding virus."

"Did he act on his own?"

"They don't know – but the feeling is that he may have been cooperating with the Muslim Electronic Army. A group of ideological Islamic hackers," he explained, when Giulia raised her eyebrows, "that targets Western interests. My guess is that there is a link between them and your good friend, Mahfuz."

Giulia shuddered – that bigoted old man who had fed Giordano's precious writing to the flames as callously as the Inquisition had put his body to the stake. "So all the threats, the hoaxes, the events at the Tower – they can be traced back to Islamic extremism or terrorism?"

"Yes."

"And Bookworm?"

"Mahfuz's men."

"Why?"

"To intimidate us and Al-Rafai, so that we'd keep our noses out until they finalized their attacks, and also to scare Biblia's staff."

"What happened to Father Marini?"

"My guess is that Jim and his friends intended to let him do the donkey work of identifying the gems within Al-Rafai's Bruno collection – then lay their hands on those manuscripts in order to blackmail Al-Rafai and put more pressure on Biblia. So they kept an eye on the friar. When they saw all those trips to Andreoli's room, they must have concluded that the Vatican had other plans for the manuscripts. So they waited for him outside the building on the Saturday afternoon and took him on a little ride…"

"You think they killed him?"

"Not necessarily. Maybe they just frightened him or roughed him up a bit—"

"To force him to tell them about the manuscripts and their contents?"

"Yes. Maybe his heart gave way. So they were left with a warm corpse and decided to stage a suicide. But before they get hold of the Bruno manuscript, Andreoli runs off with it, so Mahfuz's men follow us to Jerusalem, let us get it back for them – and then the rest you know."

"It all makes sense."

A man from the concierge's office came to their table.

"Special delivery, sir," he said, handing Peter a small parcel.

"Thanks," Peter said, weighing the package in his hands. "Wow, they don't hang around in this country, do they? I sent it via 9 a.m. Express and it's already here. It's actually for you."

"For me?"

"A little souvenir from Jerusalem. Be careful when you open it."

Giulia's hands tore the courier bag and pulled out a large padded envelope. She opened the envelope along the seal line and took out a box folder.

"What is it?"

She lifted the lid of the box, removed some bubble wrap inside and—

"Jesus!" Peter said, putting his hands to his ears as she screamed.

"How…" she said, with tears in her eyes.

He smiled, watching her run her fingertips down the title page of Bruno's Gospel.

"I didn't like it when I realized we were being followed in Jerusalem. And as a precaution I thought I'd send the manuscript by courier rather than carry it around with us."

"So…" Giulia said, running both hands through her hair, "so what was in the package that Mahfuz burned?"

"The blank papers at the end of the Gospel."

"You're a genius!"

"Still some way to go before I catch up with Bruno."

"Does Al-Rafai know?"

"Of course he does."

"Both of you let me have a heart attack and risk the wrath of a mad mullah?" She jabbed him with a sharp fingernail.

"Ow! We needed some authentic Italian passion to make sure Mahfuz believed the goods were the real thing."

"Why didn't you tell me?!"

"I did try to tell you later in the car, but you wouldn't let me."

"Unbelievable!"

"Listen, Al-Rafai wants you to take the manuscript with you so that you and other scholars can examine it."

"Really? What about the rest of the collection?"

"He's going to arrange for it to go out on loan to your university department in Rome. Sounds like your hands will be full for some time to come."

"I simply can't believe it. Thank you. Thank you. Is Al-Rafai coming to see us before we leave?"

"I think he's too busy making arrangements for his own swift departure from this country – and that of his family. I'm sure he'll be in touch with you again soon. Shall we start making a move?" He pointed at the manuscript and smiled. "Don't forget that."

As they approached the airport from the highway, Al-Burj rose higher and higher on their left. Peter glanced at his watch.

"Planning any duty-free shopping?" he asked.

"Shopping can wait until London."

"Then perhaps a last look at the Tower – and say bye to Chad and Chris Dale?"

* * *

Majed parked the car in an almost empty parking lot. The two Biblia helicopters were grounded, and large lorries were being loaded with crates. In the near-deserted main hall, gates and turnstiles were open, and the giant TV screens were dark. A man waved them in without checking their documents. Sweat dripped down his face, because the air-conditioning was down.

"Fast or scenic route?" Peter asked Giulia at the lifts.

"Electricity down, sir," one of the two guards said. "Only main line working."

When they emerged into the huge circular hall on the hundred and ninety-ninth floor, they met people walking in every direction with crates full of folders, office equipment and personal belongings. They went up to the suite on floor 200 using the stairs. Chad was sitting behind the desk with his back to the door and his gaze lost on the glass cupola. He spun round as they entered.

"Hey. Good to see you," he said, standing and stretching his hand out. "Take a seat. Great to hear that you recovered the manuscript."

"We'll only stay two minutes," Peter said. "We're on our way to the airport. No Chris?"

"No Chris. Poached. He's going to start working next month for Alibaba. I always thought his talents were being wasted here. He set up Biblia in Jordan from scratch – but there were so many problems: the decline of the stock, lack of resources, the incompetence of the locals… and, of course, a secret enemy in his own house."

"Does anyone know where Jim is now?"

Chad shrugged. "Syria? Russia? China? I am sure he'll crop up again sooner or later."

"So the hacking was nothing to do with Bookworm."

"They deny any involment. Although I'm sure they're pleased."

"Just a case of twisted anti-corporate idealism, then?"

Chad smiled. "People can believe that."

"Why do you say that?"

"Oh, well." Chad scratched his bald head.

"We're still bound by our confidentiality agreement."

"Ha!" Chad looked around. "Have you ever heard of a company called Woohah?"

Peter knitted his brow. "Wasn't it a very successful dot-com start-up that launched a few years ago?"

"2006. It was founded by Jim. At one point it was valued at eighteen billion dollars, and there were rumours of an IPO and of a takeover bid by Apple. But then it ran into financial difficulties. Fred Mortensen, Biblia's CEO, rescued it from bankruptcy, but Jim had to go. Fred turned the company around, and within two years he sold it to Sony for a colossal figure. Jim didn't see the shadow of a dime – while Fred used the money to set up Biblia with Jerry Dyson."

"Why did Biblia recruit Jim, knowing his past history?"

"Well, first of all he was an excellent software designer and the perfect man for the job. And then I think that deep down Fred felt guilty about the way things had turned out. I suppose he was trying to help Jim."

"And Jim's felled the tree."

"And made a couple of bucks at the same time through derivatives and short-selling." Chad grinned.

"Was he speculating on the value of Biblia's shares?"

CHAPTER 29

"Either him or someone he was in cahoots with."

"So it was all about money?"

"It's always all about money."

"So what's next? Are you still planning to have everything digitized by 2020?"

"Perhaps this sets us back a few years, but we'll get there in the end. What did Chris say? Nothing can stop progress. History moves only forward. The clock can't be turned back."

* * *

Giulia closed her book and pressed her nose to the window as the plane taxied across the shimmering tarmac.

"Sorry to be leaving?"

She looked round at Peter and smiled. "I was thinking about Jim." She brushed her hair back with a hand. "Maybe he was not driven by greed or revenge, but by a sincere idealistic motive. Perhaps he really wanted to stop the use of new technology to control and manipulate knowledge. That's what dictatorships and tyrannies do. We're in the twenty-first century – but books are still burnt in the middle of squares, intellectuals are put in prison or killed for expressing uncomfortable truths or asserting their right to free thinking. In the West we have given away so much of our privacy and so many of our liberties. They can track where you are whenever they want. They know what you like, what you say and what you think. And if you give someone the power to control you – well, in time they'll use it against you, that's for sure. Look at the National Surveillance Agency in America – the most liberal country in the world. Look at what happens to the whistle-blowers – Snowden, Assange. Maybe Biblia made up some of the accusations against Jim too – just like the Inquisition did against Bruno."

The plane began to accelerate down the runway. Giulia put her nose back to the glass, and Peter settled back in his seat, closing his eyes, listening to the engines' roar.

The plane rose in the sky, and the Tower grew smaller and smaller, until it became a grain of sand in the vast desert plain and vanished from sight altogether.

30

Coda

The embers of Bruno's pyre in Campo de' Fiori were still smouldering when another fire was started in front of the steps of St Peter's Basilica. A large heap of volumes and papers was thrown on the flames and left to burn until it was reduced to ashes.

But these weren't Giordano's books and manuscripts. Pope Clement had changed his mind and given the Master of the Dominicans, Ippolito Maria Beccaria, a special dispensation so that he and the other Holy Office consultors could subject the works to further scrutiny. However, later that year, Beccaria suddenly died, and his successor, the Spanish theologian Jerónimo Xavierre, had more pressing matters to deal with and limited knowledge of the Italian language.

It was decided that the Vicar of the Order, Paolo Isaresi, should continue the examination of Giordano's writings. When he was made bishop of Squillace in the August of 1601, he took all the material with him to the remote town in the south of Italy. But the following year he died too, and Bruno's books and manuscripts lay forgotten in a locked cupboard of the bishop's residence for years.

The cupboard survived a powerful earthquake in 1630, but was seized by one of the bands of marauding Saracens that attacked Squillace in 1648. As they sailed back to their base in Cyprus, a gusty storm blew their vessel onto the shores of Lebanon. The cargo was offloaded, the loot was sold to a merchant from Damascus and the cupboard containing Bruno's works began its journey through the lands of the Middle East.

Historical Note

THE PAPERS OF BRUNO'S TRIAL

Most of what we know about Giordano Bruno's life derives from the minutes of his interrogations in Venice and a short summary of his trial in Rome. However, the full transcripts of the hearings, the witnesses' depositions and cross-examinations, his statements of defence and all other papers relating to his case dating from the time he was in the prison of the Roman Inquisition have been lost. How could that have happened?

In February 1810, following his annexation of the Papal States, Napoleon had ordered the removal of the Vatican Archive to France. That same month, more than three thousand crates full of documents were carted to Paris to become part of a centralized archive of the French Empire. These were followed in April and July of the same year by the records of the Holy Office. The custodian of the French National Archives, Pierre Claude François Daunou, noted down the arrival of 102,435 registers, volumes and bundles, with only a small number of documents lost or damaged in transit. The estimated cost of transport, borne by the taxpayers of the Napoleonic Empire, was in excess of six hundred thousand francs, an astronomical sum of money in those days.

From the very beginning, despite the fact that the Pope was being held in captivity by the French and later exiled to Savona, the Holy See spared no effort in trying to retrieve the priceless material previously contained in its collections. It was the Vatican archivist Marino Marini (1783–1855) who was entrusted with this delicate task.

The Sacred Congregation of the Inquisition was particularly keen to recover its archive. Marini received detailed instructions from the Holy Office. The archive – he was told – was divided into five sections: Doctrinal Matters, Statutes, Criminal Law, Civil Law, Administration. "All the material in the first two categories," the Holy Office archivists wrote, "is of the utmost importance […]. The third category includes the records of criminal trials and, although it's the largest one, it is also the least important. Sig. abate Marini will use his discretion as to whether it can be left behind and sent back at a later stage – unless he is able to extract the most famous trials and send them back." As an example, he was informed of eight "famous trials", including those of Galileo Galilei, Cecco d'Ascoli, King Henry IV of France and Miguel de Molinos – but not Bruno's. As to the rest of the material, he was told that if its recovery or shipping proved to be too expensive, it might as well be burnt.

When, after Napoleon's abdication in April 1814, Louis XVIII ordered that the Vatican Archive be returned to the Holy See, Marini was sent to Paris to organize its shipment. He soon realized, however, that the cost of returning the archive to Rome would be higher than that of its removal to France, and therefore prohibitive both for the Pope and for the French King.

A first small convoy with some of the most important material was sent in May 1814, to coincide with Pope Pius's return to Rome after five years of imprisonment and exile. Louis XVIII agreed to pay up to 60,000 francs for the transport of the rest of the archive back to the Vatican. Knowing that this would not be sufficient, Marini asked for an additional 40,000 francs to get the process underway, but the French government responded by suggesting that the archive should be slimmed down and partially sold in order to finance its transportation.

There were further delays due to Napoleon's short-lived restoration to power between February and June 1815: Marini returned to Italy, and the archive – which was kept in a building used by troops as a garrison – suffered severe losses.

With Napoleon's defeat at Waterloo, Marini was once again dispatched to France, where he resumed the arduous task of getting the archive ready for shipment, personally supervising each phase of the preparations. At the end of October 1815, a convoy of 620 crates left Paris, and by Christmas that year Marini returned to Rome with the first part of the retrieved documents.

The Pope's Secretary of State, Ercole Consalvi, now entrusted the recovery of the rest of the archive to Giulio Cesare Ginnasi, a nobleman from Imola who was then living in Paris. Mons. Ginnasi, due to lack of funds and following Consalvi's directives, destroyed and sold – often by weight to "grocers" – thousands and thousands of items that were either considered superfluous or labelled as such – although in some cases the labelling had been devised only to deceive the French. Four more convoys were organized from late 1816, carrying a total of 569 crates. Some of them were damaged during their long journey by sea or land. Unhappy with Ginnasi's handling of the situation, Consalvi sent Marini back to France to help him out and even buy back some of the documents he had unwisely sold.

Two final shipments of 999 and 259 crates were arranged in the second half of 1817. In order to contribute to the transportation costs, 2,600 volumes from the Criminal Law section of the Holy Office archive – containing the records of a great number of court proceedings, including perhaps the ones against Bruno – were shredded in the presence of Marini, pulped and sold to a Paris cardboard maker for around 4,000 *scudi*. Several other Inquisition bundles and documents were sold to a paper manufacturer called Sabatier for 458 francs. The total number of volumes destroyed is estimated to have been around 4,158.

Of the 3,239 crates originally sent to the French capital, only around 2,450 were returned – many of them damaged. Since Daunou had started rearranging and recataloguing the archive, the collections came back in a badly organized and often chaotic state.

Although, looking at the evidence, it is probable that the papers of Bruno's trial may have been destroyed either accidentally or for practical reasons, many scholars refuse to believe that such a *cause célèbre* was not given special treatment, as was the case for the "Codex of Galileo's Trial", which was one of Marini's "principal preoccupations" and was famously returned to the Holy See only in October 1843.

Conspiracy theories abound. According to some historians, in the atmosphere of rabid anti-clericalism of the time, the proceedings of Bruno's trial and other compromising documents from the Inquisition archive were wilfully destroyed by the Church in an attempt to cover up their past crimes. Others are convinced that Bruno's papers were saved from pulping and are still held in some secret dungeon of the Vatican Archive, banned from consultation.

The truth is that the culling of archives was not uncommon in those days, and although the Vatican archivists would have loved to recover the whole of the collections to ensure their integrity, Consalvi's correspondence with Marini makes it clear that the Papal Secretary of State regarded the Holy Office court documents as "*cartacce*", useless bumf, and as such deserving to be shredded, pulped and sold off.

Also, it appears that Giordano Bruno, unlike Galileo, was not among the Vatican's priorities at the time. His treatises on mnemonics were now out of fashion and his philosophical dialogues in Italian had been superseded by the work of early scientists – a much more pressing and dangerous threat to religion.

But Bruno's strategy of printing his books outside Italy meant that most of his writings – despite having been put on the Index – had survived and escaped the censorship of the Church of Rome. A new wave of interest in Giordano Bruno's philosophy began in the 1830s with the publication of his Italian works in two volumes, edited by Adolf Wagner, the uncle of the famous composer. Many more editions followed, including that of some previously unknown Latin works by him. With the unification of Italy and the dissolution of the Papal States, a wealth of documents about Bruno and his times began to emerge from the archives. The first scholarly biographies were written in French, Italian and English, leading to more studies and research, and culminating with the publication in 1942, by the Biblioteca Apostolica Vaticana, of the summary of Bruno's trial, edited by Mons. Angelo Mercati – enabling us to have a glimpse, if not a clear view, of the last troubled years spent by the Nolan philosopher in the prison of the Inquisition.

On 9th June 1889, a bronze statue of Giordano Bruno was unveiled in Piazza Campo de' Fiori, despite strong opposition from the clerical faction in Rome. It depicts the friar in a resolute pose, with a stern, unyelding expression on his face. The inscription on the pedestal reads: "TO BRUNO – THE TIME HE IMAGINED – HERE WHERE THE STAKE BURNED".

His works, his ideas and the memory of his heroic life live on.

If many details have come to light in recent times about Bruno, we still know relatively little about some of the people who were instrumental in determining his fate. There are several lacunae and grey areas in the scanty information available, and this cannot fail to arouse all sorts of doubts and suspicions.

Despite having held a very high ecclesiastical rank in his life, the Inquisitor of Venice, the Dominican Giovanni Gabriele da Saluzzo, remains a mysterious figure. He appears to have been born into a noble and ancient Piedmontese family, but the dates of his birth and of his death are unknown. It is unclear why he pursued Bruno with such tenacity, nor why he secretly corresponded with Santoro in Rome and sent him a copy of the entire trial – a somewhat extraordinary procedure. Unlike his eight predecessors, who were appointed by papal briefs, he was designated by the Congregation of the Holy Office and arrived in Venice with a letter from its Secretary, Cardinal Santoro. During his tenure in Venice between August 1591 and January 1595, he proved to be a merciless inquisitor. His personality emerges with clarity in the minutes of Bruno's interrogations.

Giovanni Mocenigo (1558–1623) was the member of one of Venice's most prestigious families. There is evidence that he had been in touch with Saluzzo before his first written denunciation of Bruno. His motivations are not entirely clear. Although he publicly claimed to be dissatisfied with Bruno's lessons and worried about some of his pronouncements and beliefs, it is difficult not to suspect darker motives behind his actions. Was he an instrument of the Inquisition? Did he act on an impulse or did he help lay down a trap to ensnare Bruno? Why was he so doggedly hostile to Bruno? Was it personal hatred, revenge or the fear of a backlash if the Nolan was not convicted? Did he bribe some of the witnesses? These and other similar questions will never be answered. Claims that he or one of his brothers was working for the Holy Office in Venice as a Wise Man in Matters of Heresy at the time of Bruno's imprisonment cannot be substantiated.

The figures of Celestino of Verona and Francesco Graziano of Udine, two of Bruno's cellmates in Venice, later to be among his accusers, deserve some attention.

The cripple Francesco Graziano appears to have been a fantasist and perhaps somewhat insane as well. He had already been tried on charges of heresy in 1585 and recanted, but had been jailed again as a reoffender. In March 1593, shortly after Bruno's extradition to Rome, he was sentenced to life imprisonment. Five years later, however, he was freed on condition that he present himself every month to the Holy Office in Venice. Why was he shown such lenience if other recidivists were almost invariably punished with death?

Fra Celestino's actions, after his encounter with Bruno, are still more difficult to explain and understand. Celestino, a Franciscan friar, had been forced to recant in 1587 after being convicted by the Roman Inquisition on unspecified charges of heresy. Arrested again in September 1592, he was tried in Venice and probably acquitted, since he was confined to a Franciscan monastery in San Severino, in the Marche region. From there, in the autumn of 1593, he sent his accusation against his former cellmate, which precipitated Bruno's fate in Rome. Nothing more is heard of him until May 1599, when he wrote to the Congregation of the Holy Office to be heard on some matters of faith and was invited to present himself to Rome. In the meantime, he had also sent an anonymous letter to the new Venetian inquisitor. Its content is unknown, but it must have been worrying enough for Cardinal Santoro and the rest of the Congregation if the handwriting was subjected to examination to determine whether it had indeed been written by the friar from Verona. Was the letter to do with Celestino's old doubts in matters of faith and doctrine, or was it a confession in connection with Bruno's case? Why did he write to Venice rather than directly to Rome? It's impossible to know. Shortly after sending the anonymous letter, Celestino either surrendered himself or was conducted by force to the Holy Tribunal in Rome. He was interrogated on 9th and 11th July, and on the 15th the members of the Congregation read the transcripts of the two hearings. Pope Clement himself intervened in the trial, demanding the "strictest secrecy" in the proceedings. After an unusually quick trial, Celestino was condemned to death as a "relapsing, impenitent and pertinacious heretic". Although he was supposed to be handed over to the secular authorities, his sentence was read behind the doors of the Congregation room – not in public, as was common – and he was not transferred to Tor di Nona, but taken to his place of execution in Campo de' Fiori, on 16th September, directly from the prison of the Holy Inquisition. Why such haste and secrecy? Was Celestino burnt at night because the inquisitors didn't want to offend the sight and nose of the French Ambassador living nearby, as a public announcement later read, or because they were worried that he might have shouted out something embarrassing for the Church?

Of Ippolito Maria Beccaria (1550–1600) and Cardinal Giulio Antonio Santoro (1532–1602) a great deal is known because of the high rank they held in the ecclesiastical hierarchy, but the full scale of their implication in the Bruno affair is unclear.

Beccaria, the intransigent Master of the Dominicans, happened to be in Venice between 5th May and the beginning of July 1592 for the meeting of the chapter of his order. The date of his arrival in La Serenissima almost coincides with Bruno's arrest following Mocenigo's delation. It is impossible not to conjecture that there would have been some contacts around that time between Beccaria and the Venetian inquisitor, also a Dominican and also a nobleman. The Maestro Generale hailed from Mondovì, only thirty miles from Saluzzo, and it is therefore probable that the two prelates already knew each other and might even have been on friendly terms. Beccaria's right-hand man, Paolo Castrucci, also came from Mondovì, and he was present when Saluzzo examined Fra Domenico da Nocera regarding his meeting with Bruno. So we can be almost sure that Beccaria would have known about Bruno's trial at the Holy Office in Venice and may have tried to use his vast connections to help Saluzzo. One night at the beginning of 1593, Beccaria was the victim of a rape or an attempted rape by three friars as he was staying at the Dominican Monastery of St Augustine in Padua. The philosopher Tommaso Campanella was initially implicated in the attack, but later cleared. The incident shows that Beccaria was not short of enemies in his own fold. The General was again in Venice at the time of Bruno's extradition to Rome, and he may have played a part in the political wranglings between the Holy See and the authorities of La Serenissima. Beccaria's attendance of the Holy Inquisition meetings in the case against Bruno began only during the later phases of the trial. Before then he had been replaced as a consultor by the Vicar of the Order, Paolo Isaresi. What is surprising is the harshness he showed towards Bruno when the Congregation gathered to decide his fate on 9th September 1599. According to draft minutes for that day, he was the only one among the voting prelates who asked for the accused to be tortured "not just once or twice" and judged on the basis of the resulting depositions. This barely legible document has only come to light recently and could have been lost for ever – which demonstrates how much we still don't know about the real involvement of many of the key players in this complex story.

Cardinal Santoro, one of the chief Inquisitors-General, showed a persistence in bringing Bruno to justice and getting him transferred to his jurisdiction that is hard to explain, considering that the Nolan was virtually unknown in Rome at the time of his trial in Venice. It has already been mentioned above that it was Santoro who appears to have appointed the Venetian inquisitor Saluzzo, so it may be conjectured that he was eager to help his friend in such a difficult case. However, there is another bizarre coincidence linking the cardinal's family with Bruno's. Santoro's brother Col'Antonio, who died in April 1568, was a high-ranking and long-serving soldier, like Bruno's father Giovanni and two other Brunos who might have been his relatives, in the retinue of the Count of Caserta, Baldassarre Acquaviva d'Aragona. Is it possible that Cardinal Santoro, who was born near Caserta and was educated in Naples under Luigi Antonio Zompa (criticized by Bruno in his *Candelaio* for being a pedant), had a secret personal motive – an old, unforgiven grudge – to add to his public persecution of Giordano, when he realized who he was?

By far the most ambiguous and sinister figures in Bruno's story are Francesco Maria Vialardi (*c*.1540–*c*.1613), a nobleman from Vercelli, and the Catholic convert Kaspar Schoppe (1576–1649).

Vialardi's possible motivations for acting against Bruno are not difficult to understand. Bruno had rashly implicated his cellmate Vialardi during one of his interrogations in the summer of 1594, accusing him of blasphemy and heresy. This may have caused Vialardi many problems and probably a slightly longer stay in the prison of the Inquisition. But if there was one person Bruno didn't want as an enemy, that was the man from Vercelli. Vialardi was a consummate political informer and schemer who had worked for several powerful lords across Italy and abroad. He had been arrested in Genoa in 1591 on suspicion of being a Navarrist sympathizer and extradited to Rome in May the following year. His case dragged on for years because of delays with the cross-examination of the witnesses in Genoa and perhaps because of Bruno's accusations, but he later claimed to have been treated by the inquisitors with the utmost kindness. "I was given excellent rooms" – he wrote – "allowed the comfort of studying and every other thing. I wasn't denied the sacraments, or being in company, receiving visits and writing. The cardinals treated me with soft gloves... I was never threatened with torture." After being cleared of all accusations, Vialardi was kept in the Holy Office prison for almost two more years, since he was unable to repay the cost of his upkeep while in detention. When his debt of 300 *scudi* was finally waived by Pope Clement, he was released in June 1597 on condition of not leaving the city of Rome. Having regained his freedom, Vialardi didn't waste time in getting back to his old job as a political intrigant and informer, writing letters and missives every day, resuming old contacts and creating new ones, probably also among the high Roman clergy. In a letter he wrote on 17th September 1599, the day after Celestino's execution in Campo de' Fiori, Vialardi described the friar from Verona as an "iniquitous man who stubbornly claimed that Our Lord Jesus Christ was not our redeemer". How could he have known about Celestino if the Pope had ordered a vow of secrecy on the matter? And it is more than likely that it was he who, around the same time, sent the anonymous letter to the inquisitor of Vercelli, the Dominican Cipriano Uberti (who had visited him in jail in December 1593), with fresh accusations against his former cellmate and enemy.

It is ironic that the only surviving description of one of Bruno's defining moments – his brief defiant speech after the sentence was read to him – should have come down to us through the words of one of his detractors. After moving to Italy in January 1599, Kaspar (or Caspar) Schoppe converted to Catholicism and began to ingratiate himself with Pope Clement and other high-ranking prelates of the Roman Curia. At the time of Bruno's execution, which he attended in person, Schoppe was living in the palazzo of Cardinal Madruzzo, where the ceremony of Bruno's degradation and the reading of his sentence took place. He wrote his famous letter to Konrad Rittershausen, an earlier mentor and friend who had just repudiated him, on the day of Bruno's death. Schoppe later became friends with Campanella and tried to get some of his works – including his masterpiece *The City of the Sun* – published by Giovanni Battista Ciotti, the man who had introduced Bruno to Mocenigo. One of Campanella's works, *Atheism Conquered*, contains a prefatory letter addressed to Schoppe. In later life the German convert turned into a rabid anti-Protestant and anti-Jesuit controversialist. Izaak Walton once described him as "a man of a restless spirit and a malicious pen".

A few words should also be said about Cardinal Roberto Bellarmino (1542–1621). Most scholars tend to underplay his role in Bruno's case, claiming that he only got involved towards the end, from 1597 onwards. Yet, looking at the existing evidence, it seems clear that the trial gained a new momentum from the time Bellarmino's name makes its first appearance in the minutes of the Congregation of the Holy Office. He certainly worked very hard to try and pin down Bruno about specific points of heresy, disputing with him at a highly technical level, reading his statements of defence and rebutting his arguments by way of learned disquisition and sophisticated philosophical reasoning. After all he was a world-famous authority on matters of doctrine, and his writings (a new edition of his *Disputationes* was published by Ciotti in 1599) were read all over Europe by Catholics and Protestants alike.

It is interesting to see that a public notice announcing a delay in Bruno's execution, published on 12th February 1600, mentions that "he [Giordano] disputed many times in Germany with Card. Bellarmino". Such a claim does not appear to be substantiated. Who spread the rumour, and why? Did it come from Bellarmino himself, or a member of his entourage, as a note of triumph after the defeat of his wilful Dominican opponent? Bellarmino was made a saint by Pius XI in 1930, and his name is mostly remembered today, perhaps unjustly and inaccurately, as that of the tormentor of Galileo Galilei. The Pisan scientist was finally rehabilitated by the Church, who recognized that his 1633 conviction on charges of heresy was wrong. Such a step has yet to be taken by the Holy See towards the philosopher of Nola.

Acknowledgements

I would like to thank Mike Stocks for his comments and suggestions on the first draft of this novel, Christian Müller for his editing work and Alex Middleton and William Dady for proofreading the text. A big thank you to Roger Clarke for his help with some of the Latin passages and for his translation of Bruno's verses from *De monade* (p. 281), and to Ali Khan for his help with the Arabic. My greatest debt is to all the scholars who have devoted so many detailed and thought-provoking books, essays and articles to Giordano Bruno, in particular Aquilecchia, Ciliberto, Firpo, Gentile, Spampanato, Verrecchia and Yates. A special thank you goes to the publisher and the editors of Adelphi's multi-volume edition of Bruno's Latin works – a truly "heroic" endeavour, in Giordano's sense of the word.

If I have failed in bringing back to life the fascinating figure of Giordano Bruno in these pages, I hope I have done so honourably.